## What was I doing out here?

The trees answered me with their bulk and deep November silence. The air was crisp, clean, and I was unaccountably exhilarated, as if a weight I'd been carrying had slipped off my shoulders and left me lighter. The world seemed fresh, capable of unexpected gifts, and for the first time in a long time I felt ready to find whatever was waiting for me.

I stood up and looked up and down the trail, then began to walk, not back toward the farm, but downhill, deeper into the woods. Just a hundred yards farther down the trail I could see a shadowed heap on the ground, and at first it looked like no more than a pile of leaves in the darkness. But there was a smell to it, a dark, familiar smell, a smell as old as the world. My shins prickled and my pace slowed, and as I forced myself to go on, some primal part of me resisted, pleading with me to turn back. Cautiously, reluctantly, I edged forward.

No, I thought. Not here. Not now.

Let it be an animal, I prayed, but I could see the telltale blue of clothing as I drew closer. Denim and a white collar. Finally I reached the lump of flesh and fabric and saw the outstretched hand. . . .

Also by Lois Gilbert

*River of Summer*

# *Without Mercy*

## Lois Gilbert

AN ONYX BOOK

ONYX
Published by New American Library, a division of
Penguin Putnam Inc., 375 Hudson Street,
New York, New York 10014, U.S.A.
Penguin Books Ltd, 27 Wrights Lane,
London W8 5TZ, England
Penguin Books Australia Ltd, Ringwood,
Victoria, Australia
Penguin Books Canada Ltd, 10 Alcorn Avenue,
Toronto, Ontario, Canada M4V 3B2
Penguin Books (N.Z.) Ltd, 182–190 Wairau Road,
Auckland 10, New Zealand

Penguin Books Ltd, Registered Offices:
Harmondsworth, Middlesex, England

First published by Onyx, an imprint of New American Library,
a division of Penguin Putnam Inc.

First Printing, September 2000
10  9  8  7  6  5  4  3  2  1

 REGISTERED TRADEMARK—MARCA REGISTRADA

Printed in the United States of America

PUBLISHER'S NOTE
This is a work of fiction. Names, characters, places, and incidents either are
the product of the author's imagination or are used fictitiously, and any resem-
blance to actual persons, living or dead, business establishments, events, or
locales is entirely coincidental.

For their invaluable editorial skill and encouragement, I thank my agent, Vincent Atchity, and my editor, Audrey LaFehr, and Genny Osterlog, associate editor.

I also thank Wayne Oakes, John Thorndike, Mary Gilbert, Claire Gilbert and Billy Halsted for their affectionate, merciless advice.

# *Chapter One*

I woke up in darkness and looked at the glowing red numbers on my bedside clock. In just a few more minutes dawn would cast a pale rose light across the west wall of my bedroom. An icy wind sliced through the cracks in the windows, but I made myself stretch and throw back the covers.

It was time.

I could feel him waiting. Down in Deputron Hollow, about a mile and a half from the house, there was a spring-fed waterfall that tumbled off a sixty-foot cliff and ended in a deep, rocky pool. I'd seen him there before. I knew he liked to nibble the young grass around the pool. In the night I'd dreamed about him, hiding in the trees. Oak, beech, maple. The dusk a camouflage. The light glinting from his antlers. In the dream I'd seen him huffing, a plume of vapor escaping his dark coat and rising.

It was cold in the bedroom, cold enough to leave a rime of ice in the water glass. I stumbled around in the closet, searching for my athletic bra, long silk

1

Lois Gilbert

underwear, canvas pants, and a thick flannel shirt.
As I pulled on my boots I felt a quick glow of antici-
pation and something close to happiness, as if I were
going to meet a lover. I tiptoed out into the hall and
closed the door behind me, careful not to make any
noise that would wake the others. Walking softly, I
padded downstairs to the kitchen to eat breakfast.

The sky outside had lightened enough for me to
see the shadowed outlines of the sink, stove, and
table, and I felt my way around quietly without turning on a lamp. I shook cereal in a bowl, poured milk
over it, and ate it in the dark. Then I unlocked the
gun cabinet and lifted my Remington 12 gauge from
the rack, broke it open, and checked the breech while
the dogs whined with eagerness.

"You stay," I whispered to them. "It's not birds
I'm after." I put a handful of shells in the pocket of
my black wool pea coat, slipped out the door, and
shut it firmly behind me.

In the twilight of the morning I strode through
fields silvered with frost, my steps quick and certain
as I drew closer to the black line of woods by the
edge of the meadow. The sky held a sprinkle of stars,
while the light of day began to seep over the east-
ern horizon.

Before long the woods enclosed me, and I felt
brisk, invigorated. The buck would be there. I could
feel him in the November chill, waiting in the
bracken by the pool, waiting for the swift kiss of lead,
waiting for me to lift his body across my shoulder. I
would take the weight. I would eat him.

2

The path pulled me downhill for a mile or so, easy walking, and I breathed in the sharp air with a pang of longing for snow, for the deep silence of winter on the farm. Last night Casey Kelly on Channel 13 warned of an arctic cold front headed our way, bringing two to three feet of snow in Tompkins County, which was unprecedented for November, even in Ithaca. Cold winds from Canada regularly swept over the Great Lakes, picking up moisture and dumping it on us with monotonous predictability, but this storm was supposed to beat anything we'd ever seen before. I looked forward to it.

Just a year ago I'd been stuck in the equatorial heat of the Sudan, working as a volunteer for Médecins Sans Frontières. The program discourages doctors from serving for more than six months, but I received permission to stay for a year. I couldn't leave when there was so much hunger, so many mouths, so many starving eyes, and so few hands to help. Stubborn to the end, I remained even though the combination of dysentery, malaria, and exhaustion reduced me to hardly more than a skeleton. My breasts hung like empty bags, my rear end disappeared, and underneath the sunburn my skin had the translucent, waxy tone of a corpse. I was weak as a baby and finally incapable of walking without help. When my grandmother saw me being wheeled off the plane at the airport she burst into tears. Before we drove out of the parking lot she insisted that I move in with her so I could recuperate at my own pace on the farm, and she graciously stretched the invitation to

include my daughter Amy. I was enormously relieved. I'd left Amy with her father for a whole year,
and I was eager to be with her again. Gran never
even paused to consider how difficult it might be to
take an invalid and a teenager into her home, and I
loved her for it.

Since my return to America my grandmother had
been a saint. Her pride in me had always been palpa-
ble, and I loved the smile in her voice whenever she
had a chance to introduce me as a doctor. She understood how it could feel to return to America after a
year in the bush, to come back from the dirt tracks
and the ragged, starving refugees of the equatorial
rain forest to television and traffic jams and the smug
self-righteousness of this rich, fat, shiny country.

It was her example that had led me to Africa to
begin with: she'd written a book about a village in
Ethiopia, a village I made a point of visiting on my
first leave from the camp, and they still remembered
her there and gave me a few pounds of dura, a kind
of sorghum grain, to take back to her. For the past
thirty years she'd written books on small communi-
ties of humans, plants, and animals in remote pockets
of the world, from a poetic and biological perspec-
tive. Her book on the village in Ethiopia had been
nominated for a Pulitzer.

It took six months for my body to recover from
the year I'd spent in the dusty camp at Ajiep. I'd
been back in the States for twelve months now and
had regained twenty pounds of the thirty I'd lost in
Africa. I felt good. I was strong, my muscle tone was

back to normal, and I had enough energy to do whatever I wanted, but I still couldn't face the thought of work. I was only thirty-two years old, but I felt ancient beyond all reckoning, old the way a mountain is old, or a rock, or a river. Some essential inner battery fueling my ambition had worn out in me.

What took the place of ambition was something like hunger, a deep, irrational, pressing need that stained my days and nights with anxiety. For twelve long months I'd watched death come and go like a thief, nibbling, sucking, stealing life, its presence so common and accepted in the camp that I began to expect it to come for me, and I accepted it, then welcomed it. After all, it was an end to the pain. I began to die a little, feeling quite generous about it, as if I could give the refugees company, at least, when the kitchen ran short of food.

Coming home from that place was like awakening from a long, dangerous sleep, and when I emerged from the spell of the camp, I knew I wanted to live, and I was frightened, terribly frightened, at how close I'd come to dying. After a few months of being nursed by my grandmother I gained enough strength to hunt, and then I was out in the woods every morning, looking for food in the sky, in the rivers, in the woods. What I'd learned in the camp was that food was the most important thing, the main thing, and if you don't have food, all the medicine in the world won't save you. I wanted a larder so full that death couldn't squeeze through the door. My need was deep, crazy deep, deep enough to kill, to count the fat young bucks in the woods, the trout that lurked in the shadows of the pond, and the geese that flew overhead, and think, yes, I will take you, I will cut you from the herd, I will eat you. I want to live.

The work I'd trained for had no place in this life of hunting and gathering. Medicine held no attraction anymore. But I wanted to hunt. Hunting mattered.

In the evenings I read Gran's tattered collection of classics that she kept in cardboard boxes under the stairs: Melville, Tolstoy, Balzac, and Proust. Lately I'd been struggling through *The Riverside Chaucer*, Benson's definitive collection of Chaucer's work. The old language opened me up, and one night I was amazed to hear myself laughing out loud as I came across a particularly bawdy line. I couldn't remember the last time I'd laughed, and the sound was hoarse, dry, like a pump that had almost rusted shut.

Reading brought me sanctuary, and I discovered that the better the book, the more my time in Africa shrank to the vanishing point. I needed to make that time in the Sudan disappear, and I soon found that old books worked the best. Nothing written in the twentieth century worked at all.

I had no plans. It was enough to hunt all day, read in the evening, and then stand outside at night and watch the stars passing overhead. Sometimes I sat with Gran in the living room and listened to her old records: Bach, Mozart, Sibelius, Rimsky-Korsakov, Chopin, Debussy. Even though the records were old and scratched, we leaned back in our chairs and listened without speaking or moving, eyes closed, every pore open to the waterfall of notes, and that, too, was a kind of release, a healing that took place where words couldn't go.

Sometimes I wondered if I could ever go back to the kind of medicine I practiced at the hospital, faced with unsolvable problems that I could only refer to specialists, or the benign pathologies that bored the life out of me. The HMOs were asking their doctors for an impossible efficiency, allowing no more than two and a half minutes per patient, and there were days—especially during flu season—when I was convinced that every patient I saw was a robot who had been given a tape of the same lines, the same set of symptoms to recite. I could not face the thought of that assembly-line medicine, seeing eighty or ninety patients a day.

My thoughts drifted as I walked, and I listened to the sounds of the woods, the creak of branches, the rustling of dead leaves as sparrows rummaged on the ground for bugs and stray seeds. Up ahead the outline of the oak appeared, big as a castle, older than the United States. I'd climbed this tree a thousand times in my childhood, scaling its broad trunk like a rock wall, searching by feel for the familiar footholds on the scars and knuckles in its bark. The first branch stretched fifty feet from trunk to tip and was as big around as a barrel. My plan was to straddle the great beam of the branch, lean against the trunk, and wait in comfort for the buck to come to me.

I paused a moment between the gnarled, worn

knees of the roots to load and cock my shotgun. The metal barrel was cold, and after I finished I breathed on my fingers to warm them.

When I looked up again the buck was there.

My breath caught as I watched his silhouette flickering in and out of the maples lining the trail. He stepped lightly over a dead branch, steadily moving closer, almost close enough for me to get a clear shot. He lifted his head, looked east and west, then ambled slowly toward me, walking out into the open and calmly up the trail, hooves clicking on the stones.

It was almost too fast, too easy. I froze, grateful to be downwind. Shivering in the cold air, I pressed my back against the trunk of the oak, clinging to the shadow, hoping he would narrow the gap between us. He paused to lift his nose and drink in the mist rising from the forest floor. The twelve points of his antlers tilted back over his broad body, as if to display the beauty of his massive head and the crown of his rack. He bellowed a challenge to the other males in the woods, and the sound sent a ripple of goose bumps over my skin.

Even after he was field-dressed he would probably weigh over two hundred pounds, and I was still thin from the year I'd spent in Africa. I'd have to fetch a rope and skid him out, I thought. I felt the old urgency, the adrenaline rising in my blood, an ache like hunger, or lust. He walked closer, so close I could see the dew on his coat. It was an easy shot. He slowed, then halted, ears pricked.

I dropped to one knee and raised the gun to my shoulder.

He didn't move. He looked at me.

I felt the curve of the trigger against my finger as I drew a bead on him. Run, I thought. If he ran I would shoot him. But he didn't run. He stared at me.

I tried to see him as food, insurance against hunger, against famine. I knew it was ridiculous, this obsession with food. It was illogical. Last week I'd canned forty quarts of plums from the windfall in the abandoned orchard, and Gran cornered me in the kitchen and held me by the arms until I put my spoon down. "You're trying to feed the world," she said, and shook me lightly, the way you might shake a child who's not listening. "And you can't, Brett."

All these thoughts flowed through my mind in no time at all. The buck never moved. My gunsight had been trained on his chest for the last few seconds while he gazed at me without blinking, without fear. Every muscle in my body felt coiled and tense. I'd heard stories about bucks during rutting season, bucks so maddened by lust that they attacked cars, or barns, or people, and the longer we stared at each other the more I wondered if he was sizing me up, getting ready to charge. My finger was frozen on the trigger, and my heart was skipping like a stone on water.

He lifted his tail to half mast. I expected him to paw the ground, to toss his antlers before he lowered his head for the charge. In my mind I could already see it happening, and my finger tightened on the trigger to within a hairsbreadth of the explosion that would end the suspense.

His tail came up another notch, and then another. Now, I thought. Do it. Make my day.

The buck let out a long fart. It was huge, resonant, blatant as a Bronx cheer, the loudest display of flatulence I'd ever heard in my life. He blinked and gave me a blandly superior look, as if my farts would never compare to his magnificent example.

I started to laugh. I couldn't help it. My shoulders shook and jiggled against the stock of the gun and threw off my aim. I lowered the gun, the tension of the hunt ebbing from me like a toppled wave being pulled back to sea. Something left me in that moment, some familiar squeeze of fear, or pressure, or guilt was gone. It was over.

The buck tossed his antlers and put his head down to crop at the grass by the side of the trail. I watched him eat. Then he walked back into the trees, unhurried, tail twitching carelessly behind him. I sank back on my knees, overwhelmed by an odd relief, as though I were the one who had escaped. I shook my head. What was I doing out here?

The trees answered me with their bulk and deep November silence. The air was crisp, clean, and I was unaccountably exhilarated, as if a weight I'd been carrying had slipped off my shoulders and left me lighter. The world seemed fresh, capable of unexpected gifts, and for the first time in a long time I felt ready to find whatever was waiting for me. My chest expanded with possibilities. I could go out

West, I thought. Take Amy and see the Grand Canyon. Get a job. Start a practice. I wanted to move, to do something, and for the first time in a long time, I knew that I could.

I stood and looked up and down the trail, then began to walk, not back toward the farm, but downhill, deeper into the woods, my gun held loosely at my side. The future seemed rosy, ripe, and accessible. There was no reason to stay here on the farm, sponging off my grandmother's hospitality for another winter. I was healthy. My body was lean and hard. It was time for a change.

Just a hundred yards farther down the trail I could see a shadowed heap on the ground, and at first it looked like no more than a pile of leaves in the darkness. But there was a smell to it, a dark, familiar smell, a smell as old as the world, a smell I remembered from Africa. My shins prickled and my pace slowed, and as I forced myself to go on, some primal part of me resisted, pleading with me to turn back. Cautiously, reluctantly, I edged forward.

No, I thought. Not here. Not now.

Let it be an animal, I prayed, but I could see the telltale blue of clothing as I drew closer. Denim, and a white collar. Finally I reached the lump of flesh and fabric and saw the outstretched hand. In the Sudan I'd pointed out the dead bodies—children, mostly—to be carried to the end of the refugee camp and burned in the mass grave we'd dug by hand in the elephant grass. But I'd never seen a dead body out here in the woods of upstate New York, on my grandmother's farm.

It was a shock. It had been over a year since I'd seen a human corpse, and this one was ripped open and left crumpled, discarded like a load of garbage. His eyes were wide and opaque and stared into nothing, while his torso was twisted so that his legs flopped to one side and his arms were splayed open as if to receive the sky. As I edged closer I could see his belly had been perforated by what looked like buckshot, delivered at point-blank range, turning his front into a cauliflower of purple meat. The maggots in the cavity were motionless as grains of rice, but if the day warmed they would begin to squirm and feed. The shirt he wore was once white but now it was smeared with blood, and his denim jacket and jeans were black where quarts of it had pooled from the hot spring in his body. There was a severe contusion to the right temple and the hands were lacerated, as if he'd been dragged across rough ground. He was at least sixty, maybe seventy, a gaunt, tall man. I could see the dark blossoms of lesions on his neck and cheek, and they looked familiar somehow, another echo of Africa and all the young men I'd treated there with identical bruises. With another dull thud of recognition, I realized that they were Kaposi's sarcoma, indicating the terminal stages of AIDS. His skin was blanched from the loss of blood, and his mouth was open in one last "oh" of surprise, or pain.

I stood and stared at the corpse and wondered

how this man could have come to such a violent end when he was clearly no more than a few months away from a very different death. In spite of my training, I was confused to discover that what I felt was a kind of grief. He looked so startled, so hurt, and in spite of the damage he looked vaguely familiar, like an older version of my brother Ryan.

For a moment the eyes of the dead man seemed to lock into mine and I felt chilled, transfixed by his sightless gaze. His eyes stared into me as if he were still looking at his murderer, the horror frozen on his face. I inhaled involuntarily, and in that quick gasp of indrawn breath I caught a whiff of him. I backed up a few paces. My hands were shaking.

Gripping my shotgun more tightly, I was suddenly aware of the shadows between the trees, aware of being a woman alone in the woods. I was a mile from the house, two miles from paved road, too far away to scream for help.

A surge of adrenaline skidded through my veins and I started to run. Thoughts darted through me, panicky thoughts. This was no hunting accident. Someone had ambushed this man, someone who knew about this slender, overgrown trail on the property that led to the waterfall. My grandmother's farm covered four hundred acres of woods and pastures, taking in nearly all of Eastman Hill. A killer had walked on our land. He might still be here.

My scalp tingled with the sensation of being watched, and my legs felt like rubber as I ran. The gun banged against my thigh as I lunged up the hill.

I was desperate to reach the house. More than anything else, I wanted the sight of our front porch and Amy and Ryan and Gran around me, but after half a mile the stitch in my side slowed me to a fast walk. When I emerged from the shadow of the woods and saw the house on the crown of the hill I began to run again, straight through the mist that licked the meadow.

"Ryan!" I shouted as I neared the porch. "Amy!"

The dogs began to bark inside the house but no one came out, so I rang the cowbell we left by the front door for emergencies. My breathing was ragged and the cramp in my side left me doubled up, but I swung the heavy black bell until my brother opened the door.

"What the hell—?" he asked. He fit the earpiece of his spectacles over one ear and then cocked his head and squinted at me, his eyes still dazed by sleep.

"There's a dead man out there," I said, and pointed back toward the woods.

Ryan looked stricken. "Dead? Are you sure?"

"I'm sure."

"Jesus. Who is it?"

I shook my head, lifted one arm in front of me, and let it fall. I was still winded.

"Where is he?" Ryan asked.

"Down in Deputron Hollow," I gasped. "Almost to the spring. About a mile from here."

"I'll call Dan."

Dan was my ex-husband and the sheriff for Tompkins County, and the thought of his arrival caused a specific, familiar pain in my chest, as if a chunk of glass had lodged in an artery there.

I sat on the porch steps to catch my breath. Ryan went back in the house and Amy peered at me from the doorway, then stepped out delicately on the cold floorboards in her bare feet. Amy was wearing one of her dad's old T-shirts that came down to her knees. Suddenly my heart pounded with fear for my daughter.

"Are you okay?" she asked. She sat beside me and bumped me with her arm.

"No," I said. I put my arm around her and clutched her tightly, consumed with relief that I was alive and someone else was dead.

Amy stiffened. I felt the tension in her, the reluctance to lean.

"Are you all right?" I asked.

"Of course," she said. Her voice was careful, calm.

For a year I had tried not to care about the coolness that crept into her voice whenever we talked, but now it cut me. I felt a ferocious desire to be close to her, to protect her, to mother her, but I was beginning to wonder if it wasn't too late. Perhaps she would never forgive me for going away without her. Before I left for Africa mothering was easy, natural, but now it was like a song I'd forgotten, the lyrics jumbled, the tune uncertain.

Amy watched me, though; she watched me carefully, as if I might forget she existed, and leave her here with Gran and Ryan and wander off into the wilderness again. She kept track of my comings and goings; she wanted to know where I'd been and where I planned to be, and this gave me some small piece of comfort.

She shivered. "I'm freezing," she said.

"Let me warm you up," I said, and chafed her arms. I was desperate to hold her, to reassure myself that she was safe and unharmed, but I knew she would resist, so I resorted to an old trick.

"Do you remember when you were a baby and followed our dog into the woods?"

"Vaguely," she mumbled, like a young Marlene Deitrich, but I could sense her body soften slightly and turn toward me, the way it used to when she was a child and I told her a story, any story, about what she was like when she was younger. She was baldly curious about herself, especially the parts of her history she might have forgotten.

I went on, holding her as close as I dared. "You were only, what, eighteen months? Two? Just a baby. Barely able to walk. No one knew where you were. We were frantic. I knew you'd probably walked downhill, because walking uphill would be too hard, so I went down in the hollow and every few steps I'd yell at the top of my lungs, 'Amy! Where are you?'

"And then I heard your tiny, exasperated voice, calling to me: *'I'm right there . . .'* "

Amy pulled away and looked at me with the deep green eyes, smooth brow, and full freckled cheeks of a fifteen-year-old baby becoming a woman. In the last year her body had taken on alarmingly voluptuous lines, and I couldn't help but feel a pang of homesickness for the child she'd been.

When I left for Africa, Amy was a vulnerable, excitable thirteen-year-old, with braces and knobby knees and bright, kinky red hair. She couldn't have a conversation without semaphoring wildly with her hands, and in spite of her awkward growth spurts she was unself-conscious and easy with Dan and me. Two or three times a day she made me laugh out loud, and to see the world through her eyes was a thrill, like being thirteen all over again. She wasn't too old back then to flop against me like a puppy, arms and legs sprawled in blissful, confident, and absolute ownership of her mom.

But when I returned from Africa the braces were off and her hair had achieved the luster of a Botticelli Venus. She had become a beauty, a knockout who radiated one constant message to me: back off.

Amy hated the farm, and her mouth hadn't lost that thin, mean line in all the last twelve months we'd lived here. She would probably be mad at me forever. A year ago she was white-faced with resentment when I insisted that she leave her dad's house (where I suspected he left her alone far too much) and move back to the farm with Gran and Ryan and me. In Amy's eyes Gran was hopelessly old-fashioned, and the farm was a monument to another age, before computers.

Gran gracefully resisted Amy's suggestions for outfitting the house with a satellite dish and modems in every room. My grandmother knew who she was and what she wanted, and modern conveniences had little to do with that. It was a relief to have the wall of Gran's opposition to hide behind, to have the power of Gran's innocent obstinacy between Amy's desires and my own. Whenever Amy argued for progress I blamed her great-grandmother for the inadequacies of the house, then secretly savored our distance from the electrified world outside the boundary of the farm.

Amy and I looked out at the meadow. The sun was just beginning to paint the grass gold, but the shadows of the trees were still long and blue. The woods looked black against the edge of the field, and for the first time in my life I could feel something evil in them, a nameless, faceless presence.

"I'm going inside," she said, and delicately extricated herself from my hands. "I need a sweater."

I followed her into the house and propped the gun in the hallway, unwilling to lock it up in the glass-fronted cabinet with the five other shotguns and rifles. I wanted my Remington near me until the killer was found. Amy floated on down the hallway, and I watched the pink soles of her feet flash up the stairs on her way to her room.

Ryan was still on the phone, and I studied him while I waited for him to finish his call. Even when he was rumpled my big brother was a good-looking man, thirty-nine years old, tall, handsome, with gold-rimmed glasses, thick brown hair and delicate hands. He barely made ends meet as a veterinarian; farmers had a tendency to abandon their animals rather than pay the vet for saving them, and our barn was full of orphaned horses nobody wanted. Ryan worked occasionally as a pathologist for Midland Insurance, which helped, but he was doomed to be a terrible businessman. He was a good vet. What kept him from making money at it was that he detested currying favor with prospective clients, and hated buttering up the ones he managed to keep. Running a business bored him, and he often disappeared at odd and inconvenient hours, leaving Gran or me to take his messages and deal with his customers.

He had always been vague, absentminded, and dreamy, but when I was growing up he was like God to me: my big strong brother, guardian and protector, a young, wise foster father. It was only in the past year that I noticed he was lazy, good at slithering out of uncomfortable tasks or confrontations. I loved him, of course; we all adored him. Amy spent hours discussing pop stars, makeup, clothes, and celebrity gossip with him. He always knew the best gossip, and his taste was impeccable. He listened to Amy with the serious attention she craved, and I quickly realized it wasn't an act. He was interested in her opinions. Ryan treated her with a courtly appreciation that made me feel even more insecure about my own parenting. Was I a bad mother because I hated MTV and loved Chaucer? Should I know the names of the rock bands? Maybe. Most of the time I was glad for the envelope of family around me, and often felt that Gran and Ryan completed the parenting I couldn't provide. They anchored me to the world, and kept me from falling into the craziness I'd brought back inside me from Africa.

Ryan was the only person in the world that Gran loved without reservation. He held the throne in her heart: he was her golden boy. They shared a connection so intense it sometimes felt like a private club, an exclusive, rarified union that no amount of overachieving on my part could penetrate. In my petty moments I was jealous of Ryan, and secretly disappointed that neither my daughter nor my grandmother loved me best.

Two years ago Gran broke her arm and Ryan moved back to the farm to help her cope. It was a terrible time for all of us; I had just split up with Dan and my first impulse was to get as far away as I could from my marriage and all the familiar landmarks around it, so I signed up to go to Africa. Ryan and his longtime companion Billy Cooper had shared a house in Cayuga Heights for twelve years, but right after I left they broke up.

Billy was a jockey, short and lean as a whippet, sharp and funny and tender as another brother to me. Losing him was like losing a member of the family, although it was easy to see why he and Ryan had fallen apart. Ryan was an idiot about money, and loved to spend it twice as fast as he could earn it. He longed for shirts from Turnbull-Asser, Venetian glass, Persian kilims, luggage made of buttersoft leather. His credit cards were always overextended. Once every few years Billy would make him sit down and cut them all up, but the credit sharks would send him more within days. Ryan was born to be a gracious host, and never added up the cost of anything. After a fancy meal in a restaurant with half a dozen of his friends he would fling his Visa down on the table and invite the waiter to write in his own tip. He was bad at arithmetic and thought it was unbearably bourgeois to fuss about money, which made him an easy target.

Then the casino opened on the Onondaga reservation three years ago, and Ryan started going there almost every night. As a jockey, Billy was all too familiar with the compulsion he saw in Ryan, and begged him to stop, but Ryan was helpless against the urge to gamble. One day Billy came home and found that Ryan had hocked the Oriental rug in the hallway and two Hepplewhite end tables to pay off a gambling debt. That was it for Billy. He refused to pretend Ryan's problem was under control, and Ryan, true to form, refused to admit there was a problem.

His gambling was worse now—a lot worse. I didn't ask, but I could see the worry etched in permanent lines around Ryan's mouth. Ordinarily my brother was immaculate in a button-down shirt under a Harris tweed coat, trousers pressed, hair crisply parted on the left. Now he knuckled sleep from his eyes and rubbed his whiskers as he stood hanging onto the phone, dressed only in his bathrobe and slippers.

After a few more mumbled words into the mouthpiece, he hung up and turned to me. "They're on their way. Get ready for an invasion."

"Should I heat up the coffee?"

He held up both hands, palms facing me. "Please."

I knew how he felt about my coffee, but I wanted to put off waking our grandmother. "He was murdered," I told him.

"How could you tell?"

"There was a shotgun blast to his belly, and no gun."

He rubbed his forehead, as if in pain. "Poor bastard," he muttered as he shuffled into the kitchen to start the coffee.

I trailed after him. "Have you been down to the spring since we rode there a week ago?"

"No. Have you?"

"No. I've been hunting over toward the Buckman place. I just wondered how long he's been there." My voice sounded high and anxious and I couldn't stand hearing the note of entreaty in it, as if the child in me still expected my big brother to fix everything.

"I don't know, Brett. One thing at a time. I'll make the coffee."

I couldn't sit still, and bit my knuckles as I paced back and forth in front of the stove. "How long till they get here?"

"Dan said ten minutes. Are you going to warn Gran?"

"I'll take some coffee first," I said.

"Sit down," he said, and glared at me until I slid into a chair at the table.

Ryan filled the kettle with water, and I sat at the scarred kitchen table and watched him fit the paper filter into the hourglass shape of the Chemex coffee-pot. He ground the beans, spooned coffee into the filter, then leaned against the counter until the teaket-tle sent up a jet of steam. Gradually my heart slowed its wild knocking and I took a deep breath as he poured boiling water over the grounds.

Ryan and I were both born on the farm. Our parents died so young I possessed only one memory of my mother, and it was more sensation than memory: the fine hair on her arm, golden in the sunlight, her cool hand touching my hot, bare belly, and a fra-grance of laundry and grass. I think we were lying somewhere outside on a blanket, in an orchard, per-haps, because I remember leaves overhead. I rubbed this memory so often in childhood, trying to burnish it into a brighter, deeper, more meaningful picture that it almost disappeared. I was only two when they died. My father left no trace of himself in my two-year-old memory, and I think I missed him more because of that.

Our parents. Edward and Caroline. When Gran spoke of them they sounded like the prince and prin-cess in a fairy tale, happy, charming, good people who seemed destined to live happily ever after. In fact, their brief history was more ordinary, and more tragic. They married young and stayed on the farm to conserve money while my father worked his way through architectural school at Cornell. Caroline was Gran's only child, and I could tell by the catch in Gran's voice whenever she talked about her that she had adored my mother.

Both Caroline and Edward were killed in a car crash. Gran rarely spoke of it. I knew it hurt her whenever I brought it up, and I learned from the pain on her face to never ask her for the details of how or why it occurred.

After the crash, Gran adopted Ryan and me and raised us by herself. She was only forty-five when our parents died, and people often assumed she was our mother. I was terribly proud of her, especially after I had Amy and realized what she must have endured as a parent. During a time when women were considered incapable of living without a man, she raised us without any spouse to support her, put Ryan and me through vet school and med school, ran the farm, and wrote thirteen books.

The farm was a magical place to grow up, a private, isolated oasis of rolling fields and forests and streams, mostly left fallow and wild, a sanctuary against the development encroaching on all sides. Counting Amy, the McBride clan had lived here for five generations. The house was over a hundred years old, built by our great-grandfather, Matthew Scott McBride, in the Greek Revival style so popular in upstate New York at the turn of the century. There were two stories, painted white, with dark green shutters on every window and a long porch on the east side. Most of the tall windows had the original glass from Matthew's day, glass that was thick and rippled with the years. Every door was warped by the long upstate winters, and the staircase was worn with the footsteps of the generations of McBrides that preceded us.

The slow pulse of the house reasserted itself in the ticking of the clock in the hall and the snoring of the dogs on the rug. I could feel the safety of the walls enclosing us, the embers glowing from last night's fire in the woodstove, the stone chimney like a sentry guarding our family. My breathing was slow and even now, and I stared out the window at the rippled surface of the pond.

The house looked grand from the outside, with rock walls lining the driveway and a large weeping willow framing the house and pond. The land rolled away on all sides from the tall peaked roof of the house. The fields were mown and bordered with split rail fences for the horses, and the house looked like a jewel in its setting, proud, high on the crown of the hill, mirrored by the big pond in front of it, the grounds defined by meadows and fences and flower beds. Everyone admired it from the outside.

But newcomers invariably were disappointed when they walked inside. Except for Ryan's bedroom, the interior was dark, drafty, and dirty; the furniture was old, and none of it matched. A moth-eaten bear's head hung from the chimney above the mantel in the living room. The curtains were heavy, an old red velvet from a butchered auditorium curtain, and the bookshelves housed at least a thousand worn paperbacks. A year's worth of *New Yorkers* mixed with old copies of *Life* and *National Geographic* in a big copper bucket by the woodstove. The cupboards were stuffed with jigsaw puzzles with missing pieces and board games no one played anymore.

Ryan's office and surgery were tacked on to the rear of the house, like an afterthought. He built the office himself after he moved in, and the materials were cheap and flimsy, as if he were uncertain how long he might be staying. His bedroom, however, was clean and light and expensively furnished in custom-made fabrics and pieces of furniture made out of blond, polished hardwood. I suspected he was biding his time until a few more credit card companies solicited his business before he tackled the redecoration of the rest of the house.

Ryan poured the coffee, and I took the mug from his hand. "So you didn't recognize the man," he said.

"No."

"That's something, anyway. It would be terrible if we knew him," he said.

"It was terrible, Ryan." I warmed my cold hands on the mug. "Whoever did it is still out there."

"Maybe not. The killer could be a thousand miles away by now."

"Do you believe that?" I asked.

"I think I would prefer to believe it." He gave me a small smile. "You want me to tell Gran?"

I shook my head. Emily Ann McBride was seventy-five-years old and had been born on the farm, and we both knew an event like this would be taken as a personal affront to Gran's iron standards of acceptable behavior. She was a sound sleeper, and I was relieved she'd slept through my ringing the cowbell. Let her sleep, I thought, but as soon as I had the thought she came into the kitchen, silent as smoke, and there was no telling how long she'd been at the doorway or what she'd heard.

Gran's face was handsome, chiseled by time into a map of wrinkles that conveyed a self-assurance that had always been absolute. She was nearly six feet tall, a descendant of the Highlanders who'd made all the McBrides tall and red-haired. Her eyes were a pale blue that saw everything on the farm with the dispassion of a naturalist.

A blue enameled clip at the nape of her neck gathered her thinning hair into a river of white that flowed down her back. Gran wore a long green silk kimono, and in spite of her age her posture was regal as she swept into the kitchen. Her clothes were always rich, sumptuous to feel and graceful to look at, for she believed in cashmere, silk, wool, and good linen more than she believed in God. She looked as though she'd been up for hours.

"What are you two whispering about?" she asked. Her voice was still supple despite her age, with a low and musical lilt that spoke of old money. Her father had owned several blocks of real estate in downtown Ithaca, and she'd been raised with servants and private schools and an education at Cornell. She still had the kind of voice you would want to turn to in a crowded room, to see the face that went with it.

"There's a dead man on the path to the spring," I said.

Gran laughed out loud. "Don't be absurd."

"I'm not joking," I said. "There's a dead man out there."

"Nonsense," Gran said, extracting a cup from the cupboard. She shot Ryan an uncertain look. "Impossible."

"I'm afraid it's true," he said.

"Did you find him?" she asked, looking at me with concern.

"Yes."

"Good God, Brett." She rushed across the room to fold me into her arms, and I stifled the urge to sink into her and let the tears come. Why did I feel so emotional about this corpse? It was ridiculous, this superstitious fear that his dead eyes had seen me. I was getting soft.

"I'm so sorry, sweetheart," she said.

"I'm okay."

"Have you called Dan?"

Ryan spoke. "I just called him. He should be here any minute, along with the medical investigator and the police."

Gran pushed back her sleeves. "Let me find that coffee urn. Ten cups ought to hold them, don't you think? How many did you say? I'll get out the mugs."

Ryan opened his mouth, then closed it. He shot a

look of exasperation at her. "They won't be here for a social call," he said.

"They'll have time for a cup. Dan loves his coffee." Gran began opening and closing cupboards as Amy walked in, wearing cutoffs and sneakers and her father's T-shirt. She curled up in the chair across the table from me, her eyes unfocused as she stared out the window to the bleached fields.

"I want to see the corpse," Amy said.

I caught my breath in a reflex of anxiety. "You don't want to do that, honey," I said. "He's been dead for days and he smells foul."

"I'll hold my nose," she said.

Gran looked shocked. "I'm afraid your father won't permit it, dear."

"I'll ask him," Amy said to me.

"Okay," I said. "But put on some warmer clothes."

Amy's eyes narrowed.

"I mean it," I said.

"He was shot," Amy said to Gran, ignoring me.

"Good heavens," Gran said.

We all fell silent at the sound of cars approaching the house, toiling up the long driveway. The dogs barked and we waited for car doors to slam. After a moment I heard Dan's voice in the hall, shouting a hello toward the kitchen. I took a gulp of coffee and burned my tongue.

"Come in," Gran called as Dan appeared in the doorway. He looked terrible, thin, unshaven, his eyes shadowed with fatigue. When he took his hat off I could see a little more gray in his crewcut. Otherwise he looked the same: tall, muscular, his green eyes alert but hooded. So much like Amy's eyes, I thought, and it made me sad to see how alike they were, how closed and inscrutable they could be when pressed.

Dan and I were always extremely polite to each other, in the way of enemies who have signed a peace treaty after a long and bloody war, but I would never forget the thousands of small lies he had told me during our marriage, or the affairs he had tried to conceal. Ever since I returned from Africa he'd been puzzled by my lack of ambition, and I knew he couldn't understand why I wasn't back at the hospital, working. His judgment of me was obvious every time I saw him, and it was clear he thought I needed particular scrutiny, now that Amy was living with me again.

"Hey, folks," he said, looking at me. My skin felt alive everywhere as he looked at me, and I was suddenly aware of the coarse flannel of my shirt, the texture of the wooden table under my hand. The sight of him filled me with awkwardness, and for a moment I saw myself as he must see me, thinner, older than my thirty-two years, pale and washed out, my long red hair pulled back from my face and tied in a knot, every angle of my face and body sharpened by three years without him.

"Daniel," Gran said, her voice tender. "Please. Invite the men in for coffee. It's almost ready. Have you had breakfast? We have eggs, pancakes, sausage. What would you like?"

"I'm sorry, Emily," Dan said. "We have to tend to business first. Maybe after."

"I'll hold you to that," Gran said.

"Sounds like you had a rough morning, Brett," he said "Are you ready to show us the body? Ryan said it was a mile or so down the trail to the hollow."

I looked at my ex-husband. "Are you sure you need me along? I could tell you exactly where it is."

He held his hands out at his sides, let them drop. "We have to interview you. I figure if you walk with us we can talk, get it all over with, get the corpse out of here that much sooner."

"I'll get dressed and come with you," Ryan said.

"No," Gran said. "You stay here. I need you."

"Your grandmother's right," Dan said. "No reason for you to come with us."

Ryan nodded, and I could see relief in his eyes before he turned back to the coffee urn to measure out the grounds. I noticed Gran didn't care so much about protecting me from the sight of the corpse. She had always expected me to be tougher. I gave myself an inner shrug of resignation. It wasn't such a bad thing, to be the tough one.

Amy materialized in the doorway, dressed in jeans and a tight red sweater. She walked over to hug her father. "Can I go, Dad?" she whispered in his ear. It startled me to see her stand next to her father, so close to his own height, looking so mature, so seductive.

"Absolutely not," Dan said. He glanced at me and I gave him a tiny nod. He made a wry movement with the corner of his mouth, as if to say, at least we still have this in common.

Gran rose and plucked the sleeve of the red sweater until Amy stood beside her. Gran laid an arm over Amy's shoulder, grasped her, and held her tight.

"Keep the dogs inside," I told them. Amy's expression was cool, neutral. Gran nodded, a frightened, serious look on her face.

Dan and I left the kitchen and walked out to the porch, where he introduced me to the medical investigator and Jim Farnsworth, a detective in homicide. Farnsworth was fat, and smelled of cigars. I remembered Dan complaining about him years ago, when Dan had suspected him of stealing drugs from the evidence room. There were two other men in uniform, but no one bothered to tell me their names.

Noah's pick-up rumbled into the yard, top-heavy with stacked bales of hay. Noah was our hired hand, a lean, tall man with long caliper legs and a muscular and supple body made for horses. Ryan had hired him three weeks ago, when his predecessor quit to go work in the Alaskan oil fields.

After only three weeks I still wasn't used to Noah's presence on the farm; he was a quiet, good-looking man who went about his work with a kind of meditative calm, a relaxed grace. The confident way he carried himself intrigued me. I was attracted to him, which made me uncomfortable, so I avoided him if I could. But we had collided a few times in the barn, when I was oiling tack or brushing the horses, and he had a way of saying odd, unexpected things that lured me into conversations that embarrassed me later, as if I'd revealed too much of myself. What he said stuck in my mind. He stirred me. He made me think.

The truck slowed and came to a stop beyond the black-and-whites and the medical investigator's van, and I could see Noah's face through the windshield, his expression uncharacteristically worried, tight-lipped.

"Who's this?" Farnsworth asked.

"Our hired man," I said. "His name is Noah Greenwood."

"He live with you?"

"In the cabin next to the barn."

Noah stepped out of the truck, slammed the door, and walked up to the gathering on the porch. "What's up?" he asked.

"There's been a murder," Dan said. "Brett found a dead body on the way to the spring."

Noah whistled a low note of astonishment. "Who?"

"Nobody we know," I said.

"You might know him," Dan said, and I realized all at once that Dan wanted Noah to identify the body. It was suddenly clear to me that he was jealous of Noah, was jealous of what might happen between Noah and me, ever since Ryan had hired him.

"Why don't you come with us?" Dan asked.

# Chapter Two

Noah met his eyes and shrugged. "Sure. Lead the way."

The sun was filmed with clouds, the golden light was gone, and a stiff breeze blew on the back of my neck as we walked toward the black line of woods beyond the meadow. I was aware of Dan striding beside me, his long legs eating up the ground as we walked in the same scissored rhythm we'd shared since high school. The morning seemed unbearably sharp and beautiful out in the open meadow, but I felt a chill settle over me as we entered the shadow of the woods.

Soon Dan and I were fifty yards ahead of the others, but Dan spoke to me in a low voice, as if he might be overheard.

"How is Amy?"

I gave him a look. "She seems to be fine."

"Is she doing okay in school?"

"She's okay, Dan."

"It didn't bother you, what she was wearing?"

I thought back: sweater, jeans, sneakers. "What are you talking about?"

"That sweater—she wasn't wearing a bra. And it was cut off above her belly button. You could see three inches of skin."

"That's the style. Remember high school? Remember halter tops in the seventies? You loved them on me."

"It's a different world for kids now. There's this new date-rape drug that scares the shit out of me when I think about Amy. I see these high school girls dressing like whores, going to frat parties at Cornell where the testosterone is so thick you can smell it, and then they cry rape. I don't want my daughter to be an idiot."

"Tell her you're concerned."

Dan pursed his lips and blew out a puff of air as if something else was bothering him.

"What?" I asked.

"I think Amy's been stealing from me," he said.

I stiffened, and realized I'd been keeping my own fears from him in the hope that he didn't know about her stealing. For months I'd noticed cash missing from my wallet, usually no more than twenty dollars at a time, and it was easy to chalk it up to forgetfulness until I saw the wad of bills in her dresser. It scared me, that tidy, rubber-banded pile. Stealing money and spending it was one thing, but why was she stealing it and saving it? The Amy I used to know would never be so calculating. She was impulsive. If she blew it all on CDs and clothes, that would be more like her, and frighten me less.

"I found some money last week, hidden in her underwear drawer," I said.

"How much?" he asked.

"Two thousand dollars."

"Jeeze," Dan said. "That sounds like a getaway stash."

"She's only fifteen," I murmured, and realized as I said it how often I used that excuse to explain away anything that upset us. "She's only two," I'd say, or "She's only twelve." Would I be telling him "She's only fifty-five," when Dan and I were both old and gray?

Dan's face looked sunken in, disappointment aging him. "I hope to God she isn't stealing from anybody besides us. She could get arrested."

I raised my hands: who knows? I spent a moment with the mystery of it all. What is this thing we call parenthood? You give birth to a helpless little baby girl, you teach her to walk, and the first thing she wants to do is run away from you. And what do you ever really know about her? Nothing. Nada. Zip.

"Do you want to confront her about it?" I asked.

"No. Do you?"

"No." I sighed. "She's been through a lot, Dan."

He smiled. "She's been through us."

He didn't have to explain; our divorce wars had lasted for three years, and the final decree had coincided with Amy's arrival in puberty. We were loud and angry during the dissolution of our marriage, our fights often spilled through the night and into the morning, and her eyes had looked permanently bruised from lack of sleep. Would she ever get over the changes that had engulfed us? Dan and I had come through the other side, so maybe it was still possible for Amy. Except for Dan's suspicions of every man who looked at me, like Noah, I had no real complaints about him anymore.

"What do you know about Noah?" he asked, as if reading my thoughts.

"Not much. Ryan was the one who hired him. You should ask him. Or talk to Noah yourself."

"I'll do that," he said.

We were close to the waterfall by now, and slowed our pace to let the others catch up with us. Noah and the medical examiner were chatting in low tones, while Farnsworth was busy jotting things down on a clipboard.

Farnsworth walked up to us, giving me another chance to see what a nasty-looking fellow he was, with a sullen face going to jowls and little beady eyes. "What time did you find the body?" he asked.

I rubbed my arms, trying to warm up; it was cold under the trees. "Just before seven this morning. It was still dark."

"Any sign of violence?"

"Yes," I said. "It looked like somebody stuck a shotgun against his belly and pulled the trigger."

"Do you own a gun, Brett?" Farnsworth asked. His expression was sly, and I knew he wanted to make me squirm.

Dan's mouth tightened. "She's not the one we're after, Jim."

Farnsworth shrugged, his eyes wide with innocence. "It's a fair question, Dan. Or do you think she should get a lawyer first?"

The question ticked off an inner alarm, but I blurted out the first response that came to me. "Of course I have a gun. No one would try to run a farm without one."

Dan spoke, ignoring Farnsworth. "Did you hear any gunshots in the past few days?"

I nodded. "Half the hunters in Tompkins County have been sneaking up here to poach deer. We're lucky none of us have been shot."

"Do you hunt?" Farnsworth asked.

"I hunt," Noah said. He appeared behind Farnsworth, quiet as a shadow. "I went on a hunting trip last week."

"How long were you gone?" Dan asked.

"Tuesday, Wednesday, Thursday."

"Anybody go with you?" Dan asked.

"No."

Dan nudged Farnsworth, who dutifully wrote down Noah's response. "Did you recognize the deceased?" Farnsworth asked me.

"No," I said.

"Did you touch the body?"

"No."

"Did you see any strangers hanging around the property over the past few weeks?"

"No."

38

"You have any theories about what happened to the guy? Any ideas about how he got killed?"

I tried to think back, to picture the dead man. "There was a bruise on his right temple, his hands were scraped, and his body seemed to have been dumped by someone in a hurry. But I didn't make a thorough physical examination."

"You're a doctor, right? How long would you say he's been dead?"

"Between three or four days to a week, maybe. But that's just a guess."

We walked past the oak tree, and after another few hundred yards the body appeared before us, a dark heap in the middle of the trail. "That's it," I said, pointing.

I covered my nose with one hand, cautious of the smell and dreading the sight of those empty eyes. I hung back while the men surged forward, stepping carefully, studying the ground surrounding the body. They crouched over the corpse to take photographs and probe it with latex-covered hands.

"No ID," one of them said.

"You know this guy?" Farnsworth asked Noah.

"No," he said. I watched Noah carefully for a reaction, a stiffening of muscles, a movement of the head, a flicker behind the eyelids. But there was none. He studied the face, the wide open eyes with clinical interest.

"That lesion on his cheek looks like KS," I said.

"What's that?" Farnsworth asked.

"Kaposi's sarcoma. A symptom of AIDS."

"Shit. A faggot," Farnsworth muttered. "I'm putting on another pair of gloves."

What a prince, I thought, and glared at him as he came back toward me, his eyes on the ground. "If you could stay off the trail, we might find out where these tracks come from," he said. "Looks like a horse came through. Do you ever ride down here?"

"Sometimes," I said.

Dan came over to us, his face grim. "You need to photograph those hoofprints."

Farnsworth gave him a cool stare. "I know how to do my job."

"Then do it," Dan said, and stalked off.

Farnsworth turned back to me. "When was the last time you came down here? Before this morning, I mean."

I struggled to remember. "A week, at least."

"That's good. It narrows the field a little. This cold air can make it tough to identify the time of death."

Dan tweezed something from the dead man's shirt and stuck it in a clear plastic bag, then came back to us and held up the bag so Farnsworth could see the straw-colored threads of hemp inside.

"Looks like somebody tied a rope under his armpits and dragged him down here behind a horse."

Farnsworth's pen scribbled briskly. "So the guy was probably shot somewhere else, then brought here."

When I studied the path I saw nothing at first, but Dan pointed to traces of flattened grass and grooves in the dirt that extended from the body. Now I saw the black drops and spatters of dried blood that were only slightly darker than the shale that formed the bed of the trail. I looked at the ground near my feet and saw hoofprints scratched by the same lines, going back up the hill toward the house.

Oh no, I thought. Not that way.

"We're going to follow these tracks and see where they lead," Farnsworth called to the medical examiner and his assistants. Dan and Farnsworth broke off from the group and Noah and I followed them back along the trail, leaving the others to their work with the body.

Noah matched my stride and came alongside me, and I felt a fresh awareness of his physical presence, his height as he looked down at me. "You don't know the dead man?" he asked.

"No. He looks . . ." Familiar, I was going to say, but stopped.

Noah was silent for a moment. "He must have been rich," he said. "Manicure, designer jacket, gold belt buckle; new boots, too, custom-made. Not cheap."

"I didn't notice," I admitted. The eyes and the wound in his belly had blocked out almost everything else.

I looked at Noah, curious that he'd seen so much, and immediately saw why Dan was so jealous of him. What was it about his face? The eyes—they were a vivid, startling blue. I was drawn to his face, the sense of calm around his mouth. His body was lean but I felt its weight, as if it were anchored to the earth.

He spoke slowly, thinking out loud. "Whoever he was, he had money. He wasn't a drifter. Somebody will be looking for him."

"I hope they are," I said. "The sooner they find out who he is, the easier it will be to find who did this to him."

Noah gave me an odd look, as if he could already see a future that would be more complicated than I imagined. "Sure," he said. "They'll figure it out."

Farnsworth spoke to us sharply to keep to the side of the trail, away from the murderer's track. The men searched for blood in the broken grass, commented on scars in the dirt where a buckle or boot heel had been dragged, and we followed the spatters of blood back the way we'd come, nearer and nearer to the house.

"You think your brother might have known this guy?" Noah asked.

"I don't know," I said, and felt my back grow cool and damp. This has nothing to do with us, I promised myself. "Ryan's at home. They'll probably show him the body when they carry it out."

We came out of the woods to the meadow of uncut hay on the south side of the house. The wind was sharp as a knife and the day had turned dark even out in the open field, away from the shadow of the woods. Purple clouds shouldered their way over the hills to the east and a few thin flakes of snow fluttered down. I shivered in my coat and dug my fingers deeper into my pockets.

The faint trail of blood went straight uphill, past the house, and then it was lost in the trampled yard in front of the barn.

"Do you lock your barn?" Farnsworth asked.

"No," I said. We had always believed the five dogs would scare off any prowler, but I didn't mention that to Farnsworth. I didn't want to say anything that would incriminate any one of us. Why hadn't we heard the dogs barking? It was possible someone had come here with a dead body when none of us was here, but the killer would have had to watch the whole family to figure out when it was safe to trespass. I felt sick at the thought of someone watching us.

The men filed into the barn, and the smell of the horses gave me a thread of comfort. We had nine horses, some orphaned by owners who couldn't pay their feed or medical bills and some that were permanent boarders. The concrete floor was cushioned in wood shavings, and the air was thick with the scent of pine and manure.

Farnsworth hung back near the door when he saw the draft horses, which were the size of elephants. His reaction pleased me.

"Are those things tied up?" he asked Noah.

"They can't get out of their stalls."

Farnsworth walked up and down the length of the barn, kicking aside the shavings to search the floor. Noah nudged me and nodded toward a length of rope looped around a nail in the wall near the door frame. The rope was smeared with dark brown patches, a discoloration that I'd ignored all week, but now I realized that those brown patches had to be blood.

Farnsworth looked up and caught us gazing at the rope, and his face brightened.

"Hello, hello," he said, and pulled on another pair of latex gloves to pluck the rope from the wall. "Take a look at this, Dan. Somebody's awfully neat about putting away his tools."

"That could be animal blood," I said quickly. "We use that rope for breech births, slaughtering, gelding. Farms see a lot of blood." This was all true, but we both knew I was grasping at straws.

Farnsworth grinned at me, pleased I was defensive. Dan nodded, reluctance visible on his face, and Farnsworth took out a large plastic bag and shoved the rope inside.

"There's some more blood over here," Farnsworth said. He was so impressed with himself I wanted to stick a pin in him and watch him blow around the barn. I could feel Noah tense at my side as we walked over to view the stain he'd exposed below the shavings, in the center of the aisle. The sight of the dark smudge on the concrete filled me with a mist of fear, and I resisted the thought of the murderer who had pulled the trigger of the shotgun, so close to the horses, so close to the house.

"Nasty," Farnsworth said, as if it were praise. He

sank to his knees to scrape a sample of the bloodstain into another bag.

When he was finished he stood up. "Let's go see the house."

"We don't need to do that," Dan said.

"Come on, Dan! We got proximity. We got probable cause."

"You got nothing. Anybody could have come in here. It's a hundred yards from the house."

"Okay, okay. How about a cup of coffee, then, while we wait for the guys to roll out the body?"

"It's all right, Dan," I said. "Gran will want to talk to you."

"You behave yourself in there," Dan said to Farnsworth.

The detective held up both palms in a gesture of innocence, a big smile on his face that showed his dark teeth.

The air outside held a clean smell, and snow was falling out of the lowering clouds in flakes so large they looked like white rags. I was glad for snow, glad it would cover the blood on the trail.

Farnsworth caught up to me and spoke in a low tone. "I'd say our chances of catching this guy are pretty good, if you can fill me in on the people who have access to this place. It must be somebody who knows the layout of your farm, knows your barn, your horses. The only weird thing is why they wanted to drag the body way out there in the woods. The body's not even hidden. You take that walk all the time, am I right?"

"At least once a week."

"So whoever it is shoots the guy, borrows a horse, drags the body a mile down the trail, then leaves it where you're going to find it anyway. Fifteen yards to the right or the left of the path and chances are you'd never have seen it."

It was true. The leaves could have hidden the corpse without difficulty for months, and the rubble of fallen branches and bracken could have buried the body entirely within a few years. Why did the killer leave the corpse in the middle of a well-used trail? What purpose would that serve?

Farnsworth, Dan, and Noah crowded into the house after me, their heavy boots shaking the furniture. Gran and Ryan met us in the living room, both of them dressed rather formally, as if for a funeral. Gran wore a quilted black silk jacket over a high-necked white blouse and a long black skirt, with dark stockings and heels. Ryan wore a charcoal tweed blazer over a black turtleneck and black trousers. His posture was erect and anxious, and the smile he offered never reached his eyes.

"Would any of you gentlemen care for coffee?" Gran said. "It's already made, fresh and hot."

"I'll get it, Emily," Dan said. "Don't you trouble yourself."

As soon as Dan left the room Farnsworth strolled over to the gun cabinet in the corner of the room. My Remington was propped against the wall. He picked it up and sniffed the barrel.

"I'm afraid I'll have to ask you for the key to this

thing," Farnsworth said, eyeing the locked glass door. There was an immediate, anxious silence in the room, and my palms began to sweat. Gran's face was pale as if she'd been slapped. Ryan took the key from the hook by the door and handed it to him.

Farnsworth unlocked the glass door and took the guns from their slots.

Dan came into the room with a mug of coffee in each hand. "What are you doing?" he asked.

"We need to run some tests," Farnsworth said.

As he picked out our grandfather's twenty-gauge double-barrel Parker with the walnut stock, Dan set the mugs on the coffee table, walked over to him, and pulled the gun from his grip.

"That's a collector's item, Jim. Leave it."

"We have to check out the guns, Dan. If the victim was shot in their barn and the murderer borrowed one of their horses, he could have borrowed a gun. You know that."

"The murderer did not come in this house," Dan said, as if vehemence could make it a certainty.

"Then we'll find that out for ourselves," Farnsworth said.

"Get a court order first."

I fought down a rising panic. I didn't know if Dan was right to insist or if he was making things worse.

"You want trouble, asshole?" Farnsworth said. "If I have to get a search warrant I swear I'll turn this place upside down. We'll shred the goddamned beds if we feel like it."

"You touch my family and you're going to see me

in your rearview mirror every day of the week." The barrel of the gun was clutched in Dan's fist, and the sight of his angry face so close to a trigger made me twitch with nerves.

"Knock it off, both of you," Noah growled. Dan whirled around to face Noah, his face a picture of menace, while Farnsworth shot Dan a look of contempt and stalked off to the far corner of the room.

"Let's get it over with, Dan," Farnsworth said. "I'm doing this to protect your family. They want to cooperate. Don't make it worse."

Ryan and I exchanged a look. I knew he was having difficulty breathing, just as I was.

"Get out of here," Dan said.

Farnsworth held his gaze for a long moment, then shook his head sorrowfully. "We'll be back, Dan. We have to do this."

"You're wrong," Dan said. "You don't."

Farnsworth left the room and slammed the front door behind him.

"Philistine," Gran hissed under her breath. "I will never allow that—that hoodlum—in this house. Never."

"I'm sorry about that, Emily," Dan said. He went to the kitchen, and I could hear him dump the coffee into the sink. When he returned I could see his face was still flushed from the confrontation. He gave my grandmother a tight smile of apology, then opened the front door and gestured with his chin to Ryan. "You want to take a look at him? You might know him. The boys will be bringing him out soon."

Ryan, Noah, Gran, and I followed him out and watched from the porch when the medical investigator and his men trudged out of the woods, carrying the stretcher between them. Puffs of vapor came from the mouths of the bearers. The body was bagged in black plastic and its dark shape was dusted with snow. The clouds were so low they seemed to sit on my shoulder, and the falling snow made everything quiet. Even the dogs were hushed by the weather.

"Do you want to look at him, Gran?" I asked.

"Lord," she said. Her voice was weary. "Do you think I should?"

"You don't have to," Noah said. "It's not pretty."

Ryan and Farnsworth walked out to meet the men with the body. When they laid the corpse on the ground and unzipped the top of the bag Ryan bowed his head to study the face. I saw him recoil at the sight of those blue open eyes and back away a pace or two. He shook his head. The men looked like crows in their dark clothes, bent over the stretcher in the dusk of the rising storm.

"This is just beginning, isn't it?" I whispered to Noah. "They'll be back."

"They'll be back," Noah said.

Shortly after the men took away the body, Ryan was called out to take a look at a pregnant mare on a neighboring farm, and Gran retired to her room with a headache. It was much later in the afternoon when Amy rode into the yard on Caledonia.

I was furious when I saw her, and light-headed

with relief. She'd been gone for hours, and no one had known where she went. I'd been sick with anxiety. There was a killer out there somewhere and she'd disappeared without a word to anyone while Dan and I were in the woods with the police.

Snow coated my daughter's shoulders and whitened her hair. The day was dark; the temperature had plummeted, and snow had been falling steadily all afternoon. She wore no gloves or hat, and her red sweater was too thin for the weather.

I walked out to meet her. "Where have you been? I've been worried to death about you."

Amy didn't answer, and her silence made me feel that familiar thud of clumsiness, as if my own daughter were a stranger I was failing to charm.

"Why didn't you tell anybody you were going?" I asked, more gently this time.

Amy swung herself off the saddle and dropped beside me. She blinked against the kiss of snow on her face. Woolly flakes were caught in her hair, white on russet, and she was so beautiful in the twilight of the storm it made my throat ache.

"Amy," I said, and caught her by the arm. I kept my voice even, reasonable. "Please. Tell me where you went."

"I took the loop around the Arsenaults' place, then came up the Depot road." She disengaged my hand.

I took a deep breath and tried to relax. She was fine, after all. The danger was over.

She cast a sidelong, stealthy glance in my direction. "I have to tell you something, Mom."

I gave her a sharp look. "What's wrong?"

Amy averted her gaze from mine and brushed the flakes from her face. "I can't go back to school on Monday."

I stared. "Why not?"

"I've been suspended. For two weeks."

My heart jumped and my face felt hot, as if I were the one who had been punished. "What have you done?"

"Nothing! Candy Whittaker put something in my locker, then accused me of stealing it. They found it there and they believe her instead of me."

My heart sank. "They can't do that. I'll talk to them."

"Don't. Leave it alone. I'll keep up with my school-work. If you could tell Gran—"

"Amy, please, let me—"

"No," Amy snapped at me, her voice urgent. "I don't want you to do anything about it. Let me work it out."

"Why do you think this girl set you up?" I asked, careful to keep judgment out of my tone.

Amy shrugged. "She's jealous. I make better grades. I'm more popular."

I must have looked incredulous, because Amy said, "Never mind. I don't need you to believe me." She flashed a smile, cheerful and false. "Is Dad gone?"

"He left about an hour ago. Ryan's out too." I examined my daughter. There it was once again, that look of Dan's: the features settling into a pleasant mask beneath which I could read absolutely nothing.

He'd begun using that smile when he was sneaking out on a date and I was nursing Amy. Lying had been a staple of his conversation, a kind of default program of fakery that he called up whenever it suited him. When had Amy learned to lie? I wondered. And why had she learned it? I ached to ask my daughter about the money in her dresser drawer, the well-worn bills, too many to have an innocent explanation. But I knew it would take delicacy and patience to extract the truth from her, and this was not the time.

"You'd better dry off Caledonia and brush her down," I said.

"Can't Noah do it?"

"No, he's got enough to do. Go on."

Amy clicked her tongue at Caledonia and led the animal to the barn. In just a few hours the landscape of the farm had changed completely, from naked stubble to a lush meringue of white. The muddy ruts in the yard were smoothly covered and the house looked like gingerbread, iced in white frosting. The pond had frozen over, and snow covered the ice. I wanted it to go on snowing, and since the clouds overhead were heavy and dark, it looked like I would get my wish. Maybe by February my heart would harden to the beauty, and I would only calculate the hours needed to clear it away, but for now the snow meant no police would risk getting stuck in our driveway.

The pole barn beside the horse barn sheltered the only patch of bare ground, and the horse trailer, hay wagon, gas pump, and tractor were tucked underneath its tin roof. Hay was stacked to the ceiling in tightly packed rows behind the farm machinery, creating a wall against the wind to keep the drifts out.

I heard a vehicle grumble up the driveway, wheels spinning in the slurry of snow. I brushed flakes away from my eyes and peered at the car, sure it was Farnsworth with his search warrant, and hoped the son of a bitch would get stuck. The road was already covered in three or four inches of snow.

A black Saab purred into the turnaround in front of the house, and the man who climbed out wore a black astrakhan hat and coat. As he drew closer I could see his eyes were so dark they were almost black, ringed by long lashes that gave him an Italian beauty. He took off his hat to reveal a head of glossy curls, and I noticed his salt and pepper mustache was meticulously trimmed. His expression was anxious.

"I'm so sorry to bother you," he said as he approached me. "My name is Vincent DeLuca." He put his hand out for me to shake and I took it. He had a powerful grip, and his nails were freshly manicured.

"What can I do for you?" I asked.

"Edward's been away for three days now and I haven't heard from him, which is terribly unusual, and I was concerned, you know"—here he took a deep breath and I could see he was even more upset than I'd thought at first, as he continued to babble on—"about whether or not things had gone well, or whether or not he was still here, and if not, I thought you might be able to tell me where he went."

Maybe Ryan knows him, I thought, gauging the man's well-groomed looks and the fussy, flustered precision of his speech. I assumed he was gay. I had no idea who he was talking about. "Would you like to come in?" I asked.

"Oh my God," he said, not moving. "I just realized, you must be Brett."

"Yes," I said.

"I can't believe it's you. I knew you when you were just a baby. Is Ryan here?"

"He's out on a call right now."

Vincent searched my eyes. "Have you seen Edward? He was very sick. He wanted to come here before he became too weak."

"I'm afraid I don't know Edward," I said, smiling politely.

"Surely he told you," Vincent said. "Edward is your father."

My smile felt stapled to my face as the words bounced off me. I would not let them enter. "No. I'm sorry, you must have the wrong house."

He extracted a wallet from the inside of his coat, took a photograph from it, and passed it over. The face that smiled up at me from the square of paper was familiar, but for all the wrong reasons. I swayed on my feet as shock rippled through me.

"I think you'd better come in and sit down," I said.

Vincent DeLuca went on talking, and his tone began to slide into an upper register of panic. "I'm sorry to interrupt your day. I was just so worried. Edward promised he'd call when he got here and then I never heard from him. It's been three days. He just isn't the kind of man who wouldn't call."

I let him babble and guided him into the kitchen. The dogs had elected to wait out the storm by the woodstove, and they were sprawled out on the floor, soaking up the warmth of the embers. I stepped gingerly over their bodies to get the water boiling. My mind was still numb, opaque to his words. I was already waiting for this to be over, for him to leave.

Vincent stopped at the threshold and eyed the dogs dubiously.

"Don't worry about them," I said in a bright robot voice. "They're friendly."

He edged around the perimeter of their dozing forms, removed his coat, folded it carefully, and placed it on the seat of a chair at the table, then sat down.

I took a deep breath and busied myself with the teakettle. "There's been an accident, Mr. DeLuca."

"Please, call me Vincent," he said.

I turned to face him. "I'm afraid your Edward is dead."

Vincent was silent. The look on his face reminded me of the time Amy fell off her pony when she was five years old. The air was knocked out of her, and she blinked up at my terrified face for what felt like an hour before she could scream. When it finally came, the scream was a relief.

I waited for Vincent to register the shock, to react. Slowly his face reddened with grief and his eyes filled with tears. I began breathing again, sat on the chair beside him, and took his hand in mine.

"I'm so sorry," I said.

He shook his head. "He was sick. I knew the trip would be too much. I should have expected this."

"It wasn't his illness that killed him. He was shot."

Vincent removed his hand from mine and wiped the tears that had spilled down his cheeks with the back of his palm. "Shot? Who would shoot Edward? Was it an accident?"

Not at that range, I thought. The crater in the dead man's belly was no accident, but I didn't have the heart to tell Vincent the truth. "We don't know. I found the body this morning. They took it away just a few hours before you arrived. Why did Edward come here?"

Vincent looked at me with surprise. "Because he's your father, that's why. He wanted to meet you. He wanted to spend Thanksgiving with you."

"I'm sorry, that's impossible," I said, but I was holding the edge of the table so tightly my knuckles were turning white. It was true my father's name was Edward, but he died when I was a baby. Gran said so. Ryan said so. Everyone knew it. He'd been dead for more than thirty years.

"Brett, Edward is your father. I'm sorry he didn't get a chance to tell you that, but it's true."

I felt queasy, and shook my head. "We never spoke with the dead man, but I don't think he could have been my father. My father died a long time ago."

"No," Vincent said. "He wasn't dead. He lived in Manhattan, with me."

"What do you mean?"

He looked at me. I could see a tension in his eyes, a thread of spite, a willingness to wound me as I had wounded him. "I used to work on this farm, Brett." A ghost of a smile crossed his face. "You wouldn't remember me, of course; you were just a baby. Do you still grow hay?"

I felt a tide of dread, a rising fear of what he might say next. "Yes."

"I was hired to help with the haying, thirty years ago. Your father and I worked twelve-hour days, side by side, all that summer. I was only sixteen then. He was thirty-one."

I heard the words he was saying but I didn't want to hear any more, and my neck stiffened as if I could physically resist his version of my history from entering my ears. My father died with my mother in a car wreck when I was just a baby. Their tombstones were in the family plot next to my great grandparents Matthew and Abigail and my grandfather Clarence, right here on the farm, up in the clearing in the woods with the carpet of myrtle. My heart fluttered like a bird trying to escape a hand tightening around its wings.

Vincent held my gaze. "Your mother was completely devoted to you and Ryan. She was always busy with the two of you, and never imagined how close Edward and I were."

I tried to smile, to say something polite. "You were close to my father," I repeated.

He nodded. "Very close."

My smile felt heavy, a mask that was glued to my face. "Are you trying to tell me my father was a homosexual?"

Vincent looked down at the table and looked back up at me. The silence in the room was electric. "Yes," he whispered.

# Chapter Three

I could not believe what Vincent was telling me. My father fell in love with a boy and left us for him? Worst of all, if what he said was true, my father had been alive until last week. My mind slid out from under the weight of this information, and my smile stretched wider and wider until laughter came out.

"So why didn't he drop by before?" I asked.

Vincent shook his head and lifted his hands, then let them fall. "I wish you could have asked him that." The gesture was conciliatory, but his eyes were cold, appraising me.

I stood up and turned my back to him, ran water in the sink, then shut it off, on and off, over and over. I could not grasp this.

My eye was caught by a slight movement in the doorway and I realized it was Amy's sleeve, whisked out of sight as she pressed her body against the wall to listen to us without being seen.

"Amy," I said, my voice sharp. "Come in here."

Amy drifted into the room and approached our

visitor. "This is my daughter Amy," I said as she extended her hand to him.

"Vincent," he said, and took her hand.

"You lived with my grandfather?" she asked. Her voice was gentle and far more kind than I felt.

He nodded as his eyes blurred with tears that rolled down his face and dampened his mustache. "I'm sorry," he said. "I just can't believe he's gone."

Then he put his face in his hands and collapsed into sobs as we watched helplessly. Amy and I glanced at each other uneasily as grief ripped through Vincent and stripped him of every appearance of dignity or control. It seemed overdone, somehow, as if he were deliberately choosing us as an audience, and I wondered why. Embarrassed, we stared at the snow cascading against the window as we waited for his outburst to subside. At last he took out his handkerchief, blew his nose, and patted his face.

"I'm so sorry," he said. "This is the last thing Edward would have wanted me to do. Thank you for being so patient."

"Would you like some tea?" Amy asked.

Vincent looked at her and sighed. "Yes." Again his eyes slid toward me, slyly gauging my response, watching me.

Amy turned to the cupboard, removed three mugs, and put them on the counter, placed a teabag in each one, then turned on the flame under the kettle.

"I'm sorry," Vincent said. "I know this is an imposition." He wiped his eyes again with his handkerchief, then folded it neatly and put it back in his pocket.

Amy moved smoothly into the chair next to him. I knew she was curious. Her curiosity felt dangerous to me, as if to question Vincent at all would take us all over the edge of an invisible precipice. My senses were alert, my movements deliberate and slow as if the kitchen floor were laced with bottomless pits. I stood by the counter, arms folded tightly against my chest, unwilling to sit, unwilling to relax.

"What did Edward do in Manhattan?" I asked. In this context it felt strange to feel my father's name in my mouth, as if I were playing a dangerous game of make believe.

"He's—he was—an architect. Didn't you know that? I suppose you wouldn't. You would have been proud of him if you'd known his work. He was a world-class designer of private homes. He selected building sites, supervised everything from floor plans to the linens. People who were too busy to create their own homes trusted him with every aesthetic choice you can imagine."

"What do you do?" Amy asked.

Vincent sniffed. "I was your grandfather's assistant." His eyes darted around the walls and for a moment I saw our kitchen as he must be seeing it: the soot behind the stove, the row of tarnished copper pots hanging from a bar above the counter, the dirty braided rug covered in sleeping dogs and dog hair. The walls needed a new coat of paint, and so did the cupboards.

When he spoke again his voice was barely more than a whisper. "Edward and I have—had—a small following in New York. In fact we were supposed to have Thanksgiving dinner with one of our clients." He laughed a small laugh. "But Edward wanted to spend Thanksgiving with you this year. He said it was his last chance."

I poured hot water into the mugs, placed them on the table, and sat cautiously beside Amy. I wanted to probe Vincent's story and find the flaw that would let me escape back into the comforting belief that the corpse I'd found was a stranger, with no connection to any of us. Instinctively I felt that something about Vincent's sudden appearance here was wrong, too coincidental, too contrived.

"Why didn't he tell us he was alive?" I asked.

Vincent coughed delicately behind one hand. I could see his eyes flick over me, that same cold, measuring look. "Your brother knew he was alive," he said.

"That's impossible," I said. When Ryan looked at the dead man there was no recognition in his expression. I saw him shake his head and step back from the body, didn't I?

"They met at least twice a year. Edward gave Ryan quite a bit of money." There was an edge of resentment in Vincent's voice.

"I don't believe you."

"Ask him."

"I will."

"Edward couldn't give up knowing his son. Ryan

was nine years old when Edward left. But you were just a baby, and Edward was convinced you'd be better off if you never saw him again." Vincent's tone was light, and I knew he meant the words to cut me.

Amy gave me an embarrassed look of pity, as if she had just seen somebody spit on me.

"How could he possibly think that?" I asked. My heart felt like an anvil, and I knew that I would turn this scene over and over in my mind for years to come.

Vincent shrugged. "He was devastated by his wife's—your mother's—death, and I'm sure he felt responsible."

"Why would he feel guilty about my mother's death? It was an accident." But my voice trailed off as I realized my mother had supposedly died with my father in that wrecked car, according to Gran's history. The image my grandmother had conjured of my parents had always been cryptic and fragmented, and now the picture began to dissolve completely.

Vincent made a temple of his hands, fingertips pressed together. His voice was quiet, almost smug. "Your mother killed herself. She took sleeping pills, a week after we left."

"My mother did not kill herself." I could feel an invisible shell begin to harden around me, a carapace of denial. Vincent was lying. He had to be.

"She did," Vincent said.

"She died in a car wreck," I insisted.

"There was no wreck. There was a suicide, and families don't like to tell the truth about things they're ashamed of." He paused. "Believe me, I know."

That got through. That one little pinprick of truth pierced all the stories about my parents that I'd ever been told. What Vincent said made sense, an awful, terrible sense, and even though I resisted him and hated him and wanted to strike him as he sat so calmly at our kitchen table telling me all this, I believed him. In all my years of growing up, Gran had never spoken willingly of my parents, and when she did the details tended to vary so much that they seemed more like fictional characters than flesh and blood. They had always seemed a little too good to be true in her telling of their story, too beautiful, too nice, too perfect, too tragic. How it must have tempted her, I thought, to create better parents for us, who were both so conveniently and permanently dead. It was unbearable to think of the lies she told me. And if Ryan knew our father was alive all this time the lies were doubled, unless Vincent was a lunatic.

But Vincent didn't look like a lunatic. When I was interning on the neuro ward at the hospital, I had to diagnose disorders of consciousness, Alzheimer's, delirium, dementia, but Vincent did not seem deluded. In spite of his grief, he appeared lucid and credible. My legs began to shake under the table and I crossed them tightly to stop them from quivering. I couldn't take it in, not all at once. I had to focus on one thing at a time. The dented spoon by my cup.

The hairline crack in the wood of the table. The ticking of the stove as it cooled.

"Is your grandmother still alive?" Vincent asked.

"Yes," Amy said. "She's upstairs."

Vincent raised an eyebrow, but didn't say anything. We drank our tea. I made a conscious effort to relax my legs, which were crossed so tightly my foot was tingling. My elbows were clamped against my sides. I felt rigid, wooden.

"Did you ever wonder why you didn't keep your father's name?" he asked. "Did you ever wonder why she made you take hers instead?"

I was squeezing the handle of my mug so hard I had to consciously loosen my grip before I spoke, fearful the cup would break in my hand. "She became our legal guardian when I was two years old. It always seemed natural to me that we'd share her name."

Vincent raised one eyebrow and stared into his cup, swirled the tea, and sipped it delicately.

The image of the dead man came back to me, as it had every few minutes since I'd found him. The eyes, blue as stone, milky with death. The thinning silvery brown hair, the color Ryan's would be in another twenty or thirty years. The retina of my memory had been etched with the shocked look of the mouth in his gaunt, blanched face, the "oh" of surprise at seeing he would die even sooner than expected. The dead man. I had to stop calling him that. His name was Edward, and he was my father.

"Could you tell me what you know about Edward's death?" Vincent asked.

"No one knew who he was. His wallet was missing," I said. The words felt like stones coming out of my mouth, hard and strange.

"Ryan didn't identify him?"

"No."

"He should have, " Vincent said.

"You'll have to ask him about that," I said. I certainly would. The thought of how many lies Ryan had told me, and the depth of those lies, began to heat the frozen part of me and melt the shock. I was angry.

"When did you find Edward's body?" he asked.

Amy spoke in a small, barely audible voice. "This morning. Mom found him on the trail to Deputron Hollow, near a waterfall about a mile down the mountain."

"Do they have any suspects?"

"Just us," Amy said.

"I suppose you all have alibis," Vincent said thoughtfully.

The anger flared in me, and I welcomed it. I set my mug down hard, splashing the tea on the table.

"Of course you do," he said smoothly.

"What about you?" I asked. "Was Edward insured? Are you the beneficiary? Does his business belong to you now?"

There was a cold flicker in his eyes, and I could see him study me as if I might become an enemy. "I believe Edward had a copy of his will with him," he said.

I felt a shiver, then, a premonition of danger. "There was no identification with the body at all. Why would he be carrying a will?"

"I think Ryan could tell you," he said.

I scraped my chair back, stood up, and put my mug in the sink. "Ryan won't be back for hours." I was unnerved by the man who sat so quietly at our table. My chest was tight. It was hard to breathe in the close air, the dense silence, and I could feel unshed tears boiling up, too near to the surface.

Gran flowed into the kitchen, still dressed in the funeral outfit she'd worn for the police. She put a hand to her throat at the sight of Vincent at the table. "Who is this?" she inquired, ready to smile. Amy shot me an uncertain look.

"I'm Vincent DeLuca," he said, standing.

"Vincent DeLuca," she repeated without a trace of recognition.

"I worked here, thirty years ago," he said.

"Oh my God," she said slowly.

"Vincent knows the dead man," I said, nearly choking on the words. "He was my father."

Gran sat down heavily. "No," she breathed.

Amy's eyes darted between the two of us. There was something hungry in her gaze, and I realized she was eager to see us fight. We had presented a united front of authority to her for a long time, and if that wall cracked, it would be easier for her to slip through and do whatever she wanted.

I realized all this in the space of half a second, but I couldn't rein in my anger. "You've lied to me for a long time," I said to my grandmother, my voice trembling.

"Oh, Brett," she said, and reached for me.

"No," I said. "Don't touch me, Emily."

She winced at the sound of her name. "I'm your gran," she whispered.

"You can go to hell."

She drew herself up then, caught my shoulder, and pulled me close. Her grip was like iron. "We will discuss this later," she said in a low voice. "Take a few minutes to compose yourself. Go to the barn and check the horses. I don't care what you think of me right now, but I will not have this man listen to us argue."

I pushed her roughly away from the doorway, grabbed my coat from the hook by the door, and left without saying a word, my throat aching. It was dark outside, the clouds low and heavy. The snow blew into my face, and I narrowed my eyes and leaned into the wind. Ryan's truck was plowing up the drive, wheels spinning, leaving two ribbons of tracks in the snow. Let him deal with Vincent, I thought. Let him handle all of it.

It was only four in the afternoon but it looked like night, and another three inches of snow had fallen in the hour since Vincent had arrived. It was still coming down, as if God's own feather bed had exploded above the farm. If it went on like this we'd be snowed in for days. Good, I thought. Let it keep

Farnsworth and Dan and the rest of the world far, far away. I needed time to absorb all this.

I was used to believing that my father was dead, but I wasn't used to seeing that blanched face, those bruised hands, the hole in his belly I could put my fist through, and knowing that was my father. My father. A father who had left me for a pretty, young boy. A father who hadn't tried to see me once in thirty years. I felt a hot, searing grief that was mixed with shame. Why? Why did he leave me? Why visit Ryan and not me? Was I too ugly? Too annoying? Too what? Why would a father leave his only daughter? I could feel hot tears crowding my eyes, and a brick on my heart.

I tramped across the yard to the barn, the place I used to be able to go when I wanted no more people, no more talk, no one around to witness me. But when I opened the door I could see Noah was there, and my hands tightened into fists, as if I were the one who'd been interrupted.

Noah was lit by a circle of lamplight in Caledonia's stall, and after nodding a wordless hello he turned his back to me and continued to brush out the horse's coat. Caledonia was a massive draft horse, eighteen hands high, the color of mahogany, and the horse stood patient as a mountain in front of him, one hind hoof tipped up in drowsy pleasure at being stroked, eyelids half closed.

"You feeling better?" Noah asked me.

I glared at him wordlessly, amazed he could ask such a stupid question.

"I guess not," he said as he came around to brush out Caledonia's tail. I hovered near the stall, my body leaning toward the door, ready to leave. But I couldn't go back to the house, not while Vincent was there, and there was nowhere else to go in the storm. I watched Noah tease out the dried mud from the ends of the longest hairs of the horse's tail with the dandy brush.

He shot me a speculative look. "You want to sit down?"

I took a deep, ragged breath. Calm down, I warned myself. Focus on something else. The snow ticked against the glass in the door, and I gauged the change in temperature from the sound, warming air compressing the flakes from white rags to sugar. The granules sifted against the window as the wind swung from north to west. I looked out at the house and saw lights gleaming at every window in the middle of the afternoon. My footprints were already gone, filled in and snowed over in less than three minutes. Ryan's truck was parked next to Vincent's Saab.

I turned back to Noah and struggled to make my voice quiet and normal. "Amy was supposed to brush out Caledonia."

"I don't mind," he said.

"Let me help you." Moving mechanically, I walked over to the tack wall, plucked a body brush from the pegboard, and came to Caledonia's stall to start on the mane. Caledonia roused herself to check my pockets for carrots, then went back to her day-dreaming.

Noah divided the matted hair of Caledonia's tail into sections, and out of the corner of my eye I watched him comb the mud out of one section completely before moving on to the next. His hands were slow and patient. He didn't pull too hard; he took his time. The shaded bulb cast an orange light on his fingers as they flickered through the coarse wealth of Caledonia's tail, and I took a deep breath as I watched his movements. Order could be restored to any mess at all, I told myself, if you just take it section by section, strand by strand.

We worked together in silence for several minutes before I ventured to speak again. "You took down the crime scene tape."

Noah kept his eyes on the comb as it traveled the length of the tail without snagging. "The horses needed to be mucked out."

"I hope the police see it that way."

"We can't ignore the animals until the cops come back."

He was right, of course. But it made me uneasy to wonder how they might view his actions. The dark bloodstain in the center of the aisle had been hosed away, and there were fresh pine shavings on the floor. Outside the snow was already so deep it was obvious the police wouldn't be able to get up the driveway in a squad car for days, not until this mess melted and the road dried.

"Any news from the police yet?" Noah asked.

I shook my head.

"You have any idea who the victim was?" he asked.

"Yes." My admission was barely audible.

"Ah," he said. There was no surprise in his tone, and I wondered why it was absent.

"I saw the guy who got shot, last Tuesday, right before I went hunting," Noah said.

I stared at him, aghast. "Why didn't you say anything to Farnsworth?"

Noah shrugged, and when he spoke again his voice was gentle, conciliatory. "Farnsworth asked me if I knew him. I didn't know who he was. I was walking up to the barn last Tuesday to check on the horses one last time before I went hunting, and I heard someone inside arguing with your brother. When I came in they stopped talking. The man who was shot was in here with Ryan."

My face must have reflected my alarm, because Noah put his brush down and eyed me with concern. "I'm not going to say a word to anybody, if that's what you're worried about. I don't want to get your brother in any trouble."

I struggled to grasp the possibility that Ryan had argued with our father, probably on the day he was killed. I could feel my mind tighten and turn away from this revelation. Ryan couldn't be mixed up in a murder. It was beyond my imagining.

I went on brushing Caledonia's mane, but my breathing felt jerky and shallow. "What were they arguing about?" I asked.

"Something about money, Ryan's gambling." He looked up and saw my face. "Hell, I'm sorry. I should have kept my mouth shut." He stepped around Caledonia, touched my arm, and left his hand there. "I just thought you'd want to know."

"It's not your fault," I said. His hand felt warm on my arm, and the reservoir of grief that had been trapped inside me ever since I found the body came close to spilling over. It was almost more than I could bear, to be touched.

I swallowed, tried to make my voice nonchalant. "How was the hunting?"

He removed his hand. I could feel him looking at me, assessing me. "No luck."

"I saw a nice size buck down by the little pond the other day. I was going after him this morning," I said.

"Who belongs to the Saab?" he asked.

"Somebody who knows the dead man."

"So you know who he is? The dead man?" he asked.

"According to the guy who owns the Saab, the dead man is my father. Edward Mercy."

"But you didn't recognize him."

"No. I never knew him. He left when I was a baby."

"What brought him back here?"

"I don't know. Ryan might know," I added in a bitter tone. I put my arms around Caledonia's neck and buried my face in her mane. The brush fell out of my hand to the floor.

"Hey, now," Noah said. I could feel him behind me, his arms encircling me. I turned and let him hold me. I cried hard enough to make a wet spot on his shirt, and then I stopped, embarrassed. He pulled away to check my face, lifted a lock of my hair, and smoothed it back from my brow. He's just being kind, I thought, but I was flustered by his touch. A wave of heat flooded my neck, my breasts. It had been three years since a man had touched me with this much tenderness.

"They're going to suspect us," I said, wiping my face on my sleeve and pulling away from him. "Who else have they got?"

"What about the Saab? What's his name?"

"Vincent DeLuca."

"What's his connection to the dead man?" Noah asked.

"They were lovers."

"Holy crap," he said.

I sat on a bale of hay in the corner of the stall. I wanted to forget the father I'd found with his skull bashed in and the hole through his middle, the same father who had abandoned me thirty years ago. I knew the image would haunt me for the rest of my life, but it was excruciating to go on thinking about it now. "Can we talk about something else?"

"Of course. Sorry," he said, as if it were his fault I wanted to change the subject. "What would you like to talk about?"

I remembered telling Dan that I didn't know anything about Noah. Who was he, really? Why had he appeared so conveniently three weeks ago, and why was he willing to take on the job of tending horses for the pittance Ryan paid him, when he was clearly capable of earning a great deal more almost anywhere else? Could he have known my father? Could he have anything to do with the murder? It was time to stop living in the cocoon of my ignorance. I wanted to know everything. I didn't want any more surprises.

"Tell me about yourself, Noah."

"There's not much to tell."

"I can't believe that."

"It's true."

"It can't be. You're not from here, are you?"

"No."

"Tell me about that."

"I'm from Taos, New Mexico." He sat down next to me on the edge of the bale, too close, much too close, and I stood and backed away toward Caledonia, then smoothed her neck with my hands. It steadied me, to feel her bulk.

"What's it like out there?" I asked.

Noah leaned back against the bars of the stall. Wherever he was, he looked natural, like something growing out of the earth. "It's beautiful," he said. "Big mountains, the Sangre de Cristos. Lot of sagebrush out on the mesa, but the town is tucked up against the mountains. It's high desert, about seven thousand feet above sea level."

"What did you do there?"

He scratched his head, as if he were considering.

"I was born, grew up. Went to school. Worked on my dad's ranch."

"How old are you?"

He smiled. "Thirty-two last August."

"That's my age," I said, surprised. "What day in August?"

"The twenty-seventh."

"That's my birthday, too," I said.

Our eyes met and we smiled. A small silence sprang up between us as I searched for something else to ask him. Caledonia let out a long sigh, as if she were bored. "You have family there?"

"Not any more. My dad died last year," he said.

"What was he like?" I asked.

Noah's face was still, and when he spoke his voice was so soft I had to lean toward him, to hear him. I rested my back against the wall, halfway between him and Caledonia.

"He was hard as granite," he said. "Fair. Smart. Never cried, never touched me, never gave an inch in an argument. He was bullheaded, but he loved to learn. He always smiled this secret smile of satisfaction when I could prove him wrong by showing him a passage from a book. He revered books. He used to read Chaucer in the original, kept *The Riverside Chaucer* by his bed and read it over and over."

I gave him a sharp look. The same book was by my bed right now, where it had been for the past six weeks. Did he know that? Had he been in my room? I didn't believe in coincidence, and this one seemed too good to be true, like so many other things about him.

"What about your mom?" I asked.

"She split when I was a baby. Had too much Gypsy in her, my dad used to say, but I think it was the sixties that did it. She left us to go to San Francisco and live on a commune. She's probably dead too, for all I know."

I leaned back and propped one leg against the wall. "Why are you working here, Noah?"

He looked down at his hands. "I had to leave New Mexico after my dad died. It seemed like his ghost was everywhere on the ranch, and I just couldn't get used to being alone there. So I sold the place and decided to travel some. In fact I was headed for Nova Scotia when I stopped for coffee and saw your brother's ad in the *Ithaca Journal*. It sounded too good to pass up: work for the winter, nothing too strenuous, a cabin of my own, and horses. I was homesick for horses, and God knows, I was sick to death of driving."

I pondered this a moment and let the silence stretch between us. What he said sounded plausible. His voice was as natural as the quiet of his body, and I noticed again how relaxed he looked, leaning back, elbows propped up on the bar of the stall behind him, legs stretched out in front. It was attractive, that ease.

"How about you?" he asked.

"What do you mean?"

"I heard you quit medicine. Is that true?"

I thought about it. Had I quit being a doctor? The thought of going back to the hospital created a pit inside me, a deep, sucking exhaustion. But being a doctor was right up there with being a Supreme Court justice in most people's minds, and quitting medicine was unthinkable. It simply wasn't done.

"What does it matter?" I asked. "One doctor more or less isn't going to end the famine in Africa. One doctor more or less can't end a civil war, or overthrow the government that keeps food from being distributed." Just talking about it made me tired, and I sank down on the bale next to his.

"What do you want?" he asked.

The question tickled the edge of half-forgotten dreams: my own flower garden. A rocking chair. Season tickets to a good orchestra. Tango lessons, a grand piano, a night in Vienna.

"Plenty," I admitted.

"But you don't want to be a doctor anymore?"

I shrugged. "Maybe not."

"Give up all that education?"

"The education would always be with me."

He leaned forward then and looked at me, his hands clasped loosely in front of him, and I saw his eyes were a soft, rich blue with a starburst of paler blue around the pupils.

"Are you happy?" he asked.

I felt as though I'd waited a whole lifetime for Dan to ask me certain questions about myself, and I had longed to hear these questions, so I could have the experience of showing him that private and serious part of myself that was hidden from the rest of the world. I had wanted him to know me. The questions never came, not from Dan. But they were here now, spoken in a perfectly clear, quiet, straightforward way by Noah. I looked away, a little flustered to see his face so close to mine, his expression serious, intent, those eyes focused on me like two blue mirrors.

"When I came back from Africa I was so sick I couldn't move without help," I said slowly. "Not just body sick. Soul sick, from living so close to so much death. I'm not sure I've recovered from that part of being there. Death was everywhere, not just in the corpses, but in everyone. They were waiting to die, most of them, from starvation or dysentery or malaria or meningitis."

"That's a nightmare you'd have to live with," he said. "You couldn't fix it."

"You can't see all that suffering and dying without feeling at some point that the only responsible thing, the only honorable thing, is to join them. It's not conscious, but your fatigue gets deeper and your immune system begins to weaken and you slide into the stupor you've seen on so many faces. Especially children's faces. The largest tribe there is the Dinka tribe. They're beautiful. Tall. Half their bodies are in their legs. Three out of four of their children don't reach the age of fifteen."

My voice sank so low I could barely hear myself. I had never talked to anyone in the States, not even Ryan or Gran, about what I'd seen in the camp. They didn't want to hear it. When I first returned I felt like a carrier of some dreaded virus that could be spread through conversation. And it was hard to talk about it with most people, although now there was a peculiar, painful relief in describing it to Noah. I could feel a hard lump rising in my throat, grief for the death I'd seen then and again this morning. My voice felt tight.

Noah's eyes never left my face, so I went on talking. "I began to feel like a ghost. The doctors and nurses are like zombies, because we can't afford to feel what we're looking at. Finally I got too sick to work and came home. When Gran picked me up at the airport I weighed a hundred pounds."

"You must have gained some back," Noah said. "You look great."

I felt a flush warm my cheeks and cast a quick glance at him. "It's good to be home."

"You still haven't answered my question," he said.

I lowered my eyes, smoothed the fabric of my jeans over my knees, and considered it. Was I happy? No. Not today, anyway. I could not be happy while my father's body was being stripped and butchered in a morgue downtown.

"My ideas about happiness have changed," I said abruptly. "Happiness seems like a luxury. It seems irrelevant."

A bitter resignation flooded through me as I thought about how much the past was beyond fixing. My father was dead. Whoever he was, and no matter when he died, I couldn't spend the rest of my life blaming my grandmother for her good intentions.

Was it really so bad for her to protect me from a father who didn't want to know me? I wasn't sure. I wasn't sure of anything anymore.

I stood up. "They'll be wondering what happened to me. I'd better get back."

"Come back sometime when you can stay longer," Noah said.

I glanced at him, surprised. There was a peculiar look on his face, and I realized he was lonely.

Impulsively I reached out and touched his cheek. He smiled, took my hand in his and held it softly for a moment, then released it. The intimacy of the gesture pierced me. He was gentle, a strong and gentle man, and I was so grateful for his gentleness it shocked me and made me realize how starved I'd been for the simple pleasure of being touched by a man. "Thank you," I said, suddenly confused, and turned away to walk out the door.

When I stepped outside my breath caught at the transformation in the landscape. The blizzard filled the air with a fury of snow, blasted by a high wind that nearly knocked me over as I leaned into it. My mouth filled with snow when I opened it to breathe. Through the slitted cracks of my eyelids I could see the snow humped over the vehicles. The farm was bathed in the spectral light of snow falling in darkness, cars and tractors marooned in drifts that revealed only black slits of windshields. There was a single lamp on a pole by the barn, and the flakes in the air spun in nearly opaque, windswept spirals in the circle of light it created. The tallest evergreen along the driveway had snapped in half from the weight of the snow, and the fractured treetop hung down, clinging to the splintered trunk. The pond looked solid as a parking lot.

The Saab was still there; Vincent hadn't left.

A prickle of fear skittered down my back as I considered the possibility that we might be snowed in with a murderer. I shoved my way through the drifts, ascended the steps to the porch, pushed the kitchen door open, and slammed it behind me.

"He can't stay here," Gran snapped at Ryan.

This was the first thing I heard as I stepped back into the kitchen. I crossed the room, picked up the hatchet, and began to split kindling on the brick hearth under the woodstove. Each stick of pine struck by the blade fell into clean white halves. It was satisfying to make noise, to hit something.

Gran watched me warily, then spoke again in a softer but no less determined tone. "We can't let him stay, Ryan."

Ryan lifted his chin to indicate the snow rushing against the windowpanes. "It's over a foot deep out there, Gran. How's he going to go anywhere? You want to give him a pair of snowshoes and tell him to get lost?"

I piled the kindling in my arms and carried it to the woodstove, then dumped it with a satisfyingly rude clatter on the hearth. I was still too upset to talk to them, but I wanted them to know I was angry.

They were both standing in front of the open refrigerator, and after glancing at me to weigh my mood, they turned back to the problem of dinner. Ryan lifted the foil covering the turkey carcass from yesterday's Thanksgiving dinner. I knew there wasn't enough meat left on it to feed us all. He closed the door and sighed.

"Sweet mother of Christ." Gran sighed. "We'll have to feed him dinner, won't we? How are we ever going to get rid of him?" She stared through the hallway to the rectangle of firelight in the living room. Vincent's head was hidden by the back of his chair, but I could see his legs stretched out to the warmth of the fire. I opened the stove and shoved more wood on the coals.

"Have you seen the way he looks at us?" she asked. "He's up to something, I can smell it."

"An omelette," Ryan said. "If we have enough eggs."

"It's Vincent's own damn fault, coming here in this weather. Let him take the consequences," Gran muttered under her breath.

"Don't you think it would make him even more suspicious of us if we hustle him out the door in the middle of a blizzard?" Ryan asked.

Gran gave Ryan a long, level look. "He's not what he seems to be, Ryan. Watch yourself around him. He's dangerous."

"That's ridiculous," Ryan said, but there was no heat in his voice, no outrage or surprise.

"He's going to make trouble. I can feel it coming. I vote for the snowshoes. Let him find his own way home."

"He's too upset to make trouble."

"Well, I have no desire to dry his tears," she said.

I stood up and brushed sawdust from my hands. If I hadn't been so upset with both of them I would have agreed with her. Every instinct in me wanted Vincent out of the house. Whatever primal part of me had learned to sniff out danger was alert now, tensed, ready to run or fight. First there was a murder, and then Vincent appeared. We'd be fools if we weren't suspicious of him. Why did he come here? Was it really because he hadn't heard from Edward? When Vincent entered the house it had taken him less than a minute to make me distrust everyone I had ever loved. It was easy to hate him.

Ryan cloaked himself in silence as he washed his hands in the sink. It was clear he didn't want to talk, and he concentrated on cleaning the dirt from his fingernails as if he were scrubbing for surgery. When he finished he opened the refrigerator again and handed Gran a carton of eggs. "Crack these in a bowl. I'll cut up the onions."

"What about bacon?"

"Your heart, Gran."

"Balls. You know they'll decide cholesterol is good for you. Just give them a few years."

"Bacon is not and never will be health food."

"I don't care. I want bacon. I need bacon. I will have bacon."

"Fine. Go ahead and clog your arteries just because you're in a snit over an uninvited guest."

After Gran finished cracking the eggs she wiped

her hands on a tea towel. "Do you believe the dead man is Edward?" she asked Ryan. Her tone was uncharacteristically hesitant.

*Liar*, I thought. You know he is. I loved you and believed you and you lied to me every day of my life. The betrayal was unbearable, as unbearable as the memory of my father's dead blue eyes. I leaned back against the wall, crossed my arms in front of my chest, and looked at my brother.

"What do you think, Ryan?" I asked. My throat was tight, my voice high and strange. "Is the dead man really our father?"

Ryan sighed, picked out a knife from the drawer. "I know he is."

Gran's eyes fixed on him like two pins stabbing a moth to a board. "How do you know?"

Ryan sliced the scallions into thin silver discs and I knew the truth was about to spill out of him. Vincent's arrival must have made certain lies impossible to maintain. An avid, reckless curiosity seized me, a need to carve away the fantasy I'd been brought up to believe. I wanted to hear the truth about my father.

Ryan spoke without meeting our eyes, his knife punctuating his words as he chopped the greens on the cutting board. His voice was even, controlled, as if he had rehearsed the story. "When I was in seventh grade my homeroom teacher told me to go out to the playground because I had a visitor. I ran outside. It was a beautiful day. And then I saw Dad, leaning against the chain-link fence next to the baseball diamond. Three years had gone by since I'd seen him."

"How did he look?" I asked.

"Same as ever. He was nervous and he smiled too much, I remember that, but he looked fine. He looked prosperous."

"Did you always know he was alive or did Gran lie to you too?" I couldn't resist asking, even though I knew the answer would widen the chasm between us.

Ryan shot a look at Gran, who beat the eggs with a whisk and avoided my eyes. "I knew there was never a car crash. I knew he left us and ran away with Vincent. I assumed he was alive."

I felt empty, as if all the love they'd given me might be a lie too. Didn't I deserve to know the facts? Did they think I was some sort of doll, so delicate or stupid or shallow that I wouldn't be able to absorb the truth?

"Whose idea was it to lie to me about it?" I asked. My voice cracked. "Why didn't either of you tell me what really happened?"

"It was too painful, Brett," Ryan said. "We wanted to forget him. I didn't tell anyone—not even Gran—that I saw him that day in school."

"Oh, Ryan," Gran said, pushing the bowl away and washing her hands in the sink. "He had no right to put you in that position."

"It was a huge shock to see him. I wasn't sure I could breathe, much less walk over to him. Eventually, of course, I shook his hand and made small talk,

I forget what, exactly: how are you, where have you been, the kind of questions people ask a hundred times a day, but Dad never gave me a straight answer."

"Why didn't you tell me?" Gran asked, and her voice was full of pain.

I snorted in disbelief. "How can you ask him that, after lying to me for thirty years?"

Gran lifted her hands in surrender, and I could see she was too upset to answer. The air between the three of us was thick with hurt, and I had to swallow the knot in my throat.

"He gave me a hundred dollars that day," Ryan said. "He asked me about my teachers, and I said something that made him laugh, and then he opened his wallet and fished out five twenties."

"And you took it? How could you?" I was too loud, recklessly loud. I didn't care if Vincent heard us or not.

Ryan continued in a low, shamed voice. "I don't know. It was free money, more money than I'd ever seen or held, and it felt great, at first, as if I'd passed some test. It felt like winning."

"You saw him again, didn't you?" I asked.

"Yes, but he left that day without making any arrangement to see me, and I felt worse and worse about taking the cash. I couldn't stop thinking about it. I knew it was a bribe. Obviously Dad thought he'd purchased some little piece of me, that a hundred dollars would connect us forever, and I didn't want that connection. It was too painful to know he was out there. I hated him. I wished he were dead, to tell you the truth."

In spite of my anger I could understand how it must have felt, to be so casually visited by a father he hadn't seen in three years and then dismissed with a shabby little gift of money. I sat down at the kitchen table and put my head in my hands, confused by my sympathy, angry at how we all had been cheated. It would cut me to the heart to be in Ryan's shoes, to be looked over and abandoned all over again. If Dan ever tried to do that to Amy I would do everything in my power to make sure he never saw her again.

Ryan went on. "By lunchtime I was flashing the money to everyone in homeroom. The most popular boys in the class wanted to eat lunch with me, and I made one stupid bet after another with them. Whether the cafeteria would serve meat loaf or spaghetti, whether there would be a fire drill, whether the bus driver would say 'settle down back there' at least six times before we got to Coddington Road. I lost every time, and every time I gave away another twenty I felt lighter, as if I didn't owe Dad anything anymore, as if I could make him disappear all over again."

"Why didn't you tell the police you recognized the body?" I asked. "That's obstructing justice, Ryan. Didn't you even think about that?"

Ryan paused at the cutting board, his knife suspended, glinting in the lamplight. He sighed and put the knife down, then adjusted it until it was precisely parallel to the board, all the while avoiding my eyes.

"I don't know. It was stupid, but I was shocked to see him like that. Of course they were going to find out who he was, but you didn't know about him and I was used to keeping his existence a secret from you. I just couldn't tell you who he was in front of all those strangers."

"How often did he come to see you?" Gran asked.

He looked up at her. "He showed up every year, usually just once, sometimes twice. He told me not to tell anybody."

"Did he give you money every time?" I asked, not trying to hide the bitterness in my tone.

"Yes."

"That was the beginning of your gambling, wasn't it?" It was crossing a line, to ask him about his gambling; I knew that, but I wanted to smash the wall he'd built between me and his secrets.

He shrugged. "It made me sick to see him and take his money. On the days he showed up I threw up as soon as he left. I had stomach pains so often I carried a pack of Rolaids all the way through junior high and high school."

"Oh, Ryan," Gran whispered. "I'm so sorry."

He flashed her a smile. "Hey, it's all in the past. Come here." Gran entered his arms and he held her and whispered into the crown of her head. "Everything's going to be okay."

"I hope you're right," she said, her voice muffled by his shoulder.

I crossed my arms, leaned back in my chair, and watched them hold each other. They seemed like strangers to me, actors on a set, repeating lines for my benefit.

"Come here, Brett," Ryan said, opening one arm to me. My grandmother lifted her face from his shoulder and extended her arm to me as well.

"Please, sweetheart," she said. They waited for me, but I was caught in the bitterness of finding out I'd been lied to for thirty years. I watched them reach for me and didn't move.

The phone rang and broke the spell. "Shall I get that?" Vincent called from the living room.

Gran's face tightened as she pulled away from Ryan and wiped her hands on her apron.

"I'll get it," I said. I left the kitchen and passed through the living room where Vincent was standing at the bookshelves, idly paging through a scrapbook of old photographs. It annoyed me to see him looking at our family albums. "Those are private," I snapped, then ducked into the hallway and picked up the phone.

Dan's voice crackled over a bad connection. "Brett? Is that you?"

"Yes," I said. "Any news? Is Farnsworth coming back?" I spoke in a low voice, not wanting to be overheard by Vincent.

"The medical investigator says your John Doe was killed on Tuesday, probably between one and three in the afternoon. The police will be asking all of you exactly where you were and what you were doing then. You understand what I'm saying?"

"Yes," I said, lowering my voice in case Vincent was listening. "But he's not a John Doe anymore.

Someone came to the door a while ago looking for him. We know who he is."

"No kidding," he said. "Who is he?"

"My father. Edward Mercy."

"I thought your father was dead."

"That's what Ryan and Gran always told me, but they were lying. Ryan's seen him several times over the years, and Gran knew he was alive. Ryan says he didn't want to identify the body in front of me."

"This isn't good news," Dan said. "I don't like it."

"No," I said. "Neither do I. But Farnsworth will love it."

"Make sure you all have good alibis for Tuesday, as detailed as possible, with a couple of witnesses. Who is this guy who showed up looking for him?"

"His lover. Vincent DeLuca."

"Jesus Christ. Your dad was gay?"

"Apparently."

"I'm going to run a background check on this De-Luca. Vincent, did you say? Is he still there?"

"Yes. We're buried out here, Dan. There must be over a foot of snow on the ground. We can't get rid of him."

"I know. It's just as bad here in town, and they say it's going to get worse. The interstate is shut down, and all the stores are closed. They're expecting another foot at least. You can't even buy a cup of coffee. The networks are calling it the blizzard of the century."

"Great. We'll be stuck with him for days." My palms grew damp at the thought. If Vincent was a murderer, we were all in danger, but what I feared even more was the way he'd so easily and swiftly ripped apart everything I'd always believed about my family. His presence had turned us all into strangers.

"Listen. Be damned careful of this guy."

"When are the cops getting here?"

"They'll be back with warrants as soon as they can get a truck up your driveway. Is Amy okay?"

"She's fine," I said.

"Let me talk to her," Dan said.

"I'll go get her. Hang on." I put the phone down and took the stairs two at a time, treading lightly out of habit, walking softly down the hallway. When I pushed her door open it swung silently on its hinges, revealing Amy sitting in bed, reading with her knees propped up, her favorite comforter tucked under her armpits. For a moment I stood on the threshold, drinking her in before she was aware of my presence. I felt pricked by a needle of tenderness as I saw her in the lamplight with the glasses she hated to wear perched on her nose. She was so beautiful.

Then my eyes took in the creased, wrinkled paper that she held in her hands: a long legal-size sheet filled with cramped handwriting and bordered by pale blue and red lines. Her gaze was intently focused on the last few lines of the page as the top of the paper curved over her knees. Even upside down, I could read the large black type of its heading.

In oversize Gothic print it said: "Last Will and Testament of" and underneath, in precisely handwritten blue ink, "Edward Mercy."

# Chapter Four

No, I thought. It can't be what it looks like.

"Where did you find that?" I asked, nodding at the will.

Amy crumpled the paper in her hands and stuffed it under the comforter. "God, Mom, don't you ever knock?"

The sound of my grandmother's voice lilted upstairs from the kitchen. "Amy! Brett! Dinner's ready. Come and get it!"

"Could you give me a minute, please?" Amy said. "I need to get dressed."

Footsteps echoed down the hall, and Ryan poked his head in the door behind me. "Brett! Amy! Are you coming?"

More than anything else I wanted to rip the covers off my daughter and seize the document she'd just hidden, but I was frozen in disbelief, paralyzed by the fear of what her possession of the will might mean, and I didn't want to let Ryan know what I'd seen. The prospect of making the wrong move terrified me.

"Your father's on the phone," I said. "He wants to talk to you."

Ryan went back out in the hallway, and I retreated from her bedroom, closed the door behind me, and followed him. My chest hurt as though I'd fallen and had the breath knocked out of me. How was it possible that my father's will was in Amy's hands? My mind spun with possible scenarios that might explain how she had come into possession of Edward's will and why she wished to conceal it. Could she have taken it from Edward's dead body? I recalled how much she wanted to see the body after I'd found it. It was just barely possible that she'd saddled up Caledonia, looped through the woods, and reached the body ahead of us. Or had she found the will somewhere else? In the barn? Ryan's room? Had she stolen it from him?

It was shocking to even consider these possibilities, but I couldn't get around the fact that I'd seen the will in her hands. Whether Amy chose to tell me the truth or not, I needed time to compose myself before I asked her any questions; above all, I needed to get my hands on that will and put it in a safe place. It seemed doubtful that she would surrender it willingly. I should march right back into her room and take it, I thought, and paused on the stairs, despising my uncertainty.

Ryan looked back at me in the stairwell. "Brett? What's the matter? Aren't you coming?"

"Yes," I said, and felt a cowardly flash of relief that he'd stopped me. I could postpone everything until after dinner. I'll find it later, I promised myself. In the meantime I didn't want Ryan to become suspicious, so I hurried down the stairs after him.

In the living room Vincent was standing by the window, looking out at the darkness of the storm. "There's enough for all of us," Ryan said to him, his voice neutral. "Come on in."

Vincent followed us into the kitchen, where Ryan took his place at the table, cut the omelette, and dished out portions to the places at the table. Gran was buttering toast, and when she saw Vincent she sniffed and made a show of setting an extra place at the table. My ears were attuned to the sound of Amy padding down the stairs, then talking to her father on the telephone in the hall. She sounded warm, excited, and she laughed in a voice pitched high enough for me to hear, as if to let me know exactly how much she preferred him to me. Weeks had gone by since I'd heard her laugh, and in my present state of mind it sounded theatrical and false.

My mind raced as I chewed my food. Gran's back was ramrod straight and her knife and fork moved with exquisite precision as she carried food from her plate to her mouth. Every other word out of her mouth was "please" or "thank you." Ryan avoided looking at Vincent or speaking to him.

Amy finally joined us and sat down at her place. "Dad said Greek Peak is going to open on Thursday. He wants to take me skiing next weekend."

"Lucky girl," Ryan said.

The thought of planning a ski trip seemed ludicrous. What about the murder, and the police? What about her suspension from school? My heart sank as I realized I still had to tell Gran that Amy wouldn't be going back to school on Monday.

"Have you heard the new CD from Devil Pie?" she asked Ryan.

His face lit up. "Just a couple of cuts on the radio. Great energy. That lead singer is hot."

I looked up from my plate. "There's a singer who calls himself Devil?"

Amy rolled her eyes. "You are so unplugged, Mother. It's the *band's* name. And it's a her, not a him."

I slid a glance over toward Gran and saw that her fingers were wrapped tight around her glass, as though she were choking it. Vincent cleared his throat to make an announcement and we all stared at him, our expressions polite, attentive, and cool. The events of the day were written in the fatigue on his face, and I wondered why I didn't feel more sympathy for him. He was a bereaved spouse, after all. But the moment I asked myself the question, the answer was clear: I didn't trust him.

"This storm looks like it's going to last all night," he said. "I'll have to get my bags from the car."

It was just the excuse I'd been waiting for. "I'll help you carry them in, and then I can show you to the guest room," I said quickly, before anyone else could make another suggestion. No one spoke. My grandmother daintily patted her lips with a napkin while Ryan and Amy exchanged glances.

"Give me a second," I said to Vincent. "I'll just get my coat."

I took the stairs two at a time and walked quickly down the hallway to Amy's room. Twisting the knob delicately, I pressed the door open, then closed it behind me just enough to shield my presence. Her bed was unmade. I lifted the pillows one by one. No sign of the will. I flung back the comforter, the sheets. Nothing.

Outside the wind was drumming against the walls like a stormy sea against a breakwater, and bare willow branches thrashed against the window. The will had to be here, somewhere. I looked inside the cups of all her riding trophies lined along the top of her bookshelf. Nothing. I untacked the bottom edge of her posters and lifted them to reveal an empty wall. In her top dresser drawer I ran my hands under her underwear, her socks, her T-shirts and leggings. I found the bundle of money, but no will. The second drawer was filled with jeans and sweaters. Frantic by now, I pulled them out one at a time, shaking each article and throwing it on the floor, desperate to find the will before Amy appeared at the door.

When I extracted the last pair of jeans from the drawer and gave it a shake, the will slipped out of one of the legs, where it had been carefully rolled and pressed inside.

Clever, I thought. She's too damn clever. The care she had taken in hiding the document frightened me almost as much as her possession of it. I grabbed the will and shoved it in my pocket just as the bedroom door swung open.

Vincent stood in the doorway, taking in the chaos of Amy's clothes on the floor, the dresser drawers yawning open and empty, the bedcovers thrown on the floor. "Looking for something?" he asked.

His boldness astonished me. Why would he follow me upstairs in a house where he was certainly aware he was an unwelcome guest, and open a door to a room he'd never seen before? I came toward him, forcing him back into the hallway. "Amy borrowed something from me yesterday. I was just trying to find it." Skepticism was written on his face, but I didn't care. I closed the door behind us and moved toward the stairs.

"Aren't you going to get your coat?" Vincent asked.

"I forgot," I said. "It's on the hook by the front door."

As we started down the steps Amy materialized at the bottom, and I could feel a flush rise up my neck as we descended the stairs. "I'm sorry," I whispered as we passed her.

"What are you talking about?" Amy asked, cool and polite as if I were a stranger.

"You'll figure it out," I said to her.

Her lips compressed and her eyes telegraphed something serious, adult, forbidding. A deep uneasiness spread its wings in my mind as I glanced at her. The little girl I had known and loved before I went to Africa was gone. Amy had grown up and around her, and swallowed her whole to become another person, this frightening half-grown woman who seemed to have no aversion at all to stealing from the dead.

Vincent watched our interaction like a cat sniffing at a mouse hole. There was an alert curiosity in his face, in the single raised eyebrow. I didn't try to explain. Amy bulldozed past us up the stairs and Vincent and I proceeded to the kitchen door, where I found my coat on the hook and slipped it over my shoulders.

Once outside we plunged into the shock of the storm, where the windblown snow showered us in a relentless assault. Tucking my chin into my collar, I punched my way through the drifts to the hillock of white that hid the Saab, then swept aside the deep, icy shroud that covered the trunk. With some effort Vincent keyed open the frozen lock, tugged at the weight of snow still remaining on the lid of the trunk and opened it. He extracted a garment bag and a suitcase. It seemed like a lot of luggage, and I wondered uneasily why he'd brought it in the first place. He must have known the storm was bearing down on Tompkins County when he arrived. His timing was a little too perfect, as if he'd intended to become stranded here.

"I'll take that," I offered, reaching for the garment bag.

"No," Vincent said. "Take this one, it's lighter." He pushed the suitcase into my outstretched hand.

I led him back inside, where we stamped the snow

from our boots and continued up the stairs to the spare room. The bedroom was tucked in a corner of the house under the eaves, and Vincent stared up at the uneven planes of the ceiling that loomed close to the bed.

"You'll have to watch your head," I said.

Vincent nodded, looking resigned. "It's fine."

It was a tiny room, and the scent of Vincent's cologne and sweat drifted on the heat from his body to surround me in the small enclosure of space.

"The bathroom's at the end of the hall, on your left," I said. "If you turn the hot water on full blast the pipes seize up and make a lot of noise. Just turn it on slow."

"I'll remember."

"I'll go get your linens."

I went to the hall closet for sheets, blankets, and a towel, and when I came back I found Vincent standing at the window, gazing into the tempest on the other side of the glass.

"I would like to speak to your brother in private," Vincent said. "Would you mind asking him to come up here?"

"I'll ask him," I said. "I don't know if he will."

"Tell him it would be to his advantage to talk to me in private before I talk to the police."

My face tightened. "He might not agree."

"Please," he said, holding up one hand, palm out, facing me. "Just tell him."

Leaving Vincent in his room, I stepped next door

to my own, eager to examine the will that was crumpled in my pocket.

It looked innocuous, a worn and wrinkled paper that had been folded into a small square. I sat on the bed, smoothed it out and studied my father's precise handwriting, the flourish of his signature. Skimming the legal jargon at the top, my eyes flew to the paragraph that stated, "All of the estate when I die seized or possessed, real, personal, and mixed, wheresoever situate, I hereby give, devise and bequeath as follows:"

The first thing my father wrote in the space provided was this: "The following assets I give to my only son, Ryan McBride, after my debts and funeral expenses are paid." I took a deep breath and raced on through his methodical list of real estate, bank accounts, safety deposit boxes, cars, a boat, an airplane, mutual funds, stocks, bonds, art, antiques, all the miscellaneous property my father apparently owned at the time of his death. The real estate alone looked like it had to be worth at least a few million. My father was rich.

For a moment I had a nearly overwhelming impulse to rip it up, not just to put a safe distance between the murder and my family, but because it made me so angry that Ryan was the only one mentioned in the will. What about me? Why was it so hard for my father to acknowledge me?

There was more writing underneath the list of assets, but I threw the will down on the bedspread unread, struck by a sudden wave of uneasiness at the fact that Ryan was the beneficiary of my father's estate. The police will have a field day with this, I thought. I rubbed my forehead, trying to think clearly. I couldn't destroy it—it was too valuable; Ryan would never forgive me. I could hide it, though, until the killer was found. Where? If I left it in my room then Vincent might find it and rip it up, or Amy might try to steal it back. I decided to keep it in my pocket for the moment. It felt lethal, explosive, like a grenade that might go off and damage all of us.

In the kitchen Ryan was washing dishes while Gran was clearing away the food and wiping the counters.

"Vincent wants to talk to you," I said to my brother.

"What about?" he asked, not looking up.

"He said you two should speak in private before he talks to the police."

The plate he was washing slipped from his fingers and fell into the dishwater with a splash. "I don't know what he's talking about," he said, "but I'd better go see."

Gran stopped wiping the counter and gave him a wild look. "Why—?" she started to say, then stopped when she saw my face.

"It's all right, Gran. Don't worry," Ryan said. "I'll go see what he wants. Brett, can you take over?"

"Sure," I said, and accepted the wet sponge from his hand. Ryan wiped his hands on a dish towel and left the kitchen.

I could feel Gran's irritation mounting like a stopped-up sewer as she scrubbed at an invisible spot on the counter. "Don't," I said, and took the dishcloth away from her. "You're going to give yourself an ulcer."

She looked me in the eye, her lips tight, chin trembling. "I have a terrible feeling about that man."

"Hey," I said, giving her shoulders a shake. "Relax. We'll survive. Stay out of his way and we'll send him off in the morning."

She nodded obediently, like a child, and went out of the kitchen, looking frail and old, her shoulders stooped. I waited for her to finish climbing the stairs, heard her bedroom door open and close, and then I threw the sponge in the sink and sprinted on tiptoe up to my room.

No more secrets, I thought. I closed the door silently after me, careful to avoid the telltale click of the doorknob's release. In my closet I scrabbled as quietly as possible through the shoes and boxes and scrapbooks until I found my old doctor's bag. The back wall of the closet was thin plasterboard, and I could hear a murmur of voices from Vincent's room on the other side. Yanking my stethoscope out of the bag, I looped the clips around my neck, then inserted them in my ears and pressed the bell against the wall.

The sound was amazingly clear. "Sit down," Vincent said.

I could hear the creak of bedsprings.

Vincent spoke. "You saw Edward, didn't you? Last Tuesday, before he died."

"Yes," Ryan said.

"Could you tell me what he said?"

Ryan's voice was loud, defiant. "He wanted to move in with us. He wanted to die here, on the farm."

My heart gave a painful lurch as a cloud of confusion filled me, and my eyes stung with unexpected tears.

There was another protest of bedsprings: Vincent must have sat down on the bed, next to Ryan. "That son of a bitch," Vincent muttered.

"I'm sorry," Ryan said. "He told me things weren't so great between the two of you."

There was a pause. "You look just like him, did you know that? A younger, healthier, more beautiful version of Edward, but it's obvious you're his son."

Another silence, longer this time.

Vincent's voice: "I'm clean, you know. Negative for HIV. I haven't slept with your father in years."

My God, I thought. Is Vincent coming on to him?

Ryan spoke. "Don't do that," he said.

"Sorry. It's just that you look so much like him, the way he used to be. You're a very beautiful young man, Ryan."

"Please," my brother said. "I can't do this with you."

"I'm not that much older than you are, you know. Just seven years. You have such nice hair. Just like your father's used to feel. Like silk."

"No!" Ryan's voice was sharp. There was the sound of one of them rising from the bed.

"Do you mind if I smoke?" Vincent asked. He sounded slightly breathless. There was a click, the sound of a lighter being snapped open and shut. "So what did you tell Edward?"

Ryan's voice was jerky, angry. "I didn't want him to come here. I told him he'd have to go back to you, that none of us would let him come back. Brett didn't even know he was alive."

"He was a vain, selfish man, Ryan."

"I know."

"Fifteen years ago I discovered him in bed with a client. That was the end, for me. I never slept with him again after that. It was too risky."

"Why did you stay with him?" Ryan asked.

"I was in school, halfway through my architecture degree, and Edward was paying the bills. I needed him. And in all fairness, he needed me. I did his taxes, arranged his schedule, kept the apartment running smoothly. I was the perfect housewife, except for our sex life."

"So you stayed with him for his money." Ryan's voice was bitter.

"My dear boy," Vincent said, a smile in his voice, "surely you don't underestimate the power of money." Another pause. "Edward wanted freedom, complete sexual freedom. He'd already given up a family and his home to have it, and I knew he would give me up, too, if I stood in his way. So I gave him what he wanted."

Vincent went on. "At first I thought age would change him. But as the years went by it became clear that he needed to punish himself for leaving you and Brett and your mother. His infidelities were always flagrant, and would have killed him if . . ."

If a gun hadn't finished the job first, I thought.

Vincent continued to talk. "For the past year Edward was too sick to work, too sick to flirt, and the walls were closing in on him. He saved his strength for weeks to make this trip. I'll never know why it was so important to him to come back here. Brett didn't exist as far as he was concerned, and he rarely mentioned you. I had no idea he wanted to move back here. Christ, I never thought he'd go that far."

"He told me you had a fight," Ryan said.

"Yes, we had a fight. We had a lot of fights. Why do people cling to the myth that invalids are supposed to be saintly? Edward was a total bitch. He never let up, and I was the only one around to absorb the abuse."

"You should have left him."

I could hear the bedsprings again as one of them stood up, then the light tread of pacing. Vincent spoke. "Did he tell you anything about his will?"

"No."

"The estate is actually quite large. Worth several million, at least. He bought some rental property on Long Island that's probably quadrupled in value. His business is worth a small fortune, and his stock portfolio is enormous."

"I don't care about that," Ryan interrupted, sounding uneasy.

"Don't you? Somehow I rather doubt that, Ryan." Another pause. "The last time I saw him alive he told me he was going to cut me out of the will altogether and make you his sole heir. He was out of his mind, of course, sick and delusional; any court would see that, I think. All his previous wills list me as the only beneficiary. But last Monday he showed me a will he'd written himself. It was one of those cheap, standard issue form wills you can buy at any office supply."

Exactly what I had in my pocket. My palms began to sweat as I held the bell of the stethoscope cupped tightly to the back wall of the closet.

Vincent went on. "He filled it out in his own handwriting—handwriting, for Christ's sake. He pays his attorney three thousand a month and he resorts to handwriting. Anyway. He told me he was going to take it to his lawyer and file it with him when he returned from his trip to see you. He made me read it while he watched. It was meant to hurt me, and it did. It was so ugly, so demeaning. Full of unnecessary remarks about me . . . it was absolutely maudlin, full of the ravings of a dying, angry man. I saw that it was witnessed by two bank clerks, and the thought that two strangers might have read it hurt me terribly. But underneath all the invective against me, he made it quite clear that you would inherit everything he had."

Ryan spoke. "There was no will found on his body."

"I know the will exists. I know he brought it here. I think you have it, Ryan. I think you killed Edward so you could have it."

"You're crazy. You probably killed him yourself."

"Aren't you leveraged up to your neck in gambling debts?"

"I don't believe that's any of your business."

"Maybe not. But you need the money, don't you? Maybe you didn't want him to move in here. Maybe you knew your grandmother would never allow it. But I'm sure you wanted that money."

"You don't know what you're talking about," Ryan said.

"The mortgage, Ryan. How are you going to pay it off? Your credit is maxed out, isn't it? The bank won't help you. Does your grandmother know? Does Brett know?"

I felt a blade of cold air on my neck and pressed the bell of the stethoscope even more firmly against the wall, as if I could squeeze the truth out of my brother by listening harder. What mortgage could Vincent be talking about? The farm was in Gran's name, and I knew she would never mortgage it. Gran had always said the farm would come to both Ryan and me when she died, and I had no reason to think she'd changed her mind. But Ryan didn't own any real estate that I knew of. When he split up with Billy he sold Billy his share of the house in Cayuga Heights.

"How do you know about the mortgage?" Ryan said.

"How do you think? Edward told me, of course. He was deeply disappointed in you, Ryan. I can't think why he wanted to leave you everything."

"Please don't put that there," Ryan said.

"Then let's find an ashtray." There was a squeak of a dresser drawer being opened. "What is all this?"

"Nothing important. Things Gran can't throw away but doesn't use anymore. Tablecloths, extra napkins, my great-grandmother's silver."

Another sound, one I couldn't identify, then a squeak of hinges.

"Why is this here?" Vincent asked.

"I don't know."

"Is it loaded?"

There was the unmistakable sound of a gun being broken open. "No. I'll take it downstairs and lock it up. I'm sorry. I have no idea why it's up here." Ryan stopped talking.

Vincent's voice was cold. "Don't you think the police should take a look at it?"

"Of course," Ryan said. "If it has anything to do with Edward's murder they'll find out. As soon as the weather clears they'll be here to collect all the guns we own."

There was the creak and click of a closet door closing. Ryan spoke. "Is there anything else you need?"

"No. We'll talk again." Vincent's tone was curt, dismissive.

I heard Vincent's bedroom door open and close,

and I wriggled out of the closet and silently turned the knob of my bedroom door and pressed it open a fraction of an inch. Ryan was in the hallway with a shotgun tucked under one arm, a work shirt wrapped around the barrel. He leaned against the wall, his face white, his eyes closed, just inches from the crack in my door.

The shirt that swaddled the barrel of the gun fell to the floor, and when he picked it up I could see dark flecks streaked across the fabric. It looked like spatters of blood.

Ryan stared at the stain as if he were willing it to look like something else. It could be chicken blood, I thought, horse blood, blood from a cut or a scrape or a dog in heat. My mind scrambled to escape the obvious deduction.

He ran a finger along the inside of the barrel, then sniffed the brown smear on his knuckle. Weakness skidded through me as I watched him let the gun drop to his side. He shook his head and started toward the stairs.

I followed him at a distance, clinging to the shadows of the landing as he hurried down the stairs. Slinking down after him, I saw him stand in front of the glass-fronted cabinet where the rest of the guns were stored. I was grateful that the living room was empty. Apparently Amy and Gran had gone to their respective rooms to avoid the possibility of getting stuck with Vincent. As I stood in the shadow of the hall I watched Ryan pick up my Remington, then unlock the cabinet and lift the rest of the guns out one by one: the Browning 12-gauge pump, the Winchester .30.06, the .303 British Enfield, the .12-gauge Ithaca Deerslayer, the double barrel Parker, all of them. He carried the armload of weapons into the kitchen and dumped them on the table.

The edge of the doorway concealed me as Ryan opened the woodstove, raked the embers and added more kindling. Then he stuffed the bloody workshirt on top of the flames.

I must have gasped in dismay, because he whirled around and saw me.

"Brett! My God, you scared me. What are you doing down here? I thought you were in bed."

I moved into the room. "What are you doing?"

He looked at the guns on the table, then looked back at me. "What does it look like?"

I knew he hated to clean the guns. Who was he protecting, if not himself? "Destroying evidence, is what it looks like. That's what Farnsworth will think."

"Maybe he'll just think we take good care of our equipment."

I watched in silence as Ryan gathered a can of machine oil and rags from under the sink, then sat next to the dark, shiny pile of all the guns we owned. The lamp above the table cast a pool of light over the shotguns and rifles, and cold reflections glinted off the plunger he used to ream out the barrel of the gun he'd found in Vincent's closet.

It was hard to reconcile this image with the brother I thought I knew, the brother who obsessed over his wardrobe, manicure, and hairstyle and left his bank balance to chance. His nails were dark with gun grease now. What happened to the man who used to be my ally, my confidant, my fussy guardian? Ryan was the one I ran to first for advice on every major decision that had ever faced me. So many parts of my life held the stamp of his good, sensible counseling: marriage, divorce, motherhood, going into medicine, going to Africa. I had always trusted him, and now I was frightened to realize I didn't.

I sat in the chair across from him. "Ryan, why are you doing this? Do you think one of us has something to hide?"

He pushed his glasses back up the bridge of his nose. "I'm just cleaning them, Brett." He stroked the length of the gun with an oiled rag and polished the stock, the trigger and safety. Then he propped the gun against the chair beside him and selected another from the pile on the table.

I watched his hands move over the body of the rifle. "Tell me what's really going on."

"I can't," he said.

"Why not?"

He was silent.

"I know you argued with him, Ryan. The day he was shot."

"It wasn't what you think."

I sat at the table, the guns bristling in a pile between us. "What did you argue about?"

"He wanted me to do something for him that I didn't want to do."

"What did he want?"

"That's a long story."

"I'd like to know if my brother is a murderer," I said.

Ryan blinked, and for a moment I wished I could take it back. "You can believe what you want," he said.

"If you didn't kill him, then who did?" I whispered.

"I don't know," he said, but his voice was a level monotone, lacking any conviction.

"Vincent had a garment bag he didn't want me to carry," I said slowly. "He could have brought the gun into the house."

Ryan looked at the gun, then looked at me. "How did you know—?"

"I saw you carry it from his room," I said quickly. Of course I didn't let on that I'd listened to every word he and Vincent had said to each other.

He made a face. "It's our gun, I'm afraid."

"Do you think he might have taken it from our cabinet? He could have shot Edward with it, then put it in his room to make it look like one of us did it."

He shrugged and shook his head. "Even if he smuggled it back in here somehow, how would he have found the key to our gun cabinet in the first place?"

"It's right there," I said, pointing to the hook by the door. "It's probably been hanging there since our father lived here. Maybe Edward told him about it.

And don't forget, Vincent lived here too, thirty years ago. He could have known where we kept the key."

"Maybe," he said, but his voice was flat, skeptical.

I studied him, torn between the desire to believe him and the need to know everything, no matter how incriminating. "Please tell me about the last time you saw our father. Tell me what you argued about."

Ryan sighed. He looked depressed, beaten. "Are you sure you want to hear this?"

No, I thought, I'm not really sure of anything anymore. But I nodded.

Ryan licked his lips and began to speak. "It was last Tuesday morning. I was on my way out the front door when I saw Dad's car parked in the yard. He always drove a black Mercedes jeep when he came out here. It made me nervous when he showed up out of the blue, especially when he came to the farm. Maybe he didn't care, but I was terrified that you or Amy or Gran would see him."

"I wish I had," I said.

"Nobody was around, but the barn door was ajar, so I walked across the yard to close it, and when I got to the door I saw him standing in the center of the aisle inside the barn. There was a shaft of light from the window in the hayloft, and he was standing in the middle of it, facing me. His face was skeletal. I hadn't seen him in seven or eight months, and he'd gone downhill fast. He was at least twenty pounds thinner, and he was skinny to begin with. His skin was stretched tight over his bones, and his clothes were big on him, too big for his frame.

"I asked him what he thought he was doing here, and he said 'Is that any way to greet your old man?' I felt sorry for him. He looked so sick, and he sounded so weak. But mostly I just wanted to get him out of there, so I asked him what he wanted.

"He said 'I'm afraid, Ryan.'

"I asked him if he was afraid of dying and he said no, that wasn't it. He said he was afraid of Vincent. He leaned against the railing of the currying pen and gave me this peculiar look, as if he were ashamed of something, and then he said, 'Vincent scares me, Ryan. I'm too weak to control him anymore.'

"I told him he'd have to talk to Vincent, work it out, and he told me they'd had a terrible fight. Vincent threw a full bottle of wine at him and it smashed a window. Dad said it almost hit his head. It could have killed him. Apparently Vincent was going through the estate as if Dad were already dead. Their credit cards were charged up to the limit. Last week Dad checked his safe deposit box, which he swore had fifty thousand dollars inside it the last time he saw it, and the money was gone. He was sure Vincent stole the key, forged his signature, and took the money."

Ryan's eyes were hidden behind the reflection of the guns in his glasses. He spoke in a monotone, his hands moving with a machinelike precision over the body of the rifle in his hands.

"My God, Ryan, that man is upstairs just down the hall from my daughter. What are we going to do? How can we get rid of him?"

"Let me finish. Dad said he'd been taking dozens of pills every day, but there was no point anymore; the virus was winning. He'd stopped taking any medication. He promised me that in eight weeks he'd be dead. He said, 'I want to come back and die here, Ryan.'"

"He wanted to move in with us?" I asked, as if I hadn't heard him admit this much to Vincent.

"That's right," Ryan said. "I told him you and Amy didn't even know he was alive, and he said 'Don't you think it's time to remedy that?' I was flabbergasted by his nerve. 'Is that fair?' I asked him. 'You drop into their lives just in time to let them watch you die?'"

"'Ask them,'" he said. "'I'll abide by their decision. I want to know my daughter before I go. Maybe she'd like to know me.'"

As I listened to Ryan a twist of sadness encircled me like a wire pulled too tightly around my chest. How close I'd come to meeting my father. For a moment the chance to see him alive, to talk with him, had existed. He had wanted me.

Ryan went on. "I told him Gran would never allow it, and he said, 'Emily is an intelligent woman. I don't believe she hates me.'"

"I said, 'I wouldn't count on her forgiveness, if I were you.'"

"He smiled at me then. 'Don't underestimate her,' he said. 'We used to be very close. I always thought she was the most intelligent woman I've ever met. I still think that. I'd enjoy her company again.'"

"I asked him what he wanted me to do, and he said 'Help me. I want to come back. I want to die here.' He coughed really hard then, and at first I thought he was just laying it on thick, trying to get my sympathy, but the spasms rocked through his body for almost a full minute. It was so bad I thought he'd die right there.

"He told me not to worry about the cost of caring for him, told me he had a new will drawn up before he left the city. He said it was in his wallet. He told me he would leave me his estate if I let him move back here, and Vincent wouldn't get a penny."

"Jesus, Ryan!" I said, interrupting him. "If the cops ever hear this they'll arrest you. It's all the motive they need."

"I told him it would be impossible for him to come back here. I told him to check into a hospice if he wanted to, but it was out of the question for him to lay the burden of his dying on the family he'd abandoned. He was angry. I didn't care. I felt relieved, like I'd crossed some watershed, like he finally got the message that he didn't own me anymore."

Doubt filtered into me as I weighed the probable truth of his story. Maybe he thought it made him sound heroic, but if what he said was true, he'd taken away my last chance to meet my own father, without even consulting me. It rankled, no matter what good intentions he'd had.

"Did you take the will?" I asked.

He threw the rag down on the table and looked at me. "No."

I wished I could believe him, but I wondered if I would ever believe my brother again. Certainly not with the ease I had taken for granted just yesterday. I felt infinitely older, as if a great central innocence in my life had been blasted apart.

"Would you have wanted him to move in with us?" Ryan asked.

"In a heartbeat."

Ryan looked at me over the top of his spectacles and blinked in surprise. "Why?"

I looked away, embarrassed that I cared so deeply about the father who had left me. "You have no idea how much I always wanted to know him."

What did it matter, now? He was dead. Listening to Ryan made me restless, made me want to move, to disconnect from him, from the house. The blizzard beating at the windows and doors was claustrophobic, and the pressure of the storm only increased the tension and suspicion that thickened the atmosphere.

"I'm going out," I said.

"In this?"

"Just to the barn. Maybe there's something in the barn, some clue the police overlooked."

"I wouldn't try to play detective, if I were you." Ryan's voice was grim. Why was he warning me? Was he worried about my safety, or his own? "I'm going to finish cleaning the guns," he said. "Lock up when you get back."

I almost felt sorry for him as he sat there at the

table, surrounded by our guns, trying to clean up a mess that would never be clean. After all, he'd lost his father too. I pulled myself up from the table, found a flashlight and my coat, and left.

Without the flashlight I would have lost my way within seconds. The house disappeared behind me in a blur of snow so thick it was like walking through white curtains that clung to me, cold and wet against my face, my hair, my coat. When I finally waded through the drifts and pushed my way into the barn, the interior was dark as ink. I felt along the wall for the light switch and flicked it on, but nothing happened. The electricity was out.

The beam from my flashlight cut through the blackness, and I moved the disc of light over the backs of the horses in their stalls. Their eyes glittered as they turned to look at me, and I saw that they were already rugged up against the cold night ahead. Bridles, bits, reins, and saddles glowed against the tack wall, the leather and metal polished and gleaming. Before Noah came to us the wall had been cluttered with mismatched, broken, and dirty pieces of equipment. Why did he work so hard for so little, for a farm he didn't own? Could his motives be as simple as he claimed?

I aimed the shaft of light at the spot on the floor where Farnsworth had scraped up his sample of blood. The shavings were fresh, unstained, and I poked them aside with the toe of my boot and bent down to examine the concrete underneath. There was a brownish tinge near the grating in the floor, and I felt a chill ripple over my skin at the thought of my father's blood running down the drain.

Something rustled behind me. I stood up, not sure if the noise was real or I'd imagined it. I listened, heard nothing, and moved the beam of light toward the dark corner where the sound had come from. Nothing there but hay and shadows. My mind offered explanations: horses, storm, wind against the window. I almost accepted them.

Then someone grabbed me from behind. I was shoved to the floor, hard. Pinned flat, the wind knocked out of me, I watched helplessly as the flashlight tumbled out of my hand and flew across the floor, out of reach. I gasped for air, rolled, and clawed at the intruder. My fingers met thick leather, a sheepskin collar, then hair, long enough to pull.

I yanked.

The phantom grunted in pain, and I thought, I know that voice. I twisted toward him, panting.

"Noah?"

"Brett? My God, is that you?" His breath was warm on my face.

"What the hell are you doing?" I asked.

"I saw your light. I thought you were a prowler. Why are you out here?"

"I came out to check on the horses," I lied. His face was an inch from my own, his arms on either side of mine, his body a warm and crushing weight. We were sprawled flat on the shavings, and in the darkness I could smell the scent of him, a musky, light odor of earth and leather. A moment passed, and then another, and neither one of us moved. I felt suddenly shy, expectant, as if I were about to be kissed.

Instead he lifted himself up and helped me scramble to my feet, and then he walked over to the flashlight and picked it up. As he headed back to where I stood he aimed the light briefly toward my face, as if to check that it was really me. I squinted into the beam of light and he lowered it.

"Did I hurt you?" he asked. I couldn't see his eyes at all, couldn't see anything until the pupils in my own eyes widened in the darkness. My arm was sore, but my coat and the shavings on the floor had padded the fall. My breathing was still shallow, my pulse racing.

"No, you just scared me to death."

He handed the flashlight to me and I felt slightly better, as though I were in control of something. I turned off the light. I still felt awkward, and wanted to hide my face in the dark.

"You almost scalped me." His voice was hushed in the blackness, but I heard a smile in it.

"I couldn't stay in the house," I confessed.

"The Saab is still here?"

I nodded, then realized Noah probably couldn't see me. "Yes."

"You had a rough day." His voice was low, almost a whisper. "You need to rest."

"I can't rest." My voice was strained, and I realized that behind my words was a wilderness of pain and isolation. In the past twelve hours the people I loved the most had become strangers, and suddenly I longed to talk to Noah about all of it, to rage and weep and then cling to him and be comforted. The tears were hot in my throat, and I swallowed them. My face felt stiff. "I don't know who to trust anymore."

I could hear him breathing, slowly, quietly, in, out, steady and calm. "That's something you'll have to learn," he said.

His hand touched mine, his fingers curled around my palm. My heart pounded in my chest, and I held my breath, caught in a fear I couldn't distinguish from any of the other fears that shimmered inside me.

"What are you thinking?" I asked.

"I'm attracted to you," he said. "And I haven't been attracted to anyone in a long time."

He took me in his arms and kissed me in the dark. Softly, at first, then more deeply, sending a wave of heat down my back, bringing an intensity I wasn't ready to feel.

I pushed him away. "What do you want, Noah?"

His lips brushed my ear. "Right now? This."

"I have to go," I said.

"I like it here," he whispered.

"So do I, but I'm insane," I said.

He gave my hand a squeeze. "Let me walk you back."

The fire in the grate burned low. It gave off enough light to illuminate the living room, which was empty.

The house was silent and dark, and after climbing the stairs, entering my bedroom, and shutting the door, I yanked off my clothes in the dark and crawled into the icy bed.

My body was flooded with the tactile memory of Noah's arms wrapped around me, his lips touching mine. The sheets were cold, and a fierce pang of longing shot through me, to have his warm body beside me, to feel his arms around me, to press myself against the long, smooth curves of his chest and belly and the solid length of his legs. I wanted to smell the musk of his body, that elusive odor of earth and trees and clean air.

Then I wondered how he could have entered the barn so quietly, without my hearing him. Was he really there because he saw my light, or had he been there all along, waiting in the dark for someone else?

I punched the pillow and burrowed deeper into the covers, determined to shut out the noise of my thoughts.

# Chapter Five

When I woke up the sun was shining through my bedroom window, dappling the west wall with the latticed shadow of tree branches, but I could feel the wind sifting through every crack in the walls. The storm windows hadn't been hung yet, and the air in the house swirled with icy drafts that snatched the warmth from the woodstoves and carried it outside.

My room was Spartan: a bed, a nightstand, a lamp, a bureau, and unbleached cotton curtains that I'd left open. The light was blinding as it reflected off the snow, and sunlight turned every icicle into a prism, refracting an eye-searing brightness.

I could see from the bed the battleships of gray clouds lurking on every horizon, looming heavy and dark in a ring around the sun, but for the moment the sun ruled the sky. The shadow of the previous day's events skulked on the perimeter of my consciousness just like those clouds. My father's dead face. The lies Gran and Ryan had told me. The will in Amy's hands. I didn't want to think about any of it, but it was all there, waiting for me, lurking.

All the usual landmarks outside were obliterated by snow that had fallen in the night: the pines flanking the drive, the rock wall, the pond, the split rail fence, the chicken coop and toolsheds were all buried. Wind roared over the blank canvas of the fields and pushed the clouds back.

Take a shower, I told myself. Wash off all of yesterday and start over.

I rose from the bed, shivering as I put on my robe and wool socks and hurried to the bathroom down the hall. When I switched on the light it worked, and I registered the fact that the electricity had been restored since the night before. The pipes complained as the water ran in the tub. Adjusting the temperature until it felt hot, I lifted the stopcock for the shower, then peeled off my robe and hooked it on the bathroom doorknob. My skin still carried the smell of horse, the smell of the barn. When I saw my image in the mirror I shuddered at the matted hair and sleep-wrinkled face of the woman who looked back at me.

Hot water sprayed into the tub and the room began to fill with steam. I pulled off my socks, then stepped into the stream of hot water and let it pound down my back. It felt good. I took a deep breath, squeezed my eyes shut, and let the hot water pour over my head. The warm, steaming rain sluiced down in smooth, wet rivers all over the contours of my body, the valley between my breasts, the slope of my belly, the beginnings of wings on my back. Tilting my face back under the showerhead, I felt my hair grow heavy and black with water. I reached for the bottle of shampoo on the edge of the tub and poured a capful into my hand, then applied it to the wet mass of my hair, rubbing in gentle circles until it frothed up high and white. After rinsing I shampooed again, then massaged my body with a soapy washcloth, taking my time until the hot water ran out. It had been too long since I'd paid attention to my skin. Without the casual tactile presence of a husband or a baby I'd become as numb as a robot, a grim, hard-working, remote-controlled machine. I missed feeling my skin. I missed being touched.

After brushing my teeth and drying my hair, I padded back to my room along the gloomy corridor. The sunlight was gone. Clouds pressed low overhead, engorged with snow, and the icicles hanging from the eaves were dark as swords as they reflected the shadow of the storm. I dropped my robe and turned on the lamp by the bed, and the illumination mirrored my nude body in the glass over the bureau. I'm so young, I thought. My body was clean, rosy in the lamplight. My face was soft, my cheeks flushed from the shower. Why have I felt so old? I asked myself. I'm not old; it isn't true; it isn't real. I'm young enough to start over.

I was tired of wearing flannel shirts hanging unbuttoned over long underwear and jeans that hung too loosely from my hips. A wistful desire was awakening in me to look pretty again. Choosing what to wear more slowly than usual, I took care to inspect all the possibilities before I selected a camisole and clean underpants, light gray wool trousers and a cream cable-knit fisherman's sweater. After pulling on black suede boots, I tucked the trouser legs inside, then brushed my hair and left it loose in a red-gold cloud around my face. As I was applying a touch of lipstick I shook my head at the woman in the mirror. You look great, I thought, but why are you going to this much trouble?

I didn't have to answer. I knew why.

The shadow of the previous day's events hovered over me again as I finished with the lipstick. Edward's dead face, his eyes pleading, frozen, filled with horror. I shook my head to release the image. Someone murdered him, and it was hard to escape the thought that whoever killed him was here in the house, snowed in with the rest of us.

Vincent.

It had to be Vincent.

My hand trembled as I put the cap on the lipstick. He was in the next room, presumably asleep, and part of me wanted to wake him up, drag him out into the snow, and then barricade the rest of us inside, behind locked doors. But what if he didn't kill Edward? What if the murderer was one of us? It was chilling to speculate, and I instantly rejected the thought of Gran or Amy having anything to do with the murder. It was harder to dismiss Ryan from suspicion. Since yesterday he'd seemed totally unlike his old childhood self, the earnest young boy who had guarded me through the dangers of kindergarten.

Back then there was a big kid named Wilcox Goolrick who lived two farms over from ours. Wilcox was in Ryan's class, but he was an equal-opportunity bully and terrorized both of us. Fat, mean, pimpled, and scary, the kid had flunked fourth grade twice, and by sixth grade he was already shaving. He was built like a tractor, and he used to enjoy tying us up and leaving us in the woods, or taking our lunch boxes and feeding our sandwiches to his dog while we watched. One day he came hulking over to me at the bus stop, pushed me down to the ground, and stood on my back. Resisting him was impossible—it was like resisting a mountain, a mountain that seemed mindlessly intent on squashing me to death. I couldn't breathe. Just when I'd given up all hope of ever making it alive into first grade, Ryan dashed over, stood quivering in front of him, shouted "You shall not hurt us, Wilcox," and gave him a big push. Wilcox was so amazed by Ryan's courage—or his grammar—that he lost his balance and fell in the dirt. Ryan grabbed me and we both ran like hell. Even way back then I knew Ryan had done something monumentally brave. That phrase, "You shall not hurt us, Wilcox," became our battle cry through childhood, our private joke in adulthood.

I loved Ryan so much. I loved him with all my heart.

But he had lied to me. He had lied to the police. He had cleaned all the guns. Why? And what about the mortgage Vincent mentioned? What was the mortgage for? What property could Ryan own without my knowing about it?

If I asked Ryan about the mortgage, how could I explain how I knew about it? What if the mortgage had nothing to do with Edward or the murder and it really wasn't any of my business? Maybe Vincent would tell me, but I hated to give him the satisfaction of hearing me ask.

Noah might know. He heard Ryan and Edward argue in the barn that Tuesday, and perhaps his memory could be prodded if I asked him if either of them had mentioned a mortgage. I could go to his cabin right now and ask him. It was exactly what I wanted to do anyway.

The house was quiet, although I could smell breakfast cooking in the kitchen. Bacon. It must be Gran, I thought, and I didn't want to meet her. She would certainly ask the question I didn't want to answer: why was I dressed up? I hadn't worn lipstick in at least a year. And of course she would ask me where I was going. I picked my way softly down the stairs, avoiding the third step from the bottom, which always squeaked, and opened the front door while holding my breath, hoping the dogs wouldn't smell the fresh air and come racing from the kitchen to give me away.

The snow stretched out before me in an unbroken field of white. My tracks would be immediately visible to anyone looking out from the house, and I felt self-conscious about creating such an obvious line to Noah's cabin. I headed for the barn instead.

Floundering awkwardly through the soft snow, I stabbed my way through drifts that came up to my hips and quickly turned my legs to ice. It was piercingly cold and bright. The frigid air needled my face and the inside of my nose and made my lungs ache.

In the barn the warmth of the animals defrosted my nose slightly, but I walked straight down the center aisle and through the back door, then struggled across the drifts to Noah's cabin. Frozen to the bone, I arrived at his doorstep out of breath and feeling extremely self-conscious. A small spot had been shoveled clear at the threshold so the door could open. I stood and shifted from one foot to the other, eyeing the door and the blank, dark eye of the window. What if he was asleep? No, I thought, he must have shoveled the snow sometime this morning. Knock, I urged myself.

The door swung open without warning. "What a pleasant surprise," Noah said, smiling. "Come in, come in."

It was warm inside. My legs were freezing. I stood awkwardly, embarrassed at all the snow I was tracking inside.

"Take your boots off," he said. "Let me get you some slippers."

As I started to pry off one of the boots I lost my balance and hopped a little until he caught my arm to steady me.

"Here," he said, drawing up a straight-backed chair. "Sit. I'll help you."

My heart began to pound like a drum, glad, strong, allegro flourishes as he knelt at my feet and wrestled one boot off, then the other. I was too happy, and it was annoying to be so happy, to have to keep fighting the grin that threatened to break out across my face. Noah put the boots by the door and returned with a pair of leather moccasins. He lifted my right foot, put the slipper over my toes, nested the heel inside. The touch of his hand on my calf was unbearably erotic. He lifted the other leg and put the slipper on as I tried to push down the helium of feeling that welled inside me.

"You look incredible," he said. "I was just about to make tea. Would you like some? I have coffee, too."

"Coffee would be great."

"Make yourself at home," he said.

"Can I look around?" I asked. "I haven't been in here for a while."

"You can look at anything you want," he said, filling the teakettle. "Open the drawers, read my notebooks, look in the medicine cabinet if you like."

Exactly what I would love to do if he weren't here watching me, I thought. I looked around. The cabin used to be no more than a big shed dug into the hillside, with a stone wall bermed into the earth, but Ryan had remodeled it three summers ago.

"Nice view," I said. "I always liked it."

"It is a pretty view," he agreed. The picture window in the sitting area looked out on the lower meadows. The kitchen was in the southeast corner, with two windows overlooking the little pond.

"Is there enough space for you in here?" I asked. There was a tiny living room with a couch that folded out into a bed and a small bathroom, but the whole cabin was no bigger than a hotel room.

"It's fine," Noah said. "Easier to keep everything squared away."

I noticed that the bed was already stowed, the sheets and blankets neatly folded on top of the couch. On a bookshelf by the couch were several veterinary textbooks on horses, as well as a row of books of poetry: Wallace Stevens, Rumi, Yeats, Rilke. There was a small makeshift desk in one corner of the room, no more than a couple of planks laid across two columns of plastic milk crates. In the open space of one crate I saw a row of college textbooks on anatomy, chemistry, calculus, agriculture, and nutrition.

"Have you been studying?" I asked, examining the titles.

"Here," he said, crossing the room in three steps and handing me a mug. I took the cup from his hand and watched him covertly, my face hidden in the curve of the cup. The coffee was terrible, instant, even worse than mine. But he looked great. He was wearing a white T-shirt that hugged the line of muscle from shoulder to waist, and his jeans were pale from multiple washings. They fit him like a second skin. His face was open, clearly delighted to have me visit but I could tell he was anxious, too, a little short of breath, flustered to have me in the heart of his territory. His nervousness made me relax a little.

"I try to read twenty pages a night," he said. "An old habit my father ingrained in me. I like to know how things work. I like to learn."

"But you want to work on a farm?"

"You think the two are mutually exclusive?" he asked, a hint of coolness in his tone.

"Of course not," I said. "My grandmother lived on this farm all her life and she's the smartest woman I know."

"Farming is the closest thing to playing God that I can think of," he said. "You have your own garden of Eden to mess up."

"What do you think of our farm?"

Noah sat on the couch and gestured for me to sit beside him. "You really want to know?"

"Sure," I said, and sat at the far end, holding my cup demurely on my knees.

"It's a mess."

I must have looked startled, because he hurried to explain. "The woods need to be cleaned up. There's dead wood from the past fifty years piling up, so thick you can't walk through the trees. You're going to have a catastrophic fire one of these days, if you don't remove some of it."

"What about the rest of the property?" Surely he was impressed by how pretty it was, how the house was framed by the pond, the trees and fields.

"The barn's foundations are rotting—you can see it's an old stone foundation from the couple of feet that are visible above ground, and the mortar is crumbling. If the house was built the same year as the barn it probably needs its foundations shored up too. The whole barn is riddled with termites and dry rot. You need new beams."

I felt reprimanded, as though a teacher were giving me a less than passing grade on a prize project. "Anything else?" I asked with some impatience.

He heard it in my voice. "Sure, but maybe I should write up a list, if you're really interested. I could go on and on."

"Mmm." I believed him.

"Sorry. I get carried away. It's a gorgeous piece of land," Noah said. "The mature hardwood trees you have are worth a fortune. It's rare to find a piece of land this big that's not farmed or logged to death. You have some rare species here, spotted salamanders, all kinds of frogs, owls, turtles. It's a biologist's dream."

I knew he was only trying to soften his criticism. He was probably right about the termites, the foundations, the beams, everything—I'd heard Gran moan about the cost of maintaining it often enough.

I put my mug down on the coffee table to signal a change in the subject. "I wanted to talk to you about the argument you overheard between Ryan and my father," I said.

"Okay," he said, facing me, turning his body to put one arm over the back of the sofa. His hand was next to my shoulder, almost touching it.

I took a deep breath. "Did either of them mention a mortgage?"

He raised his eyebrows. "No, I don't think so. Why?"

"It was something I overheard Vincent say to Ryan."

"I didn't hear much. It sounded like Ryan was in over his head with gambling debts. But a mortgage—I don't recall anything like that. Could he have mortgaged the farm?" he asked.

"The farm is in my grandmother's name," I said. "I can't believe she'd give it to Ryan without telling me." Even as I spoke I could hear how ridiculous it sounded, how naive and trusting, how easily I believed, even now, that my grandmother and Ryan wouldn't keep a secret from me.

A memory darted through me, bringing a sliver of suspicion with it. Right after I flew to Khartoum to begin my sabbatical with Médecins Sans Frontières, my grandmother broke her arm when she tripped over the vacuum cleaner cord. Ryan moved in with her because he and Billy had split up, but it was good timing for both of them. She sent letters to me in Africa telling me how indispensable Ryan was, now that she couldn't drive a car or lift anything, and how glad she was to have him living with her. I didn't dwell on it much at the time because I was drowning in the crisis of caring for a starving village, and a broken arm seemed mild and easily curable in comparison. In a distracted way I was glad my brother was there for her, even though I still felt the tiny reflex of jealousy when she praised him.

But now her gratitude seemed dangerous. Could Ryan have charmed her into cosigning a loan, using the farm as collateral? Unfortunately, it fit. If there was a mortgage on the farm, it would explain Ryan's conversation with Vincent: the accusations Vincent had leveled at him, the implicit admission (or at least lack of denial) in Ryan's voice. It would account for everything I'd overheard.

I turned back to Noah, pasted a smile on my face, and tried to blot out the thoughts about the mortgage that were beginning to send tendrils of panic running down my spine. As he studied me I warmed under his gaze, and forced myself to remember where I'd left the conversation.

"I'm sorry," I said. "I shouldn't be trying to involve you in the family drama."

There was concern on his face, and longing. "You can involve me anytime," he said. He put his mug down on the table, next to mine. He was sitting so close I could see the stubble he'd missed shaving on the corner of his jaw. My heart shimmered with a delicious turbulence.

"I want to hold you, Brett," he said.

I shook my head and looked down. "It's a small world on this farm, Noah. I'm a mother, a sister, a daughter. This isn't a good time to start something with you."

"Come here," he insisted.

I blurted out the truth before I could stop myself. "I'm afraid."

He reached out and touched my arm, and his intention was unmistakable. He slid his palm slowly upward. He took his time. I could feel the heat of his hand through the weave of my sweater.

"I want to kiss you," he whispered.

My heart was beating so loud in my chest I was afraid he could hear it. He put his work-roughened palm against the side of my cheek, and his hand was warm. He tipped my face up and looked into my eyes, and then he kissed me.

His lips brushed mine, feather-soft at first, then firm, warm, insistent. For one soft, delicious, impossible moment, something in me buckled and collapsed, as if I'd been hiding for a long time inside walls that were toppling now, and caution disappeared. I put my arms around his neck and kissed him back. It was wonderful to be crushed against his chest, to feel the rough warmth of his face pressed against mine, to forget the farm, the murder, Vincent, everything. The wind battered the glass in the windowpane, and I thought, let it snow for a hundred years. Let me have this.

He eased his body next to mine until we were braided together in a tangle of legs, arms clasped around each other's waists, faces pressed together. When he finally leaned back to look at me his eyes were like two chips of blue sky.

"You're an incredible kisser," he said.

I met his eyes and let him see the desire in mine.

He pulled me close and I could smell rich, masculine odors of sweat, leather, and shaving cream. The back of his neck was as weathered as tree bark, permanently darkened and seamed by the sun. I touched his face and pushed his thick, dark hair back from his brow, where it stuck out in uneven wisps, as if he'd cut it himself. His face relaxed under my touch, and a lazy smile drifted over his lips, as if we had all the time in the world.

"You sure remind me of a girl I used to know," he said.

I tweaked his nose. "That's not a tactful thing to say, under the circumstances."

"We were in tenth grade," he continued, unperturbed, snuggling down deeper in the couch, tugging me closer. "She sat ahead of me in geometry class. Every time a lock of her hair fell on my desk I got hard. I just about lived for geometry class."

I laughed out loud. "Did you ever tell her that?"

"No. She belonged to the captain of the football team, and he tended to beat up on her admirers."

Noah leaned back and went on talking, his voice a low rumble that vibrated in my ear as I lay my head on his chest. "I was so shy back then I was invisible. I probably couldn't have said anything to her even if she'd been available. I never joined any clubs, never volunteered anything in class, and never talked to girls."

"You should have told her you wanted her."

He looked at me and smiled his lazy smile as he twirled a tendril of my hair around his finger, then kissed it, his eyes never leaving my face. "I want you," he murmured.

I put my arms around his neck and felt a rush of heat in my bones, my breasts, my belly, in the warm loosening of my thighs when I kissed him. The dark events of yesterday shrank until the world became no more than sensation, where surfaces were velvet and the atmosphere was full of breathing. My lips touched his lips, our kisses a delicate surprise, a discovery. He tasted like peppermint. His tongue was warm from the tea.

I wanted him, the hard roughness of him, the thrust of him, the whole of him. I wanted him to see me naked and suck the tips of my breasts and lick the bumps of my spine. I wanted to be purged, cleansed, exorcised, and I wanted him to do it. My breath came hot as I touched the outer whorls of his ear with the tip of my tongue. He shivered.

"I want you," I whispered.

We both stood up from the couch and he began to undress me, lifting the hem of my sweater, exposing the camisole underneath. I unbuttoned his jeans and pushed them to the floor while he unzipped my trousers and I stepped out of them. When we were naked I looked at him and saw that his face reflected a curious mixture of anxiety and yearning, which was close to how I felt. Noah went into the bathroom and came back with a foil-covered package.

"I could pull out the couch and make up the bed," he said.

"No." I kissed him. He reached out to cup my

breast, and I pressed closer to him. We stood naked together, his belly pressed to mine, his hard shaft between us. My skin felt electric, shimmering everywhere that he touched me, and my legs began to tremble.

He guided me backward until I tumbled down on the couch, and then he ripped open the foil wrapping on the condom and fit the latex sheath over the crown of his cock. The smooth, hard globes of his biceps enclosed me, and I could smell soap on his skin as he pressed the length of his body against me.

I wrapped my legs around him. He entered me in one fluid motion, and I gasped, unprepared for the volume of pleasure, the familiar, luscious fullness, the same liquid response I'd felt as a teenager. Relief and pleasure cascaded through me in waves. His buttocks tightened in my palms as he began to fuck me, hard, and I moaned and arched my hips to receive him. He hammered against me, insistent, persevering, pounding the core of me, as if to force the darkness out. The air around us felt charged, and the need to reach climax rose in me so quickly it felt like a force of nature, the opposite of gravity, a pull from the sky, impossible to resist. We came at the same time, groaning, laughing, and I thought this is good, this is incredible, how could this not be a good thing?

A knock came, loud, at the door. Then louder, hard as a shotgun blast on the window.

A face was pressed against the glass, and in one horrified moment I realized it was Amy. I saw recognition dawn on her face, and then a great rage distorted her mouth as she began to scream through the glass. "You slut!" she yelled. "You fucking slut! How dare you!"

I struggled to pull myself away from Noah and cover my nakedness. Noah snatched what clothes he could find while I grabbed a saddle blanket hanging on the back of the couch and wrapped it around me.

Amy was marching resolutely away from the cabin, straight back to the house as I raced out the door. "Amy, stop!" I called after her, but my daughter charged across the meadow without looking back. I ran toward her, plunging through the deep snow in bare legs and feet, struggling to keep the blanket in place.

When I finally reached her I tried to grab her by the arm and caught a mass of her hair instead. Her head snapped back, and she gave a shout of anguish. Appalled at my mistake, I stood frozen to the spot, still clutching a fistful of her hair as she whirled around to face me, her lips drawn into a tight, furious line. I let go and tried to back away, but the snow was too deep and Amy was too quick.

She drew back her right arm and swung at me with her fist, her whole body engaged in the delivery. *Wham!* The blow smacked me on the face with a power that jolted me. It was amazingly painful, and I tottered, stunned by the blow, and fell down into a drift. What an arm on that kid, I thought with an odd little thrill of pride that was quickly swallowed by shock. My cheek tingled from the impact, and I could tell it would result in a bruise that would last for a week.

The snow was unbearably cold, numbing my feet, legs, and belly where the blanket had fallen open. From a long way away I could hear Noah shout, stop, stop, but the sound of his voice seemed to come from an unimaginable distance. I couldn't move. My eyes were open, and I saw the blue shadowed hollow of the snowdrift pulse like a beating heart, in tempo with the throbbing in my head.

By the time Noah arrived at my side, Amy was halfway back to the house. "Brett? Can you move?" he asked, leaning over me.

My face hurt, and my body felt as though it had been run over by a train. Amy had never hit me before. No one had ever hit me before. It hurt a lot, much more than I ever thought it would. Slowly, delicately, I traced the superciliary arch and the orbital bone above and below my eye. Nothing was broken. "I'm okay," I gasped. I felt numb. I'm really okay, I thought. This is just another thing that happened. I'll be fine. I can handle this.

"Come on," Noah urged. "Come back to my cabin."

I sat up and let him lead me back to the cabin. It was warm inside. My head was pounding. Noah helped me into my clothes and made me lie on the couch with a pillow under my head and two blankets tucked around me, and when he was sure I would stay there he went to the stove to put the kettle on. I was glad he was there to make a fuss over me; I needed someone to make a fuss, just as much as I needed some time to figure this out.

As I lay on his couch staring at the ceiling I tried to think of how I was supposed to react, what I should say to my daughter. My insides felt wobbly, my eye ached, and I realized Amy could have done some damage. Consciousness took effort, and I knew I was slipping in and out of shock. I'm okay, I chanted dully inside my mind, I'm okay.

Noah brought me another cup of his terrible coffee, pressed the mug into my hands, and told me to drink, and I did, mechanically. The cup clattered against my teeth. He tucked the blankets more securely around my legs and sat beside me on the couch with my feet in his lap.

"Did she hit you in the face?" He rubbed my feet to restore some warmth.

I nodded.

"Can you count to ten?"

I counted off the numbers.

"You remember who our current president is?"

"I'm okay. I'm not concussed," I lied, automatically protecting her.

"I'm sorry." He shook his head, opened his mouth as if to say more, then closed it.

"It's all right. I probably deserved it."

Noah's expression remained soft, concerned, but his voice was hard. "Don't ever say that again, Brett."

My eyes filled with tears as the shock faded. "I'm not a good person, Noah."

"Me neither. But we don't deserve to get beat up for it."

I sipped my coffee. "Why was Amy here? Why did she have to see us like that?"

"She probably saw your tracks and came over to investigate. I've noticed she keeps a close eye on you. She doesn't want to lose you."

"But I was careful," I moaned. "I went through the barn." But that wouldn't be enough, I realized. It was true; Amy did keep a close eye on me. In spite of her chilly attitude, she didn't like it when I disappeared without telling her where I was going, and she could be hysterical if I failed to return from town or a hunt exactly when I promised.

Noah gave me a rueful smile. "I can't tell you how sorry I am."

I placed the mug on the floor, leaned back on the pillow, and covered my face with my arm. "I'm the one who should be sorry."

"It's not your fault."

"We have to leave the farm, Noah. We have to get away from here."

"Fine with me. Where do you want to go?"

"I'm not talking about you and me. I mean Amy and me."

He removed his hand from my ankle. "I see."

"I've neglected her. I left her to go to Africa, and I stayed away too long. I know it was a mistake, now. A terrible mistake. It seemed so noble, and Ryan and Gran encouraged me to do it, but who knows why they wanted me out of here? It was probably more convenient to both of them to have me out of the way. No one told me to think about Amy, and what my leaving might do to her. Not even Dan."

I realized I was babbling now, but I couldn't shut up. "I never should have gone. She didn't want me to go. I have to make it up to her."

"What about you?" Noah asked.

"What about me?" I wasn't sure what he meant.

"What about what you want, what you need? Do you really think you're going to be any good to Amy if you can't figure out that part of the equation? Can you show her how to be happy if you're not?"

"I can. I will. I have plans."

"What plans?" His eyes never left my face.

"I want to move out west. Colorado, maybe," I said, embarrassed by his scrutiny.

Noah was silent for a few beats, and I could see the disappointment on his face. What did he expect? That we could live happily ever after here on my grandmother's farm? With a growing resignation I realized how much baggage I carried with me from the past, how complicated it was, how burdened with lies and distrust. And now I had a daughter who hated me. It was too much for any man to cope with. It was almost too much for me.

I pulled my feet away from him and struggled to sit up. "I can't talk about this right now. I need to see if Amy's all right."

Noah looked irritated. "Amy just beat the crap out

of you. Why don't you leave her alone until she real-
izes what she's done? Let her come to you."

"She won't." I pulled myself up from the couch,
and the movement made me dizzy. "She's in more
pain than you think." I worked my feet back into
their boots, and every change in my position brought
on a violent pain at the base of my skull.

Noah stood and took me in his arms. "You want
me to walk you back to the house?"

"No. I'm fine, really."

"I'll come up later and see how you're doing."

I sighed and leaned my head against the door
frame. How nice it would be to relax into those arms,
to sink against that chest, to let him love me. To let
myself love him. I studied his eyes, the pale starburst
around each pupil, and wondered: how do you decide who you trust?

"Thanks for the coffee," I said.

Noah touched my face with his hand, the callused
palm warm against my cheek. There was longing in
his face, and that powerful loneliness.

"Good-bye," I said.

The cold felt good. It cut the dizziness and soothed
the ache in my skull. I made my way unsteadily
through the blinding storm toward the lamplit haven
of the house. When I entered the kitchen door I saw
my grandmother scraping grease from the frying pan
into the compost jar.

"Brett McBride, I want to have a chat with you,"
she said when she saw me. "Your daughter came

waltzing in here and said she saw you fucking Noah—her words, not mine. Is that true?"

"Yes." I groped for a chair, sat, and held my head in both hands. I felt like I was going to throw up.

"What's the matter? Did that man hurt you? I swear, if he hurt you—"

"Amy hit me," I said.

"She what?"

"She hit me. I'm going to have a black eye in another couple hours. I should put ice on it but I'm too damn cold already."

"How in the world—?"

"She saw us through the window at his cabin. I ran out the door and when I reached out to stop her I accidentally grabbed her hair and yanked it. She turned around and socked me."

"Oh my sweet Jesus," Gran breathed. "I had no idea. She really hit you?"

"Knocked me down and ran away," I said ruefully, running a hand along the tender side of my face.

"Didn't you try to stop her?"

"No."

"You mean you just let her hit you?"

"Yes."

"We can't have this, Brett. I'm going to speak to her right now." Gran unwrapped the tea towel she'd tied around her middle and threw it on the counter. "That child has just about shredded my last nerve."

"Gran, wait. I can handle this."

She paused and looked at me, her features burning

with self-righteousness. "I don't care what you've done, Brett. Your daughter has no excuse for this barbaric behavior. I won't let her treat you this way."

"What are you going to do?" I asked, alarmed at the fire in my grandmother's eye.

"You'll see," she said, and swept out of the kitchen.

"Gran, wait," I said, and dragged myself up to follow her. The floor felt uneven, as if a giant hand were tipping it this way and that. "Please." I caught up to her, grasped the hem of her jacket, and pulled. "If you love me at all, let me do this by myself."

She whirled around to face me, her lips tight as a sewn line, her cheeks flushed, her eyes bright with outrage. I could see she was deeply upset over the events of the past two days: the murder, the suspicions of the police, Vincent's presence in the house, and my indiscretion with Noah. It wasn't just Amy's violence that sent her over the brink, ready to lash out; it was all too much for her.

"I can do this," I said gently, insisting.

Amy lay on her bed, face up, hands at her side. When I closed the door behind me she turned to face the wall.

I approached her cautiously, sat on the bed, and looked at the side of my daughter's face. Amy was so pale I could see the blue vein at her temple, beating like a tiny drum, telegraphing her rage. I knew I had to watch myself, take it slow, and avoid saying anything I'd regret later.

"Talk to me, Amy."

"No," Amy said.

"You hit me. No matter how angry you are, you can't hit people."

Amy's voice was cool and hard. "Maybe I should tell my father about this. Maybe he'll have a problem with a hired man who's fucking you. Maybe he'll arrest him."

"Maybe he will."

"Noah doesn't love you." Amy's voice was sarcastic. "He knows you're easy, that's all."

I was stung by the possibility of truth in her statement, but I cleared my throat and shook my head, as if to dismiss her words. "I'm worried about you, Amy. I know you're angry with me, but hitting me is way over the line. Tell me what's going on."

"Why should I talk to you? Remember the last time we had one of our mother-daughter talks? Right before you left for Africa?"

"I'm not sure," I said.

"You said I could have a new computer."

"I don't remember that."

"No, you wouldn't, would you? You were too busy planning to leave."

"Is it a computer you want? Is that why—?" Why you've been stealing money, I wanted to say, but I didn't dare open that can of worms.

Amy's voice was tight with anger. "You don't care anything about me. You don't even know me anymore. Why should I talk to you?"

"Because I'm your mother. Because I love you. I'm

sorry you had to see Noah and me like that, but that's no excuse for hitting me."

"I can't believe you! You tear up my room, you go through all my things, then I see you fucking him like an animal." Her voice was choked with unshed tears. She closed her eyes and shook her head. "I don't trust you anymore."

"I'm sorry for that. But I'm not too happy with you either. How did you get that will? Did you steal it?"

"I don't want to talk to you," she whispered.

"This is serious, Amy. Serious enough to put your uncle in jail."

There was a long silence between us as Amy looked out at the snow ticking against the window. "I used to feel sorry for you," she said in a faraway voice. "When you got back from Africa you were so sick. All you talked about was food. Killing food, growing food, finding food. But you barely ate anything. I was so worried about you. I felt like I had to be here to take care of you, to keep you from dying. But you've got Noah now. He can take care of you. I'm just in the way."

My eyes burned. "You're my daughter, Amy. You could never be in the way."

"I don't want to live with you anymore. I want to go live with my dad."

I felt the sledgehammer blow to my heart. "Oh, Amy," I said.

Her voice was weary but determined. "Dad told me all I had to do was ask, and he'd take me back. Well, I'm going to ask him. I'm through with you.

I've had it. If Dad wants to know why I'm leaving, I'll tell him to ask you. Okay?"

"No, it's not okay," I said. "You have to give us another chance. I'll do whatever it takes. I'm willing to meet you halfway. Can't you do the same?"

"I don't think so," my daughter said, looking at me as if I were already part of a past she'd rather forget. "Please get out of my room."

I put up a hand to cradle my face, which was throbbing. The ache at the base of my skull was blooming into a larger pain that shot currents of fire down my neck, and a wave of dizziness struck me. It was time for a tactical retreat, time to lie down, think this through, and take a fistful of aspirin. With as much dignity as I could muster, I rose from her bed, walked out, and closed the door behind me, then staggered down the hall to my room.

There were always battles, I thought, easing myself down on the bed. You've been here before, and the lesson has always remained the same: don't lose your temper, and don't sink to her level. Never give up being Mom.

I had a sudden vivid memory of the doctor bag Gran gave me when I decided to go into med school. For one solid week when she was three, Amy was obsessed with it. There were rows of scissors, needles, and forceps neatly arranged inside the smooth leather reticule, all of them sharp and shiny and alluringly dangerous. She wanted to play with them in the worst way, and there was no way I was going to let her. One afternoon she spent a full fifteen minutes sobbing her heart out on my bed after I insisted for the umpteenth time that the bag was not a toy.

"I make you disappear, Mommy," she said darkly, after the tears finally subsided.

I smoothed her hair back from her hot little forehead. "How are you going to make me disappear?"

"I say the magic word."

"What's that?" I asked.

"Applecadabra," she said, as menacingly as she dared.

The magic words had grown stronger over the last fifteen years. They were more frightening and more powerful than I ever expected them to be. But I was still here. And I was still the mom.

# Chapter Six

I tapped lightly on my grandmother's door and swung it open. Gran looked up from her desk and smiled anxiously. "How did it go?" she asked.

"Not good," I said. Gran nodded wearily and indicated the chair in front of the desk.

I sat down and let my head fall forward until my cheek rested against the surface of the desk. My neck ached. My eye hurt. My whole body felt as though it had been tumbled in an avalanche. The storm had returned with an even greater fury, and the house groaned as the wind pummeled the walls. The windows were unnaturally dark as the clouds thickened and disgorged the snow that whispered against the glass.

Gran's fingers had been resting lightly on her Royal typewriter, an old manual that she refused to replace with anything electric. After I sat down she leaned forward companionably, one elbow propped to the side of the Royal, and touched my cheek.

"You've been crying," she said, her voice soft.

"Amy says she wants to live with her dad."

"Would that be such a terrible thing?"

I sat up and gave her a look. "Of course it would be a terrible thing. It would be wrong."

"Why?"

"I don't know," I admitted moodily.

"I think it would be good for both of you," she said.

"How can you say that? She's only fifteen. I've left her alone long enough. I should never have gone to Africa right after the divorce. It was selfish."

"In Ethiopia girls are often married by the time they're fifteen. They have their own households, their own children. You were only two years older than she is now when you gave birth to her."

"It's not a recipe for success in my book," I said.

"It worked for you, though. Once you had Amy you were unstoppable. Everyone predicted such dire things when you married Dan and went ahead with the pregnancy, but you turned out fine. Amy is more like you than you think. She needs autonomy. There isn't anything here she can control; she's at the bottom of the pecking order. I've watched our Amy for the past twelve months, and, Brett, she's not happy."

"But Dan leaves her alone all day and every other night! That can't be a good thing for her." I glared at my grandmother, feeling irritable at her unexpected indifference to what I knew would be a huge mistake.

Gran continued to look at me, her eyes soft with compassion, but there was also an unyielding certainty there. She knew what she knew, and I wouldn't change her mind. After a while I couldn't bear her scrutiny and let my gaze wander around the room, which had always soothed me with its familiarity and fertile clutter. It was the largest room in the house, large enough for three tall windows, four bookshelves, a dresser with six pot-bellied drawers, two overstuffed chairs, her Hepplewhite writing desk, and a spool bed. The floor was layered in Persian carpets, bought long ago when such things could be had for a fraction of their present worth. The smell of mothballs mingled with mildew and old books.

Lamplight flooded the litter of objects scattered across her desk: a hummingbird's nest held two eggs the size of peas inside a gray sack of whisker-thin twigs; a howler monkey skull sat between small framed pictures of Ryan and me. Chunks of amethyst, quartz, and feldspar held down stacks of papers, and a desert tortoise carapace she'd found in the Mojave perched on top of her OED.

"I have too many things," she said, catching my eye as I made my visual survey of her desk. "I know it's junk. I can't stop from wanting to surround myself."

"You've been a great mom to me," I said. "I just wish you hadn't lied."

Her eyes swam with sudden tears. "Oh, Brett, I wish you didn't have to go through this sordid business of having the past thrown up in your face."

"Why did you do it?" I asked.

Her mouth went slack and I noticed with a little

shock how old she looked when she relaxed her face.
"You were happy, growing up. I didn't want to tamper with that. Then you were pregnant." She shook her head. "You were so determined to do everything, to have Amy and a marriage and a degree in medicine. I wanted to support you any way I possibly could."

"You did," I said. "But you should have told me the truth about my parents."

"I know. Of course. It's obvious now, isn't it? But the pain and mess of that year your parents fell apart was beyond imagining."

"Tell me about it," I said. "I need to know."

Gran sat back and rubbed her forehead, as if the memory gave her a headache. "I was utterly powerless to break the spell Vincent cast over Edward. It was like watching a witch, to see how that boy could hold Edward's gaze."

I studied her face. Her words came slowly, as if the truth took effort.

"He was the most beautiful sixteen-year-old I'd ever seen," Gran said. "Smooth. Ripe. Wildly sexual. He aimed his beauty at Edward even at the dinner table, licking his lips and biting into a buttered biscuit in a parody of eating, staring at Edward with those bedroom eyes."

"Why didn't my mother do something about it?" I asked.

"She didn't think it was possible for Edward to love anyone else, especially a boy. In some ways your mother was fairly unimaginative. Her mind ran in a single track, and anything outside that track was discarded. She loved Edward so much she couldn't imagine he might be tempted by Vincent."

"Tell me about her," I said.

Gran's eyes lost their focus then and her face softened as she directed her thoughts inward, to the past. "She was devoted to you. You look so much like her, Brett. She was about your age when she died. You have her hair, her eyes. She was stunning. Like a painting. A Titian, or a Renoir. I think she wanted to be a good housewife, but she wasn't. It was a family joke, how poorly she cooked. I remember one morning I came down the stairs and saw her standing at the stove, reading a book, stirring oatmeal that was burning up right under her nose. I mean it was absolutely black charcoal, and the smoke was so thick I thought the house was on fire. That was how much she could lose herself in reading. She burned most meals because she would try to read and cook at the same time.

"She loved reading fiction, any kind of story. The classics, especially, just like you. She didn't have any particular ambition to get a job or move out of this house. She was intelligent, but she was timid, and she hated to talk to strangers. She liked being a wife. That was enough for her. Or it would have been, if she could have held Edward's attention."

"What was my father like?"

"He was greedy, darling. He was just too damned greedy. But it hurt to lose Edward, more than I could ever admit to anyone. I adored him. We all did. He reminded me of a fair-haired Errol Flynn—a strong, well-made man, handsome and intelligent. When he moved in he filled this house with noise and life, though he always seemed edgy here. The farm confined him.

"But he was a wonderful man, Brett. Talking to him made me realize how delicious words could be, how they could convey the most subtle and powerful observations. It made me drunk to talk to him. Our conversations were incredible, full of laughter, surprise, sparks.

"But when he left, the humiliation was fatal for your mother. She had no defense against a blow like that. She took after her father, your grandfather Clarence, who never saw the world in anything but black and white. She simply didn't have the resources to understand what had happened, or survive it."

"What did you do after she died? Did you tell my father she was dead? Did he try to take us away?"

"I sent him a clipping of her obituary, but I never heard from him."

I winced. "So you had no choice, really. You had to take care of us."

"Brett, I loved you and Ryan as if you were my own. Even if Edward had wanted you I would have fought to keep you."

"But your own daughter had just died! You must have been devastated."

"I was. The day after Caroline died I chopped down the pear tree in the front yard. It was a beautiful tree, fifteen feet tall and covered in blooms, but when I was done there wasn't a piece of wood left that wouldn't fit in the woodstove."

"How did you ever get over her death?" I asked, certain I could never get over the death of my daughter. A loss of that magnitude was unthinkable, beyond comprehension.

"Within a month after Caroline's death I booked my first trip overseas. I packed you and Ryan off to my cousin Ned and his wife Charlotte down in Binghamton—do you remember them?"

"No," I said. My first real memories of people didn't come until later, when I was three or four, so I had no recollections of the drama surrounding my mother's death.

"And then I flew to Nairobi. I wasn't afraid of anything anymore. I wasn't afraid of writing, or leaving the farm, or showing the world what I really thought. Up until Caroline's death I'd been afraid of all those things, but after she died, there was nothing left to fear. No shame, no rejection, no exposure or humiliation could begin to rival the pain of losing my daughter. It took that kind of recklessness, that sense of having nothing left to lose, for me to risk writing the words that were in me."

I nodded, suddenly weary of her recital of how things had worked out for her. In another minute she'd be talking about her awards, her travels, her nomination for the Pulitzer, and I had heard all those stories before.

She caught the look of fatigue on my face, and came abruptly back to the present. "What I can't understand is what in the world was Edward thinking? Why did he resurface?"

"Maybe he wanted his family back," I said.

"That would be impossible." Her gaze slid beyond me to the window, her expression serene and implacable. It irked me.

"Why? I would have loved the chance to meet my father, to know him. Ryan's been meeting him in secret for the past thirty years. Why couldn't he have moved in with us?" There were a thousand questions I wished I could ask him. Did he hunt, or travel, or play an instrument? Did he love old books and music? Was he driven in the same way that I was driven? Did he regret leaving me, at all? Then there was the most important question, the only question that really mattered: why did he give me up?

My grandmother made a face as though she were sucking a lemon. "Finding out about Ryan and Edward confirms some of my worst fears about Ryan."

Relief blossomed in me at her words, as I realized she could finally see the feet of clay in Ryan, her golden boy. "What?" I asked. "That he can be sly?"

"That he's weak."

"You think Edward purchased his silence," I said.

"Yes, exactly. If he could do that then what else would Ryan do for money?"

Someone rapped on her bedroom door, startling both of us. Gran rose to her feet, crossed the room, and opened the door.

"Mind if I come in?" Vincent said, and walked past her. He gave me a curt nod, then edged over to stand at the window and look out over the buried cars. He was sleek as a cat, I thought: aloof, tidy, predatory.

"Sit," Gran said, gesturing to the overstuffed chair by the window. She returned to her seat behind the desk, as if to distance herself from whatever he had to say. "What can I do for you?"

"You've done well for yourself, Emily," Vincent said, settling back in the chair as if this were a social call. "I see your byline every other month in the *New Yorker*. They seem to have quite a fetish for you."

Gran crossed her arms against her chest and waited.

"But your parents left you some money, didn't they? And the farm, of course."

"If you're here to review my history, Vincent, I have better ways to spend my time."

"Edward did well, too. Did you know? He was featured twice in *Architectural Digest* last year."

"Really?" I asked. I felt a spark of pride, which quickly died when Gran shot me a look of disapproval. I would look up the issues later, I thought, irritated at her impulse to squash information about my father, even now, when she was in the middle of confessing it.

"Yes," Vincent said, flicking a sideways glance in my direction. "He left a sizeable estate. Altogether it's probably worth a little over six million dollars."

The figure was close to what I'd guessed from reading the will, but hearing it spoken out loud made my pulse race. My grandmother's face remained smooth as stone.

"So many friends died, you know. AIDS. He inherited a lot from those friends, and earned the rest. He was a hard worker, our Edward."

Gran's eyes narrowed. "So you're rich now."

Vincent's lips tightened into a smile that never reached his eyes. "That's why I wanted to talk to you."

"Me? Why?"

"Have you seen Edward's new will?"

She stared at him, granite-eyed, giving nothing away. My chest felt tight, and I could feel a prickle of sweat break out on my back. Last night I'd slipped the will inside a rip in the lining of my suitcase. I had to find a safer place for it, I thought, sure that Vincent wouldn't hesitate to search any of our rooms. He was probably looking for the will when I asked him to stop paging through our photo albums the night before.

Vincent went on. "Edward wrote a new will, giving the bulk of his estate to Ryan. It was silly of him, really. We had a fight. He was angry at me and wanted to do something extravagant to teach me a lesson. He wrote the will himself and had it witnessed, but it was never filed. His lawyer phoned the day after Edward left Manhattan to visit you. The lawyer said he'd missed his appointment to record his new will. That's why I came up here—Edward never missed an appointment. I knew something was wrong."

A slow smile crept across my grandmother's face. "Afraid you won't be paid for all the time you spent on your belly, Vincent?"

His voice was soft, but the threat was unmistakable. "I intend to inherit Edward's estate, Emily."

I remained silent. My grandmother's expression hardened, tight as a vault.

Vincent went on. "Edward was out of his mind with worry about Ryan. And he was so sick. The will won't hold up in court."

"Ryan never needed Edward's money, or his worrying," she said. "Ryan makes a very comfortable living."

"Did you know Ryan mortgaged the farm?" Vincent said.

If I had been standing I would have staggered and fallen. The suspicion had skittered across my mind, but I'd ignored it, deflected it, refused to let it in. But when Vincent said it out loud I knew it had to be true. I turned to my grandmother.

"You gave him the farm," I said, daring her to contradict me.

Gran looked nervous for the first time since Vincent had entered the room. Her voice was low, pleading. "When I broke my arm I was absolutely helpless, Brett. I couldn't type, or drive, or cook, or even dress myself. I was so depressed I could barely get up in the mornings. You were in Africa, and Ryan was all I had. When he realized how desperate I was, he stayed with me, day and night. If it weren't for him I don't know what I would have done."

"So you gave him the farm."

"I deeded the title over to him. It was really no more than a gesture at the time, since it didn't give him anything more than he already had. But I wanted him to know how much his being here meant to me. He was a godsend, Brett. And old-fashioned as it may seem I like the thought of a McBride living on here, to continue with the tradition of the farm. While I was recovering I had a lot of time to think about these things, and frankly, I felt very close to death." She pressed her lips together. "I still do," she added in a whisper.

"What about me?" I asked. My voice was raw, and the betrayals of the past two days filled me with an anguish so deep I felt as if the foundations of my life had turned to mud. My mind whirled with unanswered questions. How could my grandmother sign the farm over to Ryan without even thinking of me? She was a woman, too, damn it. Did she still believe in something so archaic as primogeniture, and was that why her grandson was her only heir? Was I so negligible, no more than an afterthought?

She plucked nervously at the cuff of her blouse. "You were in Africa. You wanted to see the world. I didn't want you to feel tied down."

"So you gave the farm to a gambling addict?"

"Don't say that. He's going through a bad patch right now, but he'll pull through."

"I'm afraid not," Vincent said. "He signed the farm over to the Bank of America in exchange for two hundred and fifty thousand dollars. He's missed the last five payments. They've already started foreclosure proceedings."

"That's impossible," she snapped. "Who told you such a thing?"

"Edward told me. Face it, Emily: Ryan's gambling losses are huge, and time is running out. The bank will own the farm in another two weeks if they don't get their money."

"This can't be true. I don't believe it." I could see the struggle in her features, to hide her shock.

But I knew it was true. Ryan hadn't denied it when Vincent asked him about the mortgage; instead he'd asked Vincent how he knew about it. For the past few weeks Ryan had been withdrawn, depressed, and haggard, and whenever he made polite conversation I could feel the effort behind it. Now it all made sense.

Vincent shrugged. "I'm sure the police will agree it provides Ryan with a motive for murder, if he thinks he can inherit Edward's estate. Any bank in the state would be willing to front him the money if they knew he had that kind of legacy coming to him. And Ryan told me he met Edward on the day he died." He smoothed his mustache with his index finger and cast a sideways glance at me. "In the barn, actually. Where the police found all those bloodstains."

Gran stared at him while the clouds swirled and thickened outside until the last scrap of light was smothered. A cascade of thunder rippled the air and rattled the walls. The three of us sat in the cold gloom. No one spoke.

Finally Vincent coughed delicately and leaned forward. "Edward made the mistake of telling Ryan about his new will. Then Edward was shot to death. Seems more than a coincidence, wouldn't you say?"

Gran sighed and removed her half glasses, rubbed the bridge of her nose with her thumb and forefinger. I felt a sudden, crushing fatigue that turned my bones to lead. To be in the same room with Vincent exhausted me.

"What I find even more interesting," Gran said, "is that you knew Edward was coming here, and you knew he changed his will. That certainly sounds like a motive for murder to me. Of course I can see how much you'd like to frame my grandson for it, but you won't get away with it."

"If I murdered Edward, why would I be asking you about the will? I'd have it."

"Perhaps you do, and you want to make sure no one else has a copy. Or"—and here she lifted an eyebrow—"perhaps Edward had the sense to hide the will somewhere on the farm before you killed him."

He smiled at her. "Edward's estate is mine, Emily. And I intend to have it."

"I have nothing more to say to you." Her voice was quiet, edged in contempt. "Now get out."

As soon as Vincent left the room and we heard the tread of his heels going down the stairs, Gran jumped up and strode out into the hallway. She entered Ryan's room without knocking, her anger unleashed enough to make her skirt snap. I followed at a trot, determined not to miss whatever transpired between them.

Ryan sat up straight, startled from his reading, blinking at this sudden intrusion. Entering his room was like entering another house altogether, because this was the only room that was kept impeccably clean. The plants in the window were lush with health, the fabric of the upholstered chairs and bedspread harmonized with the curtains, and the hardwood floor had been waxed to a high gloss. For the thousandth time his room made me wonder how someone so meticulous could be so sloppy about money.

Gran spoke without preamble, her voice strained. "Vincent told us you mortgaged the farm. Is it true?"

The blood drained from Ryan's face as he closed his book and laid it carefully on the table. He couldn't meet her eyes.

"Have you lost your mind?" I asked him. "How could you put us in this position?"

"It was surprisingly easy," he said, his voice soft.

"How much did you lose?" I asked.

"Everything. I owe the bank two hundred and fifty thousand dollars."

Gran sat heavily in a chair and buried her face in her hands.

"How much time do we have?" I asked him.

"Two weeks."

Gran looked up at him. "Can't we just pay them the interest? We might scrape that much cash together in two weeks."

Ryan looked out the window. "It's gone beyond that stage, I'm afraid. They've rescinded the loan. We have to pay it all."

"We can't," she said. Her face was white.

"Don't you have money?" His voice was bitter. "You're a celebrity. How do you pay for all those trips? All those shopping sprees in New York?"

"It's gone," she said. "I spent it. There was always more fame than money." The air went out of her then and she sank back and let her hands fall in her lap.

"What about the stocks your parents left you?" he asked.

"I cashed those in long ago so I could send you and Brett to Cornell. And God knows the farm has never paid for itself," she said.

"Then maybe it's time to let it go," he said.

I sat down heavily on his bed. It was a terrifying thought. The farm was home, and it had nurtured me with its living presence ever since I'd been born. The hundreds of acres of unlogged hemlock, fir, hickory, and oak were where I had learned to hunt, to listen, to be still, to be. This place was in me. It had touched me, marked me like a wound.

"I'd rather die than lose this place," Gran said, sitting up. "My father spent his life building this house. Planting the trees. Digging stones out of the pastures. He and my mother are buried here. I can't give it up."

He lifted his hands and let them drop. "I'm sorry. But we'll have to."

"How could you do this?" I whispered. Where was the brother I loved and cherished and needed, the boy who was so fussy and precise about his clothes and his grooming, the boy who extended that fuss and precision to me as if it were the most natural thing in the world to advise his little sister that plaid skirts didn't go with striped blouses, that red and orange were difficult colors to combine, that patent leather could be overdone? I relied on him with the faith of a true believer. He used to brush and braid my hair every morning, inspect my clothes for lint, and make sure the pleats of my skirts were razor sharp. He was the one who got a pained look on his face and said "No, honey," when I wanted to wear a plastic rose in my hair. I'd always trusted his judgment, until now.

He shook his head. "I can't explain it."

"Try," I said.

There was a long, painful pause, and when he spoke his voice was tight with shame. "It began with gratitude," he said. His smile was wry, bitter. "The manager at the casino, Malcolm Electric Warrior, had a horse. Not a valuable horse, but an old bay thoroughbred, twenty-five years old, the horse he grew up with, practically a member of the family. Anyway, the horse collapsed last spring, and Malcolm called me because he'd heard I was a vet with a light touch, good hands. The horse had a twisted bowel, and I did the surgery, but its age made it a delicate operation. When the horse recovered, Malcolm was grateful, and he invited me into the back room at the casino for the no-limit poker night. He gave me a two-thousand-dollar stake, free and clear above my fee."

I gave a snort of disgust at the transparency of such a gift.

Ryan raked his fingers through his hair and continued. "My credit seemed infinite, and the first night I went there I was on a streak, I couldn't lose, and in two hours I was up eighty thousand dollars. Then the table went cold." He shrugged. "For the next three weeks I tried to win it all back, but the hole got deeper and deeper. First I went down eight thousand, then thirty-six thousand, then ninety thousand. It seemed unreal. I couldn't stop. Not when I'd lost so much. When I went back the fourth week, Malcolm told me his horse had died.

"He was furious. He claimed I should have told him the horse had no chance of surviving the surgery and had him put down. After threatening me with a lawsuit, he told me I'd have to pay off my debt or he'd have a lien taken out on my bank accounts and property. So I went to the bank and mortgaged the farm."

Ryan bit his lip and a dark flush crawled across his face as the silence swelled in the room. He seemed unable to go on.

"But you couldn't stop there," I guessed.

"No," he said. "I couldn't stop. I knew I'd be poor

for the rest of my life if I didn't win it back. Malcolm extended my credit, and I tried. God knows I tried. But I lost everything."

I stared openmouthed at my brother, struggling to absorb the catastrophe he had visited upon us. When I looked at my grandmother I could see her eyes well up with tears as her chest rose and fell with quick, uneven breathing. Ryan grew visibly restless under her gaze and rose from the bed and paced the room.

"Ever since I moved back here, do you know how many clients I've lost?" he asked, darting a nervous glance at Gran. His voice was loud, defensive.

She brushed away tears with the back of her hand. "Are you complaining, Ryan?"

"My practice is dying out here, Gran. It's too isolated; half my clients have left me since I came to the farm. It's no good. I can't make it here. I need a place closer to town."

"It takes time to attract new business. You have to be patient," she said.

"I'm almost forty years old. I can't wait. Gambling the farm away was no accident, Gran. I don't want the farm. I don't want it."

She was wide-eyed with shock. "This is not a gift you can toss in the garbage, Ryan! This is your inheritance. Your mother was born here. I was born here. This farm is wider and deeper and bigger than you."

"It certainly is." He turned away from her to press his forehead against the windowpane. The sky outside was ugly. Wind buffeted the window, and I could feel frigid air blowing through the cracks.

"The farm is more than any of us can handle, Gran. It's a ruin. The foundation is a mess. The beams are all shot. The well is too shallow, and the pump won't last another year."

"We have four hundred acres of land, Ryan. Land with history."

"It's just dirt."

His words left me breathless, amazed he could be so callous.

"It's my home." There were tears in Gran's voice, a rare pleading.

Ryan turned to face her. "I wish that were enough for me. I really do."

"It's enough for me." My voice was choked with feeling. "I'll go back to the hospital. I'll shovel coal, clean toilets, do anything to keep this place going. Just tell me what to do."

"It's too late," Ryan said.

"There has to be a solution to this," Gran said. "What if you go bankrupt, Ryan? Won't that protect us?"

"No," he said. "I checked. The property is too valuable. There's too much land."

My grandmother rose from her seat and paced the floor, distress radiating from every move she made. "This can't be happening," she said. "There must be a way out."

"I've tried to see it," Ryan said, "But I can't."

Gran's face was wild with panic. "This is all Edward's doing," she cried.

I spoke up then. "No it isn't. It's Ryan's." I shot

him a glance of contempt, irritated that she was already trying to shift the blame somewhere else.

Gran ignored me, took a deep breath, and when she spoke again her voice was cool, controlled. "We have to find Edward's will. If Vincent is telling the truth, it could save us."

A tingle of fear crept down my arms, and my anger shrank until it felt like no more than a hard little stone in my belly.

Ryan laughed bitterly. "The police will love that. If we find a will leaving everything to me, I'll become their number one suspect."

"That's right," I said.

"Not if we find the murderer first," Gran said.

"We know who the murderer is, don't we?" Ryan asked. "Proving it is another matter."

"I think Vincent killed Edward," I said, hoping to distract them.

"Of course he did," Gran snapped. "Have you seen the will?" she asked, staring straight at me.

My hands tightened, and I struggled to let them relax again in my lap. Why was she asking me? What did she suspect? "No," I lied.

"Edward had it with him when he came here," Ryan said. "It's got to be here somewhere."

"I agree," Gran said.

"I think Edward may have hidden it somewhere before Vincent killed him," Ryan said. "Vincent seems awfully concerned that we might have it, which makes me think he knows it's here. Edward came here in a black Mercedes jeep. Vincent must have hidden the jeep somewhere around here after he shot him. Do you think the will is in it?"

"I doubt it—Vincent would have already searched the car, wouldn't he? I think the will is more likely to be in the house or the barn," Gran said. "We should begin by going through the house. Brett? Could you look in Amy's room?"

"Absolutely not," I said. "You have no idea what you're getting into."

"All right, we'll do it without you," she said. Her tone was eerily calm.

"Be careful," I said. "If you're right about Vincent, we're living in the same house with a murderer."

"Yes," Gran said, her eyes cold, musing, distant. "We are."

# Chapter Seven

Seventy-five-thousand years ago glaciers advanced southward from Canada toward New York state, bulldozed the trees and topsoil down to the bedrock of Devonian shale, and carved out the holes that would become the Finger Lakes. A waterfall had been created on the farm by this glacial scourge. Down in Deputron Hollow, just past the spot where I'd found Edward's body, a spring-fed creek tumbled off a cliff into a deep, rocky pool.

There was a cave concealed behind the upper arc of the waterfall, with a narrow ridge that threaded the vertical wall of the gorge and led into the cave from the top. In the summer I often edged my way along the lip of rock to stand in the open cavern behind the curtain of falling water. It was one of my favorite places on the farm then, a welcome niche of coolness in July. Now the cave would be cold as the arctic, but protected from the blizzard by its ten-foot overhang. This was where I planned to hide Edward's will.

I strode through the woods, snowshoes strapped to my feet, Edward's will in a Zip-Loc bag in my pocket, hard granules of windblown snow peppering my face. Even though the storm was still pressing down, it was a relief to be out of the house, away from the bruised feelings and multiple simmering resentments. The air was stingingly cold and fresh, laced with a hint of woodsmoke from our chimney, and as I hurried down the trail my snowshoes made a whisper of crystals in the silence.

I knew I had to hide the will outside, away from the house, where no one would find it, and I knew I had to do it now, when the snow would cover my tracks. Until we found proof that Vincent or someone else had committed the murder, it wouldn't be safe to produce any evidence that my father had wanted to leave his estate to Ryan. As soon as the police discovered the truth about Edward's visit, they would certainly believe Ryan had the opportunity to kill him, and the will provided too much motive.

The sun that stabbed through the low ceiling of clouds when I woke up this morning had disappeared in five minutes, and it looked like it would be days before we saw it shine again. It was dark. The storm continued unabated, and now it was headlining the national news. Emergency weather bulletins flashed on the television screen every few seconds, telling us that snow was expected to continue falling over the next twelve hours and accumulate to a total of thirty to thirty-six inches. Already the drifts were piling up to more than ten feet be-

tween the house and the barn. The storm was breaking all records for any November in history.

Trotting over the surface of the snow in my snowshoes sent shooting pains down my neck, but it felt
good to jog in the brisk air. The dusk of the blizzard
cast a deep, intimate silence over the snow-
cushioned brush.

My face was sore. Amy was tall for her age, muscular from years of riding horses, and feeling the
effect of her fist made me freshly aware of her
strength. Could Gran be right about Amy? I wondered. Was it really time for me to let go?

Years ago, when I went to pick her up from her
first day in kindergarten, her teacher pulled me aside
and whispered to me that Amy had walked up to
her at the end of the day and said, "Thank you, I
had a very nice time, but I'm not coming back."

As we were driving home I asked her how her
first day of school had gone.

"It was okay," she allowed. I waited for more.
"I'm the smartest one in my class," she assured me.

"Really," I said. "Did your teacher tell you that?"

"No," she said. "I noticed it myself."

Maybe she'd always been smarter than I thought.

But would it really be better if I accepted the fact
that she was grown up enough to make her own
choices about her life, and let her move back in with
Dan instead of fighting to keep her? I didn't like the
resentment she'd adopted as a permanent mask since
she'd come to live on the farm, and I liked it even
less that she felt responsible for me, that she was

afraid I might die without her. Still, I didn't want to give her up, not yet, and maybe that was all she really needed to hear from me.

But oh God, I didn't want to give up Noah either. A quick little sensory shiver passed through me, a breath of heat at my core, as the memory of his body filled me. I longed for him. I was desperately attracted to the long lean hardness of him, his strong face and kind eyes, and I felt torn at the thought that I might have to lose him to keep my daughter.

I pushed these thoughts away and hurried down the slope, eager to reach the waterfall before anyone at the house noticed I was gone. The trail where I'd found Edward's body yesterday was unrecognizable, shrouded in white. No animal tracks were visible in the blankness of the snow—the thickly falling flakes instantly disguised any footprints, including my own. The woods were quiet as the grave, dark and still and blurred by the snow that sifted down from above. Time lost all meaning in the twilight of the storm, and it occurred to me that except for one brief glimpse of sun that morning, the farm had been caught in a perpetual dusk ever since I'd discovered my father's body.

Tall pillars of rock guarded the waterfall, and I could see them now, looming above the cliff. As I made my way carefully toward the edge of the precipice I could see that the waterfall below was beginning to freeze into thick, solid ropes of ice. The cave looked like a black hole behind the stalactites of icicles that fringed the top of the waterfall. Hesitating, uneasy about entering the cave along the skinny ridge leading down, I could see the path was erased by snow, and one false step could send me hurtling over the rim of the cliff.

I took off the snowshoes to give my feet a better grip on the ledge, and cautiously inched my way down the spine of snow-covered shale that hugged the side of the chasm. The windblown snow dashed against my face, nearly blinding me. My back was pressed against the icy shale. Groping my way along without looking down, I had to stamp through the mounded snow underfoot with every step, compressing it into a slick, uneven track.

A block of ice hidden under the surface threw me off balance, and my upper body tottered for a moment over the abyss until I could slam back against the cliff. My breath came in shallow gasps. I can't afford to fall, I thought. It would be days before anyone found me, and if the fall didn't kill me, waiting for help certainly would.

Finally the snowy ledge broadened and I ducked under the overhang of dripping icicles to stand on the floor of the cave. The rock walls inside were black, coated with ice, and I crouched for a moment to catch my breath. The icicles and cold running water made a pale, translucent wall on one side, protecting me from the noise and wind of the storm.

Taking the plastic bag that contained Edward's will out of my pocket, I placed it on the floor of the cave, then gathered several loose rocks and built a cairn over it. When the cairn was a foot high I stood up and took a deep breath, as though I had let go of a dangerous weight. The will would be safe here. The blizzard would cover my tracks. No one would ever think to look for it in the cave, and I was determined to leave it here until the murder was solved.

Somehow I was still nagged by doubt that Vincent would have blown Edward away with a shotgun. Why not poison him at home? With so much easy access to Edward's medication, why risk such a messy, indiscreet murder? Of course Vincent might want to frame Ryan for the murder, but the method seemed too brutal, too spontaneous, too unlike Vincent's fastidious nature. Besides, I couldn't forget the sight of Vincent's face when I told him about Edward, the utterly convincing shock in his eyes. The grief was exaggerated, but still, I found it hard to believe that he knew Edward was dead before I told him.

And where did Amy find the will? She could have stolen it from Ryan's room. They spent hours in his room together, gossiping, listening to music, reading movie magazines. Maybe she helped herself to it when he was out. How else could she have found it? Ryan had seen our father, argued with him. Ryan had the opportunity and a damn good reason to kill him and take the will from him. The thought settled on me like winter, and I shivered.

In the past two days my beliefs about Ryan had suffered a seismic shift that left me feeling miserably disoriented and alone. My brother had always been my friend, my ally, my only sibling, a reflection of the history I thought we shared. When I was a little girl I worshipped him, followed him everywhere and copied the way he stood, the way he walked, the way he combed his hair. When he played veterinarian with our pets I was the one to hold the cat's leg straight while he splinted and bandaged it. He was the first one I went to when I found out I was pregnant with Amy, and he was the one who said I should go ahead and have the baby, if that was my heart's desire.

But yesterday I learned that he'd lied to me all my life about our parents, and the size of that lie made everything about our relationship suspect. And then there was his gambling—where did that dark urge come from, and why was it so uncontrollable that he gambled away his inheritance? He was capable of ruthlessness; I'd seen it an hour ago, when he told Gran the farm was just dirt. I felt a cold trickle of doubt about Ryan. How far would he go, to be rich?

More to the point, how far would I go to protect him?

The answer was clear the instant the question formed in my mind: I would do anything for Ryan. I would walk through fire for my brother, lie to the police or a judge or a jury. I would do whatever I could to keep him out of prison. I loved him.

Even if he killed our father for his money? a nasty little voice in my head inquired. Would I look the other way for a murderer? The question nagged at me, and I shoved it to the back of my mind and focused instead on getting out of the cave and back to the top of the cliff without falling over the edge.

I threaded my way up the ledge while the cold hammered steel nails into the marrow of my bones. Strapping on the snowshoes had to be done without gloves, and the bitter air made my fingers stiff and clumsy. Finally I was ready to go, and forced myself into a jog as I worked my way uphill through the woods, back to the edge of the fields surrounding the house.

As I drew closer to the house I saw every window lit from within, an array of blazing beacons in the dusk, and my throat tightened at the thought of losing this, my only home. Every beam and board and shingle was engraved on my heart. Gran, my mother, Ryan, and I had all been born here, and the walls had soaked up over a hundred years of McBride quarrels and laughter. Now that the pipes grumbled and the walls sighed with drafts the house seemed more precious than ever, like a grandfather who complains of arthritis but still gives the best hugs. The house was part of the family, and it would be almost impossible to leave it.

My bedroom window was as bright as the others. That's odd, I thought. I was sure I'd turned that light off. A dark shape appeared in my window and I felt a shimmer of dread as I recognized Vincent. He was standing in my bedroom, illuminated by the overhead lamp as he came close to the window and pressed his forehead to the glass. His features were shadowed by the storm, and a tingle of fear stippled my skin as I finally understood what he was doing.

He was watching me.

At the back door I knocked my boots against the wall to clear the snow caked on them, then entered the kitchen. Ryan was standing in front of the stove, and when he turned to greet me his eyes registered shock as he openly gaped at my face.

"What happened to you?"

I touched the skin around my eye and realized it must have blossomed into a visible bruise while I was in the woods. "I guess it was too fresh for you to see it earlier," I said. "Amy and I had a fight. She hit me."

"Jesus, Brett. That's a little bizarre, don't you think?" he said, regarding my black eye uneasily.

"She saw me with Noah," I said, out of an old habit of telling him everything.

"And?"

What did it matter if he knew? It seemed pointless to hide the fact, now that Gran and Amy knew. They would certainly tell him.

"Noah and I were making love."

"I see," he said, and a flicker of something—worry? disapproval?—crossed his face.

I needed to get upstairs. "I just saw Vincent in my room."

Ryan gave me a sharp look, and I could see a sudden, taut anxiety in his eyes. "Are you sure? How could you see him? You were outside."

"The light was on. He was standing at the window, watching me."

Ryan glanced at the darkness outside the kitchen window, the flakes blowing sideways, tapping at the glass. "Is he still up there?"

"I'm going up to see." I turned to leave just as footsteps approached and Vincent entered the kitchen. His eyes were focused on the back door, and he wore his overcoat. He brushed past me without speaking until I caught his sleeve and yanked it.

"Where do you think you're going?" I asked.

He looked at me, lifted his arm, and removed my hand as if it were a piece of litter. "Out," he said.

"I saw you in my room."

He smiled. "So you did."

"What were you doing there?"

"Probably the same thing you were doing in Amy's room last night," he said.

Warmth seeped into my face, making my bruised eye throb. "You had no right to go in there."

"Yes. I know. Would you excuse me?"

"Where are you going?"

"I'd like to look at the murder scene in your barn, just in case there's some little clue that might have escaped the notice of the police."

"Let him go, Brett," Ryan said.

"I don't think so," I said, grabbing another fistful of his coat. I looked at Vincent more closely and saw his pupils were like pinpricks. His skin held the same waxy glow I'd seen a hundred times, a thousand times, sometimes in patients, sometimes in friends, sometimes in doctors. "What are you on, Vincent? Coke? Speed?"

"Maybe you should take a little something for yourself, Brett. Wake up and smell the blood on your brother's hands." He laughed then, a high, screechy cackle, and the sound was so weird I stepped back.

"You're insane," Ryan said, and took the knife from the cutting board and held it clenched at his side. His face was white.

The room glowed with a murderous hostility, and the thought came to me, unbidden, that one of them was the killer. It had to be Vincent. Please, I thought, addressing whatever ghosts were watching us. Let it be him, and not my brother.

"I'm not afraid of you," Vincent spat at Ryan. His eyes were bright as ice.

"Knock it off," I said. I lifted my chin toward the door. "Get out."

Vincent pulled on his gloves and vanished out the kitchen door without another word. I tried to take a deep breath, but my lungs felt squeezed tight. The air was still thick with tension.

"He could be planting evidence against us," Ryan said.

"I know," I said.

He put the knife back on the counter, and I saw his hand was shaking.

"I think he's looking for the will," I said.

"Gran is in the barn, doing the same thing. She'll keep an eye on him."

"Why aren't you looking for it?" I asked.

"I started to," Ryan said. "And then I thought, fuck it. I don't want Edward's money. He was wrong to try to buy me. If Gran finds the will and by some miracle the police find the murderer instead of nailing me for it, I'll give the money to her. If she wants to stay here on the farm she can hire all the help she needs. But I'm moving out."

"When?" I asked.

"When the weather clears. I'll get an apartment in town and file for bankruptcy."

It was too much to take in, the thought of Ryan leaving the farm, going bankrupt. I felt charged by the confrontation with Vincent, restless, eager to move, to do something.

"I'm going up to see if Vincent took anything from my room," I said.

Ryan nodded, and I hurried out of the kitchen, through the living room, and up the stairs. My bedroom door was open.

Nothing seemed out of place on the surface, but I could tell each object in my room had been shifted, peered under, examined; the bedspread was smoother, as if the bed had been taken apart and remade, and the hairbrush on my dresser was turned down instead of up. I never left it turned down. It gave me a dirty feeling to know Vincent had touched my hairbrush. It made me feel a twinge of guilt, too, to know how Amy must have felt after I'd ransacked her room.

I sat on the bed and waited for the adrenaline to recede while I looked at the room. As far as I could tell Vincent hadn't taken anything. There was so little to take. I owned almost nothing: no furniture, no appliances, not even the sheets on the bed were mine. When I went to Africa I distilled my belongings to two suitcases and a doctor's bag, and since I'd been back I hadn't bought anything but food and clothes for Amy. It would be easy to pack.

If I gave up the farm, Amy and I could start over.

Hope began to kindle inside me, warming into a glow of desire for escape. I still had a little money. It was the farm that was the problem, after all. It was the farm Amy hated, not me, and I knew I could convince her to go with me if we moved to a trendy place like Boulder, or Santa Fe, or Jackson Hole. It was a familiar dream, the dream of leaving and starting over. The last time I'd felt it was after the divorce, when I flew off to Africa, desperate to shed Dan, marriage, even Amy. But this time it felt right. I could take her with me. I could be a good mother. She would be happy. I realized I was clenching my fist and uncurled my fingers.

But first there was the mystery of my father's murder hanging over all of us. My father hadn't wanted me, and I knew I didn't owe him anything, but I suspected that I would have to know how his life ended before mine could be resolved. Waiting for the police to tell us who murdered him seemed too slow, too passive, and besides, I was tired of waiting for people to tell me the truth. I was ready to find the truth for myself, no matter what the consequences.

Vincent's room was right next door, and I knew he was in the barn.

I went out into the hall and stood in front of his door, listening to the pulse in my ears. The thought rose in my mind like the ghost of my father, demanding recognition: leave this alone. Leaving it alone was probably the right thing to do, but my hand went to the knob, twisted it, and pushed. The door swung open.

A copy of the *Wall Street Journal* lay on Vincent's bed, and when I picked it up I saw it was yesterday's edition. It seemed like a lifetime since Vincent had arrived, but it had only been twenty-four hours. His suitcase was open next to the bed, and I dumped the contents on the floor: socks, briefs, T-shirts, and a shaving kit. Lifting the kit up to the bed, I unzipped it and saw more pills than I would have guessed, some in bottles, a few in glassine envelopes. Was he a hypochondriac, or just another addict? I picked up one of the prescription bottles to read the label and saw Amy standing in the doorway, arms crossed against her chest, watching me.

"Making a habit out of this?" she said.

I'd had enough of her thin-lipped resentment, but I didn't want to argue with her now. "Vincent is on drugs. I don't trust him."

"Like you trust anybody."

"I don't have the time to fight with you now," I said, tossing the bottle into the bag. "If you want to help, start looking."

Amy didn't move, but I saw a flicker of interest in her eyes. "What are you looking for?"

"Anything. A weapon. His checkbook. A diary with a detailed confession in it would be nice."

"You think he killed your father?"

I looked at her. "Yes. I do."

Amy didn't reply right away. Her eyes were different now, the same shade of green, of course, but worried, and not as cold as before. "He'll kill you if he finds you here."

I turned from the mess on the floor and opened the closet, pulled out his garment bag and threw it on the bed. She watched me as I extracted two suits from the bag, one navy, one charcoal. In the breast pocket of the navy suit there was a credit card receipt from the Holiday Inn in Ithaca, dated for the twenty-fourth, twenty-fifth, and twenty-sixth of November. Just this past week: Tuesday, Wednesday, Thursday.

"What does it say?" Amy asked.

"He lied," I said. "He was in town when Edward was killed." I gave her the receipt. She looked at it, handed it back to me, and I stuffed it in my pocket.

I went back to the closet and pulled out his robe. It was made of heavy striped silk, with a lining of lighter silk and a black satin collar. In the pocket was a small gold pillbox, and when I snapped it open I saw it was full of white powder. I licked a finger and touched the powder, then tasted it.

"What is it?" she asked.

"Cocaine," I said.

"Mom, we have to get out of here." She bent down

and shoved his belongings back in the suitcase, then closed the lid and snapped it shut. I didn't bother to tell her it had been open when I found it.

"Leave it," I said. "Go to your room and stay there. I want to talk to your uncle."

She gave me a look and I saw the fear in her eyes, a fear that meant she needed me. I reached out and touched her cheek. "Don't worry," I said. "Everything's going to be all right. Sit tight. I'll come up later. We need to talk."

When I returned to the kitchen Ryan was drying the dishes. He gave me a wary look, and I leaned against the counter, trying to look casual. I wanted information, and I didn't have much time before Gran and Vincent came back.

"Look at this," I said, and handed him Vincent's hotel receipt. "Did you know he was in town?"

He read the slip of paper, handed it back, and looked up at me. "No, I didn't."

I believed him. We exchanged a look, a complicated glance of relief and fear. It was only circumstantial evidence, but it took some of the pressure off Ryan.

"Please, Brett, don't say anything to him," he said. "I'm afraid for you. I'm afraid for all of us."

It was bizarre to consider how stuck we were in a scene where we didn't want to be, marooned like plastic figures in a snow globe. I wanted to challenge Vincent, to accuse him, if only to break the tension created by our forced togetherness in the storm. But Ryan was right. I didn't want to end up like Edward.

"Did Gran find the will?" I asked, aiming for a neutral, innocent tone.

"No," he said. "She's still out in the barn." The peel spiraled from the blade of his knife.

"You're not going to help her?" I asked.

He shrugged. "I'm beginning to think Dad must have destroyed it."

I watched Ryan cut up the apple. Why was he giving up so easily? He went through money like water, and always lusted for the things money could buy. He was a collector, a connoisseur, a man who could differentiate one vintage of burgundy from another in a blind tasting.

I pretended to accept his words at face value. "I'm glad you quit looking."

Ryan finished peeling the apple, cut it into chunks, and tossed the chunks into a saucepan on the stove. His movements were mechanical as he picked another apple from the bowl without meeting my eyes, and when he spoke it was only to change the subject.

"I miss Billy," he said.

I missed Billy, too, but wondered why Ryan was bringing him up now.

"He just broke up with that lawyer he was seeing." Ryan sighed and shook his head. "I doubt he'd come back to me. I can't really blame him, either. I've been an idiot."

I didn't contradict him. My agenda was different, time was short, and the questions were crowding forward in my mind now that I had him alone. "Do you know anything about Noah?"

"No. He's from someplace in New Mexico, isn't he?"

"Did he give you any references?"

"He did, but I never checked them out. I think they're still in my office. I interviewed him in the barn, while I was changing the bandage on Stagger Lee. Noah wrapped it and Stagger Lee didn't kick once. That was all the interview I needed. He's got a great touch with the horses."

Typical, I thought. Fussing over references would be too petty for Ryan, like dickering over a bill. It disturbed me to realize how little any of us knew about Noah, and how quickly we'd all accepted his own account of himself. All the great con men inspired trust, didn't they? The abyss of his unknown history yawned around him like a moat.

"I'd appreciate it if you'd find those references and give them to me," I said.

"Sure. No problem. That is, if I have them."

I picked up one of the apples from the bowl on the table and polished it on my shirt. "What will the bank do with the farm?"

Ryan shook his head and stirred the bubbling applesauce in the pan. "Chop it up into parcels and sell it at auction. I don't know. Create subdivisions. Log all the timber and sell it. Whatever they want. They'll own it."

I could hear the apples hiss in the pan. The kitchen filled with the smell, a deep, luscious fragrance. The smell of autumn. The smell of home. I could not absorb what Ryan was saying. It wouldn't fit. It was one thing to imagine running away from home, but to picture the farm divided and sold to strangers was impossible.

"I'm sorry, Brett," he said. His glasses were misted over from the steam of the cooking apples and I couldn't see his eyes. "But we'll all have to leave soon."

"Did you know our mother killed herself?" I asked.

"I knew. I was the one who found her."

"Jesus, Ryan. How could you not tell me?"

"You were two years old! How could I tell a two-year-old that her mother overdosed on Nembutal?"

"I'm thirty-two now. How could you keep it a secret for thirty years?"

"Would you really have been better off knowing? Should I have told you when you were a little girl? In high school? When you were pregnant with Amy? There was never a good time to tell you, Brett, and I was prepared to keep it a secret forever. I thought I could protect you."

Gran and Ryan had both kept their secrets to spare me grief, but being deprived of the truth about my history felt like a theft. My pulse quickened with resentment. If my grandmother decided to stay and fight for the farm, I didn't have to stay and help her. It might be good for her to face the consequences of giving the farm to Ryan. It was her mistake; I didn't have to make it right. It would never be right. As for my father, I was almost certain Vincent had killed him. I didn't have to stick around to prove it. Just that fast, I made my decision.

"Amy and I are going to move out," I said.

He looked blank. "When?"

"As soon as the snow clears."

He stared at me, absorbing this for a moment, then raised an eyebrow. "Amy won't want to leave her father."

That was the crux of it, all right. Dan would be furious, but I knew he'd have to give in if Amy wanted to go. It was Amy I needed to convince.

Ryan picked an apple from a bowl of fruit on the table and began to peel it over the sink. "It's a good idea to leave, Brett. It's time."

"I'm going to start packing," I said. Action of any kind was preferable to feeling trapped by the storm. There were boxes in the cellar.

Ryan nodded and continued to stir the simmering apples.

The door to the cellar was in the corner of the kitchen, and when I opened it and descended the wooden steps I was immediately aware of the chill below and the dank smell of earth and old vegetables. The cellar walls were made of stone, and the dirt floor was bare except for a few scattered pieces of slate. It was dark as a tomb until I reached the string dangling from the naked bulb in the ceiling fixture and pulled it on.

Snow filled the window wells and sealed the interior from any outside light. The wooden bins along one wall held potatoes, turnips, beets, onions, while rows of canned tomatoes, plums, pears, apples, beans, and pickles filled the shelves above. Cartons were piled haphazardly in a corner by the water heater, no more than blocky silhouettes in the gloom. In another corner there were three ten-gallon containers of gasoline and a drum of kerosene. If the power went out again we'd have to bring out the kerosene lamps, and I made a mental note of where the kerosene was, just in case we needed it. At least we had plenty of fuel.

I picked up three empty boxes and balanced them in a stack, then climbed the stairs to the kitchen just as Gran entered it.

"What are you doing with those boxes?" Her voice was so close behind me my heart nearly stopped, and I dropped them.

"Packing," I said.

Her hair was mussed, as though she'd been rooting through closets. "Where do you think you're going?"

"We have to pack, Gran," Ryan said. "We won't be able to stay here."

Gran brushed invisible cobwebs from her sleeves. "Don't be ridiculous. We're going to find your father's will. If Vincent thinks it's here it must be here."

"Even if you find it, Amy and I are still going to move," I said.

Gran ignored my words and lifted my chin to examine the bruise around my eye. "That's quite a shiner, Brett."

I tugged my face away. "I'll get over it."

"The only rooms I haven't searched are yours and Amy's," Gran said. "Have you looked in your bedroom yet?"

"Yes," I said, bending down to restack the boxes. I didn't want to meet her eyes. "No luck."

"Would you mind coming up with me to ask Amy if we could look in her room?"

"I don't think that's a good idea, Gran."

Gran shook her head. "No matter what happened between you two, I need to find that will. There's just too much at stake. And, Brett, it's not a good idea to let her get away with this sort of behavior. You have to stop protecting her. I have no intention of hurting Amy, but that girl is out of control. Hitting you is unacceptable, and she has to face up to that."

"I told you before, I'll handle it," I said.

"It's not just the violence that worries me, honey. Ever since she moved in we've all noticed that certain things have been disappearing in the house. I'm missing several pieces of jewelry and at least two hundred dollars. Ryan, didn't you tell me you were missing some cash last week?"

He shrugged an apology in my direction. "It's true, Brett. I had eighty dollars in my desk drawer and now it's gone."

Gran shook me lightly by the shoulders. "We can't ignore that kind of behavior. To ignore it is just another kind of neglect. She needs to know it hurts us."

I felt my face grow warm. "It's a phase. She's compensating."

"What if Vincent believes she has the will? What if she stole it from his room? She could be in danger."

"Vincent won't hurt her." I spoke out of bravado, but the thought of him threatening her flooded me with adrenaline.

"He'd hurt any one of us to get his hands on that will. We need to talk to her, Brett, for her own protection."

"No," I said. "She's been through enough."

"Then I'll do it without you," Gran said. Her spine straightened, as though she were steeling herself for something unpleasant, and then she swept out of the room.

The three of us stood in the hallway, outside Amy's door. I knocked. "Open up, Amy. It's important."

We heard her footsteps approach. The door swung open. Amy glanced at us, then headed back to the nest of rumpled bedding where she'd been listening to her Walkman.

"Amy, we need to have a talk," Gran said.

"So talk," Amy said, propping herself up on one elbow to look at her great-grandmother. Her face was bland, smooth, expressionless. She looked like Gran, I realized, even though they were sixty years apart. It was something in the eyes, in the determination there. They were an equal match.

Gran's voice was smooth as velvet, but we could all hear the iron underneath. "Your grandfather left a will that gives his estate to Ryan, Amy. Apparently there's only one copy of the will. If we don't find it before Vincent does, we're going to lose the farm."

Amy flicked a glance at me and I moved my head in a barely perceptible negative.

"What's that got to do with me?" Amy's voice was quiet, controlled. There was no surprise in her expression when she heard we might lose the farm. I wondered if she'd overheard Ryan telling us about the mortgage, or was it simply that she didn't want to give Gran the satisfaction of appearing surprised?

Gran sat on the bed. "I'm worried about you, Amy. If you have the will, Vincent could hurt you."

"You think I have Edward's will?" Amy looked directly at me. She leaned back and smiled, obviously enjoying my discomfort. My mouth was dry.

"We've all noticed certain things disappearing around here, Amy," Gran continued in a soft, serious tone. "Stealing from us is one thing, but if you stole Edward's will, you could be in real danger. You have to give it to us."

I saw two bright pink circles appear on Amy's cheeks, and knew she'd been mortally offended. Insults can burn so much hotter when they're true.

"You can go to hell," she said.

Gran's voice remained low and sweet. "I'm only trying to protect you."

"I'm not afraid of you, Emily. Now get out."

"Ryan, Brett," Gran said. "Take Amy out of here. I intend to search this room."

"No," Ryan said, and I loved him in that moment more than I ever had.

Gran faced him, her eyes burning. "You will do this for me," she said, jaw set, teeth clamped, every word bitten off.

"No," Ryan said. "This is not the solution."

Gran stalked over to the door and turned to face her great-granddaughter. "I want that will," she said, and her voice was very different now.

"Go fuck yourself," Amy said. She sounded un-afraid, cold as an assassin, but her face was dark with emotion.

Gran vanished into the hallway, her heels clicking angrily all the way to her door, which slammed so hard it rocked the walls.

"Come on, Brett," Ryan said, plucking my sleeve. "Amy doesn't need us here."

"You go. I need to talk to her," I said.

Ryan glanced at me, then looked at Amy, who gave him a small nod. He walked out and closed the door quietly behind him.

Adrenaline pumped through me as I tried to choose the right words. Pick your battles, I thought, and let the silence stretch between us until the high color faded from Amy's face. She began to fidget. I stood by the door, hands locked together, willing myself not to overreact.

I came nearer and sat on the end of her bed. "That was a little over the top, don't you think?"

"Should I have told her that you have the will?" Sarcasm dripped from her words.

I let that pass and held her gaze. "Amy, I have to know. Where did you find it?"

She made a face and looked away, and for a second I could see the little girl I knew, the vulnerable little kid who was locked up inside the teenager before me.

"Just tell me the truth. I promise I'll never punish you for telling the truth."

Her head drooped. "You won't like it," she mumbled.

"Whatever it is, I need to know."

"I wanted to see the body," she said, picking at the knuckle of her left thumb.

My lungs felt as if a giant hand were squeezing the breath out of me. "But you couldn't. We told you that you couldn't."

"I did."

"No," I breathed, shaken by the possibility that she'd seen her grandfather's body, that horrible, bloody, maggot-infested corpse I'd left in the woods.

She spoke in a voice so low I had to strain to hear her at all. "I took Caledonia and cut through the woods, then came up the back way to the waterfall."

"You got there before us? You must have been flying."

Amy shrugged. "Caledonia was ready for a good run. I let her, that's all. The corpse was right in the middle of the trail, where you said he was. So I looked at him."

"Did you take his wallet?" I asked, trying to keep my voice level.

Amy looked at me. "Yes."

I let my head sink into my hands. "Oh, God," I breathed.

"I didn't mean to keep it," she said. "I just wanted to see who he was. But I could hear you guys coming down the trail and I got scared and left. I didn't have time to put it back."

"Was the will in his wallet?" I asked.

"Yes. But I didn't even know it was there until later, when you caught me reading it. I just wanted to look at his stuff, figure out who he was, where he came from. You won't tell Dad, will you?"

"I don't know," I said. I began to imagine the lies I would have to tell, to cover up what had happened. "Where is the wallet now?" I asked.

Amy's face flushed. "I threw it in the pond, before it froze over. It had some credit cards in it."

"Did you keep the cash?"

Her ears were a bright pink. She nodded.

"Amy, why have you been stealing money? Is there something you want to buy?"

"I want a car," she whispered.

I exhaled, suddenly aware I'd been holding my breath. "You don't even have a license yet. You're underage."

"I went in last week for the test. The DMV has a special thing for kids who live in the sticks—we can get a license at fifteen. I passed. I got the license."

"Why do you want a car?"

Amy's lips trembled, and her eyes grew bright with tears. "I want to go somewhere else."

The taste of ashes filled my mouth. "You mean you

want to live with your dad? Or were you planning to run away?"

She shook her head and I could see the misery in her hunched shoulders, the despair in her face. "I'm not happy here," she said. "I've told you this a million times, and you just don't care. I hate school. And the farm is too far away from town, too far for me to go to parties or go on a date or have anybody come over. We don't even have cable."

I started to speak and Amy cut me off, the words nearly choking her in her rush to spit them out. "You just moon around here in ragged old clothes and hunt and listen to Gran's scratchy records. You're a doctor, Mom! Why aren't you working?"

It startled me to hear my daughter scold me for not getting a job, and before I could think of how to respond the words came flooding out of her again.

"I thought being grown up meant getting it together, figuring out your life. But you don't do anything! And you hardly ever talk to me."

"Me!" I spluttered. "I try to talk to you all the time!"

"I can't talk to you about anything normal anymore. You don't want to hear it. Ever since you got back you can't be bothered listening to me talk about clothes or makeup or music. You hate everything I like. MTV. Video games. If you knew my friends you'd hate them too. You even hate Dad."

"What's your father got to do with this?"

"You know he still wants you. He could take care of you."

Oh, Amy, I thought. No amount of money will ever buy you that happy ending.

"Your father and I are not getting back together. Not ever."

"Not if you're screwing that cowboy," she muttered.

"Get used to it," I snapped.

"How would you feel if I were the one screwing him?" she asked. "He's looked at me, too, you know. I've seen him stare. What would you say then? Would you be happy for me?"

My stomach twisted at the thought, but I kept my voice calm. "Noah and I are adults, Amy. We have the right to make our own mistakes."

"I don't like your mistakes," she said.

"I'm not too crazy about yours, either," I said. We glared at each other for a moment, then stared moodily at opposite corners of the room.

When Amy spoke again her voice wobbled and she sounded five years younger, on the verge of tears. "Ever since you left Dad you've been falling apart. You went flying off to the other side of the world and came back half dead. I was so afraid you were going to die, and now that you're healthy I'm afraid you'll take off again. Either way, I get left behind."

"Oh, honey," I said, and felt a fresh wave of sorrow hit me. "I'm not going anywhere without you."

I crawled up beside her then and gave her a hug. Her body felt so much bigger than the child I remembered, but I drank in the warmth of her with a feeling like hunger. She was no longer the plump infant I'd guarded so ferociously, no longer the skinny tomboy, all knees and elbows and shyness. She was nearly all grown up, and we had so little time left. In less than three years she'd be off to college. I wrapped my arms around her shoulders and kept them there even though I could feel her tighten and resist, taut as a bowstring. I knew she was holding her breath.

"Breathe," I whispered in her ear.

There was a long, ragged, indrawn breath, and then I felt her explode into a series of shuddering sobs. She was a big girl, but she still cried the same way, hard and hot and loud. Her tears scalded me, and I felt a raw shame, to be the source of so much pain. Finally she pulled away, took a Kleenex from the bedside table, and blew her nose.

I nudged her over so I could lean against the head-board. The smell of her clean skin mingled with Clearasil and the funky odor of gym socks under the bed. Her bedding was grainy with dropped crumbs, and when I brushed them away my hand felt the smooth round button of a loose M&M. I held it up, brushed it off on my shirt, popped it in my mouth, and ate it.

"Mom," Amy said, and giggled. She wiped her face with the back of her sleeve.

I snuggled closer and risked leaning my head against her shoulder. "I remember when you were six." I kept my voice low and slow, a bedtime story voice. "Way back then it seemed like you were from some other planet, some other place, some other time. Wise beyond your years, Dan used to say. Anyway, one Saturday morning you crawled into bed with us and you whispered in my ear. 'I had a dream,' you said. Your dad was still snoring.

" 'What,' I said, still half asleep.

" 'I dreamed I was a chef for a king,' you said. 'I was supposed to pray over all the animals I had to kill for his table, to make the meat sacred.' "

Amy stirred next to me. "You're making this up."

I held up two fingers. "I swear. But it was what you said next that surprised me the most. 'One day I forgot to do it,' you said, 'and I was really scared I messed up. Then I thought, that's okay, all food is sacred.' "

She sank down further into the pillows until her head touched mine. "You're so crazy," she said, but there was affection in her voice.

I let out a sigh and pressed my cheek against hers. "Sometimes you astonished me, baby. You still do." I thought of my black eye, her lightning fist, and smiled. "I'm sorry I pulled your hair."

"I'm sorry I hit you," she said.

I snorted. "Who taught you to throw a punch like that?"

"Dad," she said. "He took me to the gym a few times." Amy took my hand and laced her fingers into mine. "I'm tired of being mad at you."

I took a deep breath and for the first time in days felt that everything really would be all right. "Me too."

"It's just been so weird, ever since you found that body. Ever since Vincent came here."

I took a tendril of her hair and twirled it around my finger. "He is weird."

"I saw him pick up the phone in the hall this morning. He just stood there listening. I think Ryan was talking to somebody on the extension in his room, and Vincent didn't even care that I saw him listening in. He gives me the creeps."

"Honey, this will all be over soon. And then we'll move."

"Where are we going?" she asked. I stroked her hair and felt a little starburst of relief inside me at the way she said "we." It made me giddy to be talking to her as if we were more than enemies, as if we were what we were: mother and daughter. Family.

"Wherever you want," I said.

She let out a sigh. "Where did you hide the will?"

"In a safe place," I said. "If the police find it before they figure out who killed Edward, they'll arrest Ryan. I'm glad you didn't tell anyone that I have it."

A strange look crossed her face, and I felt a pin-prick of alarm. "What?" I asked.

"Ryan asked me if I'd seen it," she said. She looked at me, her eyes anxious.

"When?"

"Maybe two hours ago. I told him you had it."

Great, I thought. At least he kept his mouth shut about it and let Gran go off on her wild-goose chase. He must know how dangerous it would be if the will surfaced now. I just hoped we could go on stone-walling Gran.

Then doubt slid over me, like a cold drop of water running down my back. How practiced my brother was at hiding things. Standing there in the kitchen, stirring his apples, telling me he didn't care about the will, had given up looking. And all that time he knew I had it.

Ryan, what have you done? The thought shuddered through me like a snake, and I closed my eyes as if I could cast it out by refusing to see.

# Chapter Eight

Stars appeared over the farm, pinpricks of ice in the blackness, a glittering sign the storm was finally ending. When the moon rose above the bank of clouds the wind exhaled one final blast, a great, long sigh of exhaustion, and the clouds rolled on in tatters to drift and dissipate over the hills to the east.

Noah came in through the kitchen door and I was so glad to see him it set off inner warning bells that I chose to ignore. You don't know him, they chimed in my head. But he's here, I thought. He promised to look in on me, and he kept his promise.

Noah's face creased into a smile as I crossed the room, and he took me in his arms and hugged me. His cheek was cold from the air outside, bristly with five o'clock shadow. We stood swaying together, my arms wrapped around the bulk of his body in his sheepskin coat, his arms circled around me. Inhaling the comforting scent of leather and horses, I felt his chest rise and fall. He didn't pat my shoulder or signal any withdrawal or impatience. He held me, and

I settled and grew quiet inside, like a tree after a windstorm.

"Is everybody asleep?" he whispered. The living room was empty. Everyone had retired to their rooms hours ago, fleeing from the effort of making conversation while Vincent was in the house.

"I hope so," I said, my lips moving against his cheek. "Where have you been?"

"In the barn. Compared to your houseguest, I prefer the company of the horses right now. Is Vincent upstairs?"

"Everybody is. They went to bed early."

"Good," he said. "I'm glad you're still awake. Are you feeling okay? How's the eye?"

I kissed him instead of answering. His lips were cool against my mouth at first, but we kissed until they were warm. Finally I broke away. "Can you stay awhile?"

"I'd like nothing more."

"Let me take your coat."

Noah let me slide it off his shoulders and hang it on the hook behind the door, and when I turned around I laughed for no reason except for the bubble of gladness that rose up in me, just to see him here in the kitchen. He grabbed me in a bear hug and we crab-walked sideways into the living room and fell in a sprawl on the couch. His body was warm and the curve of his arms fit me exactly as we slumped together, reclining in front of the fire.

"Vincent was in the barn this afternoon," Noah said, nuzzling my face.

"I know. He's a strange one, isn't he?"

"He's crazy as a bed bug."

"Gran is sure he's the killer."

"She was there, too, for a while. He tried to get a rise out of her, but she didn't fall for it. Finally she left, and after she was gone he walked right up to me and tried to feel my butt."

I laughed out loud. "The nerve!"

"When I told him to quit grabbing me he got really hyper, started pacing up and down and going on and on about your family."

"I saw him in the kitchen, before he left, and he was high as a kite."

"On what?"

"Cocaine."

"How do you know?"

"Hey, I'm a doctor. His pupils were like microdots."

"Sorry. I should have known better than to ask."

"Plus I found it in his room."

"God, Brett, be careful. He's a maniac."

"Why? What did he say?"

Noah shook his head and looked embarrassed. "You don't want to know. When I told him I didn't want to listen to his ranting and raving, he tore the barn apart looking for your dad's will. Dumped the oats out of the bin, tossed every bale of hay out of the loft. I didn't even try to stop him. He was crazed."

"Vincent is sure the will is hidden somewhere on the farm. It names Ryan as the sole beneficiary of my dad's estate, which is worth several million, according to Vincent."

"He told me. After he searched the barn and couldn't find it he said you must have it," Noah said.

"Me, specifically?"

"Yes. You."

I felt a constriction around my ribs, a tightening of apprehension. "Did he tell you Ryan mortgaged the farm?"

He nodded, gave me a look of sympathy. "I'm really sorry about that, Brett."

I swallowed. I couldn't talk about it yet. "My grandmother is in denial. She's sure we'll find the will. According to her fantasy, Ryan will inherit Edward's money, the farm will be saved, and Vincent will be arrested for murder."

"Brett, Vincent has a gun."

"A gun? How do you know that?"

"I saw it. He keeps it in his overcoat pocket. Looks like a Colt, nine-millimeter."

"Did he threaten you with it?" I asked.

"He took it out and checked the clip right in front of me. It's loaded. He didn't point it at me or anything, but he definitely wanted me to know he had it."

I felt a twist of nausea. "I don't like the sound of this at all." For a moment I thought about rousing Vincent out of bed and driving him from the house, at gunpoint, if I had to. Let him sleep in the barn. It was warm enough out there; he wouldn't freeze. But then what would he do? He might shoot me, or any one of us. A showdown would be a lot more dangerous than letting him sleep.

Noah tightened his arms around me. "Can I stay with you tonight?"

The thought of Amy flashed through my mind, and I knew she would never forgive me if she discovered us sleeping together. I shook my head and lay my cheek against his chest. "It's been a long day."

"We don't have to do anything—I'd just feel better if we were in the same bed."

I smiled inwardly at the thought of trying to sleep next to Noah without doing anything. No way, I thought. He was just too irresistibly doable. "I talked to Amy," I said.

"How did it go?"

"Not too bad. Gran confronted her about her stealing and Amy blasted her. But then we talked. It was good."

Noah shook me gently. "I want to be with you tonight. You'll feel safer."

More than anything, I wished that I could ask him to stay. For the first time in my life I was frightened to go to sleep in the house where I was born. "I'll be fine," I said.

Noah circled my shoulders with his arms and tugged me closer. How good I feel with him, I thought. Why do we trust people? What makes us decide to trust? My body felt safe when he touched me, as if honesty was a warmth that all my nerve endings could detect.

"Noah, you're too good to be true," I murmured into his neck.

He laughed. "Hardly."

"What's your worst flaw?" I asked.

I could feel his smile as he kissed me. "You're nuts if you think I'm going to tell you that."

I stiffened under him and pushed him away. "Why? What are you hiding?"

"Nothing," he said, soothing me with his slow hands.

"Tell me."

He sighed. "Okay: I admit it, I'm stubborn."

"Stubborn? That's it?"

"Believe me, it can be aggravating. Sometimes it takes a lit stick of dynamite to get me to change my mind, and that's made a lot of people irritable over the years."

"What's your best quality?" I asked.

"Same thing, probably. I stick by my friends. I'm a rock."

"Were you ever married?"

"No," he said, but his eyes held a flicker of something, regret, loss, sadness, something personal.

"Who was she?" I asked.

He was silent for so long I wondered if he was going to answer. Quietly, I waited for whatever bad news was coming, while the dogs filled the silence with their snores.

"Her name was Sofía," he finally said.

"Pretty name," I said, waiting for more.

"She was Hispanic. Beautiful. Long hair, long legs,

eyes like a doe. We went out for about three years after I got home from college. She was a hardheaded girl, determined to be a writer. She had four poems published in a national anthology by the time she was eighteen. She was good."

His eyes were wistful, filled with regret.

"Why didn't you marry her?" I asked.

Noah let his head fall back on the upholstery. "I was born half a mile away from her family's ranch, but to them I was always an outsider, a white, a gringo. Their family had lived in the valley for over four hundred years. They were Catholic. I wasn't. Her brothers didn't want her going with a gringo. When Sofía told her family we wanted to marry, her brothers were furious. The four of them ambushed us one night in a parking lot in town. I think they only wanted to frighten me off, but the youngest one got overheated and fired his gun. Sofía pushed herself in front of me and the bullet went straight through her forehead. She was killed instantly.

"We all went to the hospital with her body. When they asked me what happened I lied to protect the boy, told the doctor it was an accident, told the police the same thing when they came around to investigate. I couldn't see the point in sending this kid to jail for the rest of his life. There was enough tragedy in that family for one night."

"What happened to him?" I asked, half expecting the hotheaded little brother would wind up in jail anyway.

"He's a priest," Noah said. "He has a parish twenty miles up the valley, in Questa."

"Was the family grateful to you for saving him?"

"No. They blamed me for her death. When I went to her funeral they didn't invite me back to the house for the wake. I was still an outsider. The gringo."

I leaned over and kissed him. The fire cast a glow on our bodies, and I could hear the grandfather clock in the hall ticking out the seconds. The warmth of him flowed into me, a sturdy, penetrating heat that made my limbs feel like butter. I could love you, I thought.

"I've dated some women since then," he said. "But I never felt anything like this."

"Like what?" I wanted him to put it in words.

"You know what."

I knew, but I wanted him to say it. If he felt it, too, then I wasn't alone. "I could love you," he said.

My skin tingled everywhere as I pulled him to me. "Me too," I said, and kissed him.

After a long embrace we pulled apart to catch our breath and straighten our clothes. I felt giddy as a teenager on her first date, breathless and unable to stop smiling.

"Why did you and the sheriff break up?" he asked.

That brought me back to earth with a thud. "Somebody sent me a letter."

"Who? Another woman?"

"She was a waitress at Denny's."

"What did it say?"

I would never forget the contents of that letter, the

plump, open handwriting, the way she dotted her i's with little circles. It was written on cheap blue stationery, with pink flowers running down the left side. I leaned back and stared at the fire, remembering the morning I opened it.

"It began by telling me where my husband had been every Thursday night for the past year. It ended with 'Pleeze give up your husbind so we can love each other like God intended, thank you, God bless you and I will pray for you at church, sinceerly yours, Samantha K.'"

Noah gave my hand a sympathetic squeeze.

"I showed the letter to Dan and he tore it up." I remembered how his fingers shook, how the letter was reduced to shreds. "He denied everything. That was his real mistake. When I realized I believed her instead of him, that was the moment I knew the marriage was over."

"Did you suspect anything before you got the letter?"

"I had bad dreams," I said. "I ignored them."

Noah's hand slipped under my sweater and brushed the curve of my breast. The pull I felt toward him was so strong it felt like high school all over again, and reminded me of the burning longing I had carried for Dan, the deep, physical yearning in my womb to marry him and make our baby. I was older now, and I knew where that pull could take me, but Noah's mouth and hands and warmth drew me into that sensory world where time stood still. It was better than music, better than books, and I wanted to stay there forever. I laughed under him as he pushed me down and smothered me in his arms, and we went on kissing each other until the house seemed like the safest place in the world.

By the time Noah left it was late. I brought my gun upstairs and placed it under the bed, within arm's reach. It helped. My sheets were so cold it felt like a punishment to crawl under the covers, and when sleep finally came it was restless and filled with bad dreams.

In the middle of the night I dreamed a snake was sitting in a chair by my bed, talking to me, hissing in my ear.

"Shhhh."

The voice was barely a whisper, so close I could feel its breath on my ear as I fluttered up from sleep. And then a hand clamped tightly over my mouth.

"Get up," the voice urged. "Don't make any noise." My eyes flared wide enough to see a face leaning over me in the darkness. It was Vincent.

Something cold and metal-hard pressed behind my ear. A gun. The dream vanished, and my awareness coalesced into heart-pounding consciousness. Vincent had a gun, and he was holding it against my head.

"Shhh," he hissed again. I whimpered, and he jabbed at me with the muzzle of the gun.

"Get up," he insisted.

I didn't dare reach for my Remington. Rising from the warmth of the bed, I saw Vincent outlined in the twilight from the window. He was wearing his coat.

The gun was pointed straight at me. "Get dressed," he whispered.

Guiding myself in the dim light with one hand outstretched to touch the bedpost, the dresser, the wall, I wobbled over to the closet.

"Why are you doing this?" I asked, as loudly as I dared.

Vincent struck me across the face with the gun. It was a stunning blow, much harder than the punch Amy had thrown at me. I reeled, and he seized me before I could fall. He covered my mouth with his hand. "Don't make any more noise or I'll hit you again. Now get dressed. We're going to take a little walk outside."

I glanced at his face. Outside, now? The snow was at least three feet deep out there.

"Dress warm," he whispered, grinning.

He's insane, I realized. He's gone over the edge. I tried to think clearly. I needed my gun, but I couldn't reach it. If only I could scream, but he would hit me, or shoot me. My face throbbed from the blow he'd struck, and two of my teeth felt loose. My lungs were tight, my breathing shallow, jerky, and I was so frightened my hands trembled like dead leaves.

Dressing myself as slowly as I dared, I pulled on heavy wool trousers and tucked my nightgown into the waistband, then put on a sweater, socks, and boots, coat and hat. If he intended to tie me up and leave me out in the woods to freeze to death, I wanted to give myself a fighting chance for survival.

Vincent gestured with his chin toward the door.

"Quietly," he said, and poked me in the back with the hard snout of the gun.

We descended the stairs and I came down heavily on the squeaky step, but the cold weather had shrunk the wood and it failed to emit its usual groan. Where were the damn dogs? The blizzard must have sent them into a stupor, I thought, or else Vincent had drugged them.

He opened the front door and forced me out into the snow, then closed the door behind us, releasing the latch without a sound. The cold air stung my nose and cheeks.

"Where are we going?" I asked, my voice climbing into an upper register of panic.

"Shut up," he said, and pushed me with the gun, hard enough to topple me forward into the snow. He yanked roughly on the back of my coat to set me upright, and I struggled to keep my balance as I fought my way through the drifts that pressed against the house.

The clouds parted to reveal a gibbous moon, and in its eerie blue light the meadow looked like the aftermath of a war. Black limbs were strewn, half buried in snow and ice. The wind had created a frozen landscape of towering drifts, waves, and depressions, and the meadow seemed to float in the pallor of the moonlit night. Skeins of snow skimmed the surface, like sand blowing across a desert.

We entered the dark funnel of the trail to Deputron Hollow. Each step was an effort as I punched my way through snow that came up to my hips. Adrenaline coursed through my veins in angry impotent surges, but the cold drew all the warmth from my body in minutes. I'd forgotten gloves. My face was already numb. When I spoke my lips felt like pieces of leather sewn too tightly to my face.

"Why are we out here?" I asked. I tensed, expecting him to hit me again, but he spoke in a singsong, little-boy voice.

"I saw you," he said.

"I don't understand," I said, although I did.

"You found the will in Amy's room, didn't you? But you didn't hide it anywhere in the house or the barn. I checked. I think you hid it somewhere down this trail." His voice was high, coked-up, and speedy.

I tried to think clearly. The cave might be the perfect place to escape from Vincent. The path along the ridge was narrow, the footing treacherous. He wouldn't dare follow me in. I could hide there, wait him out.

"Did you kill my father?" I asked.

Vincent giggled. "I could have. But I didn't."

My voice came in gasps as I floundered forward through the deep snow. "I think you did kill him. I'll tell the police."

Vincent, following in my footsteps, had breath to spare, and his voice suddenly dropped to a normal octave. "You're incredibly naive, for an educated woman."

I felt a shimmer of fear skim my back at his reasonable, relaxed tone. He wasn't that stoned, which meant he was alert, and more dangerous. "What do you mean?"

"Oh, please. You place far too much faith in your brother, Brett. He sold you out. He wants Edward's money. He killed your father for it."

I lurched through the snow, hurrying to avoid the jab of the gun in my back. "You're wrong," I said. "Ryan doesn't care about the money, or losing the farm. He told me so himself."

Vincent snorted. "He's lying to you, Brett. He lied to you all along, didn't he?"

"How would you know what Ryan really wants?"

"I listened in on the extension in the hall when he called the president of the bank at home this morning. Ryan told him he'd just inherited a large estate from his father. He said he'd go in on Monday with a copy of the will. They made an appointment for nine A.M."

"But Ryan doesn't know where the will is," I said.

"Wake up, Brett! Everyone knows your kleptomaniac daughter took it. Even your granny knows that. And frankly, dear, you're not good at playing spy. You tore up her room looking for it. It was obvious you found the will. Ryan's not stupid. I overheard him when he had his little talk with Amy, and she told him you had it. He trusts his baby sister. He knows you'll hand it over to him eventually."

"If Ryan killed my father, why did he leave the will on his body? Why not take it?"

"Think about it. If the police discovered the will on Edward's body, they'd ask the same question. It was a calculated risk, leaving the corpse out in the open like that. But it was on private property, deep in the woods, miles from a road. Ryan knew you were the most likely person to find the body. And you did. He just didn't expect little Amy to get there and snatch the will before the police could retrieve it."

Vincent's voice simmered with contempt. "He's been a busy boy, that brother of yours. He spent the morning calling in favors from friends. He has an alibi all lined up for Tuesday, when he was murdering your father."

I fought the sinking sensation in my gut. "But he found the gun in your room. You planted it there, didn't you? You wanted to frame Ryan."

"Ryan put it there to frame me, but I found it before the police could. He didn't count on the storm keeping the police away this long. He didn't think I'd search my room and find it lying in the bottom of the closet under a pile of rags."

"You're insane."

"No, Brett, I'm not insane. I'm just greedy. I want Edward's money. I want his cars. His boat. His plane. The house in East Hampton. The penthouse in Manhattan. Once I destroy that damn will it all comes to me."

"You don't even care that my father is dead," I muttered.

"Of course I care. I was genuinely upset, at first. You saw me—I fell apart. Did you think that was just an act? It wasn't. I was shocked. But it didn't take long for me to realize that I'm going to be rich now that he's dead. Besides, in the past year Edward was horrible to me, and he was sick and he smelled awful. Now I'm actually quite grateful to your brother for killing him."

Anger began to build in me, and my heart started to pound with fury. It gave me an agitated warmth as I pushed through icy banks and climbed over broken tree limbs. I nursed the anger; it was better than panic. Vincent kept poking me with the gun. My face hurt from the blow he'd given me, and I could feel my lip puffing out from the bruise on my jaw.

After a long struggle through the sea of drifts we came to the end of the trail at the top of the cliff. The rotting moon shed enough light to illuminate the ravine, but the waterfall was silent. It must have frozen, I thought. The rock pillars at the top of the chasm protruded from the snow like black teeth. Vincent carried the gun loosely by his side, relaxed, confident, assured of the outcome of our jaunt.

"Edward's will is down there," I said, panting from my exertions.

"Where?"

"Let me go. I'll get it and bring it back to you."

He laughed. "I don't think so. Tell me where it is."

"It's in the cave under the waterfall."

Without warning Vincent struck me again on the face with the gun, and I flopped into the snow, limp, stunned, bleeding. As I knelt with my head down, the blood from my mouth turned the snow dark, drop by drop.

"If this is a trick, I'll kill you," he said.

I heaved myself up, feeling like a bag of broken glass. It was too much. My face hurt. Every joint in my body was aching. It was too cold. I couldn't do this anymore.

Vincent pointed with the gun toward the lip of the cliff. "Stand over there."

"Why? What are you going to do?"

"Move," he said.

Frantically I tried to think of an option beyond dumb obedience. Vincent thinks he's in control, I thought. He's not expecting me to fight back. I kept my head down and stumbled past him. As he gave me another sharp, mean jab with the gun, I lunged at him. Shoving him as hard as I could with my body, I pushed until he swayed backward and toppled to the ground, his free arm snaking out to grab my collar and yank me down on top of him. Vincent's coat flapped around us and tangled our legs together as we slid toward the cliff in a perilous embrace, with the gun wedged flat between us.

An explosion kicked us apart as the gun went off. Vincent screamed. "You bitch! You could have killed me!"

"Good," I grunted, and rolled on top of him again, desperate to rip the gun from his hand. Vincent elbowed my face and snatched the gun away. As he tried to take aim at me I bit his wrist as hard as I could.

"God damn you!" He tried to fling me off, and the gun flew out of his hand and fell like a stone into the drift. My body was still pressed against his in the marshmallow depths of the snow. I couldn't run away. I didn't have the breath, or the strength. For a moment we lay there, close as lovers, panting to get our breath back.

Finally Vincent heaved me off and struggled to draw himself up on his hands and knees. I punched at his face and missed. There was no strength in my arms anymore. He scrabbled in the snow and came up holding the gun, the hole of its barrel filled with snow, pointing right at me.

Noah's voice bellowed behind us, thirty yards up the trail. "Stop! Stop or I'll shoot!"

Vincent turned and raised his arm to aim at Noah. He fired.

A cold fury entered me as I realized I wanted to kill Vincent. Not just stop him or hurt him or have him arrested. I wanted to kill him.

He was standing over me, straddling my legs, peering up the trail toward Noah while I lay flat on my back underneath him. His coat was open, giving me a perfect target. Pulling my legs up to my chest like a heavy coiled spring, I released them, kicking out and up, shoving him hard in the crotch. He grunted, fell on his back and slid down the steep slope until his head was within an inch of the precipice.

Got you, you bastard, I thought as I slithered toward him on my belly.

His head came up. He lifted the gun and took aim at my face. I saw the perfect little black O, then grabbed his foot and pushed him hard toward the drop-off.

Vincent fired. I felt a sting, a burning shock in my cheek.

He scrambled wildly for a purchase on the soft slope, but the snow broke off and tumbled into the chasm, carrying him headfirst into the gorge. He wailed all the way down, his arms windmilling, clutching air. The gun clattered on the rocks, and finally I heard the dense, mushy sound of his body thudding heavily against the bottom. Then there was silence.

Noah was still struggling to reach me, and I could hear the harsh, labored sound of his breathing as he approached. I lay full length on my belly and peered into the chasm. By the light of the moon I could see Vincent's coat spread open like a dark pool of ink around his body as he lay inert on the snow. Heart pounding, I stared at the black shape below me. It was still.

My cheek burned where Vincent had shot me, but the rest of my face was numb. A wave of grief overwhelmed me at the thought that I might die because of his greed.

Noah finally reached the rim of the gorge where I lay gasping. He dropped to his knees, and I felt his arms lift and hold me. "My God, Brett," he said, rocking me.

"Vincent shot me." My eyes welled up.

"Your cheek is bleeding," he said, his voice urgent.

He tilted my face to examine the wound. "It looks like it grazed you. There's no sign of a bullet hole."

I touched my cheek gingerly, felt the contour of the burn and realized there was no point of entry for the bullet. Noah was right. The bullet had just grazed me. My whole body went limp with relief.

"How did you find me?" I asked.

"I woke up and I knew something was wrong. I couldn't go back to sleep. I got up to check on the house, and there were fresh tracks leading away from it, toward the woods, so I followed them here."

"Where's your gun?" I asked.

He held up his empty hands. "I don't have one."

I remembered his threat to shoot Vincent. "He could have killed you."

Noah looked over the edge at Vincent's body. "Do you think he's dead?"

Now that I knew I wouldn't die I felt a savage satisfaction at Vincent's fall. "If he's not dead now, he will be soon," I said. Once his body temperature fell below eighty-six degrees, he wouldn't survive. The cold would kill him as surely as a bullet.

Noah shook his head and sat back on his heels. "I'll need help to carry him out. It's too steep. Maybe Ryan and I could rig a block and tackle over the edge and haul him up, or hike up from below the falls with a stretcher. It's going to be a bitch in this snow."

"Leave him," I said.

Noah looked at me and nodded slowly, his face shadowed in the moonlight. We both knew what it meant to leave him. "You need to get warm," he said. "Can you walk?"

"Wait," I said. Slowly, painfully, I pushed myself up and began to plod through the drifts to the ridge that led to the cave.

"Brett, for God's sake, what are you doing?"

"Stay there. I'll be right back." I began to edge my way along the precipice. The snow was sloped high against the wall of shale, creating an even more treacherous path than the one I'd navigated hours before. But I was numb to the danger. I felt a shutting off inside, a click of refusal to entertain any doubt about the outcome of my plan. With Vincent so conveniently dead, it was time to give my grandmother and my brother what they wanted.

The will was there under its cairn, safe and dry in its plastic bag. I scattered the rocks, picked it up and put it in my pocket.

About an hour later I was lying on the couch in the living room, swaddled in blankets in front of the fire. Ryan gave me tea and a tablet of Demerol, and I gratefully encircled the steaming hot mug with my chilled hands while Gran adjusted the heating pad under my feet. Noah was perched in a straight-backed chair by the fire, while Amy sat on the floor with her back against the couch, her cheek against my leg.

Crisis united us for the moment, and it was sweet to feel the weight of Amy's head leaning on me, her touch as warm and clinging as it was in the old days.

Now that the danger was past a great weariness crept into my limbs, and I could hardly keep my eyes open. Amy was obviously tired too. Her mouth was slack, her eyelids drooping.

"So Vincent confessed that he killed Edward," Ryan said, repeating what I'd told them. There was skepticism in his voice, but there was also an undercurrent of yearning to believe my story.

"Yes," I said. It was almost true, wasn't it? Hadn't Vincent admitted he hated Edward? Of course he killed him.

"Thank God he's dead," Gran said, tucking the blanket more tightly around my feet.

"What do we tell the police?" Ryan asked.

"The truth," I said.

He sipped his tea and regarded me thoughtfully. I knew my face was puffy with bruises and streaked with a burn from the bullet, but the painkiller he'd given me had reduced the throbbing. I felt pleasantly blurred.

"But why on earth did Vincent kidnap you and take you outside in this weather?" Gran asked.

"He knew I hid the will in the cave under the waterfall," I said.

The mug in Ryan's hand quivered for a moment before he clutched it with his other hand. "Where is it now?"

"In the pocket of my coat," I said.

Gran's face was incandescent as she jumped up from the end of the couch and strode into the kitchen, where Noah had hung my coat on the hook by the door.

"Hallelujah!" she exclaimed. The will fluttered triumphantly from her fingers as she entered the living room. "Bless you, Brett. Bless you, Edward Mercy, you poor man. Or rather, you rich man. Ryan, the farm is saved."

Desire flooded Ryan's face, a visible, half-embarrassed lust. "Let me see it," he said. Gran handed him the will and he scanned it quickly, his face breaking into a smile. "If we needed any more proof of Vincent's guilt, this is it. Dad says here that if there's anything suspicious about his death, he wants the police to arrest Vincent."

I wished I could feel relieved, but I only felt a great lassitude, a heaviness in my limbs. The sedative was working.

Amy looked at me. "Are you going to be all right? I'm so tired I can't keep my eyes open."

I nodded. "Go to bed, honey. Sleep as late as you want."

She stood up and bent to kiss my forehead. I held her in a tight hug, reluctant to let go.

"I love you," I whispered.

"Ditto," she said, and gave me a squeeze before she released me. "Good night," she called out to Gran and Ryan, who barely lifted their heads from the will to acknowledge her leaving.

Noah came over to me on the couch and spoke in a low voice. "I'm going back to the cabin so you can get to bed. Don't stay up too late."

"I won't. Thanks, Noah. I owe you."

He smiled, then whispered in my ear. "I'll be sure to collect on that as soon as you've had a good night's sleep." He straightened, then nodded at Ryan and Gran, who gave him a dismissive wave.

"Good night," I said, and watched him exit the room, then heard the click of the kitchen door closing after him.

Gran was perched on the arm of Ryan's chair, and both of their heads were huddled over the will, the sudden wealth transforming them into very happy people.

"We need a new tractor," Gran said, sitting up, looking years younger, but making an effort to appear serious as she smoothed her robe over her knees.

"Done," Ryan said, waving his hand as if it contained a magic wand, and they both giggled out loud, unable to contain their glee. "And I'm going to renovate the house, Gran, from top to bottom. New roof, more insulation, repaint, replumb, redo the bathrooms, the floors, the furniture, the foundation, everything. God, it will be nice to have money again. New clothes, a new car. The best of everything."

He wanted the money, I thought. Vincent was right. Everything Ryan had said about giving the money away was a lie. At that moment I realized how much I'd been hoping that he was a changed man, a man who could tell the truth, walk away from his father's blood money and turn it all over to Gran, the way he said he would. But that was just another pretty story. So many words had passed between us over the years, and so many of them were lies.

"Do you think Billy would help with the decorating?" Gran asked. "I'd love to have him here."

The smile never left Ryan's face. "I think he might, yes." His eyes were soft with pleasure as he contemplated the future. "Is there anything you want, baby sister?" he asked me. "A new car? A clinic? Private school for Amy?"

For a brief moment a different kind of life flashed before my eyes, a life filled with all the soft comforts I'd ever dreamed of: a house of my own, a beautiful coat, a fat checkbook, the chance to travel with my daughter. And all of it would be paid for with my father's money. Blood money.

"I need to ask you something, Ryan." I looked at my grandmother. "Could you give us a few minutes?"

Gran raised an eyebrow and looked at my brother, who became very still. She nodded at him and he smiled uncertainly.

"If you must," she said. "I'll turn in. I'm going to have to take a pill to get to sleep, though."

"Me, too," Ryan said, and gave her a wink.

Gran stood and bent over me to kiss my cheek. "Thank you, darling. I can't thank you enough."

I nodded, squeezed her hand, and tried to smile reassuringly.

After Gran left the room, Ryan came over to the couch and sat down at the end, facing me. "I meant what I said, Brett. Anything you want, just ask."

I studied my brother. What an amazing man, I thought, to hide the truth from me for so long. And yet I knew exactly how he must have felt. Tonight I had killed someone, too, and I knew how satisfying it could be.

He tilted his head and looked at me. "You know, don't you?"

"Yes," I said.

He leaned back, closed his eyes briefly, took a deep breath, and let it out. When he opened his eyes he gave me a long level look. "What do you intend to do?"

"I want to know why." My eyes never left his face. "Did you hate him that much?"

Something crossed his face, surprise, or sadness, and then he blinked and gave me a faint smile. "It's the oddest thing, Brett, but ever since he died I haven't had the slightest urge to gamble."

"Since you killed him, you mean." My heart throbbed painfully, sluggishly. I recalled the shocked expression on our father's face, still frozen there three days after Ryan shot him. The mess of intestines spilling out of his body. No one deserved to die like that.

Ryan winced, and his words came slowly, painfully. "Every time I saw Dad I felt sick. Gambling must have been connected to that instinct to purge after I saw him, because I swear I haven't had the slightest desire to go to the track or the casino since he died."

So murdering your father healed you? I thought, but held my tongue.

He shook his head. "It's true. I did hate him. I was sick of being manipulated by him. He was a sly son of a bitch. Charming on the surface but rotten underneath. Like syrup over puke."

"But why kill him right before he was going to die anyway?"

Ryan shrugged. "He said he would tear up the will if I didn't agree to let him move in with us. All that money would have gone to Vincent."

"So you shot him in cold blood? Just like that?"

A wave of scarlet crawled up his neck and suffused his face, and when he spoke his voice was choked with feeling. "What difference did it make? He was going to die anyway. Yes. I shot him in cold blood."

"No." The voice was my grandmother's. She materialized in the dimly lit doorway and flowed into the room, her face haggard with pain. "Don't say that, Ryan. I won't let you."

"Get out of here." My brother's voice was harsh, tight. "You don't need to listen to this."

She sat between us on the couch, and patted Ryan on the knee. "It's all right, sweetheart. I won't let you carry this burden. There's no need."

"What are you talking about?" I asked.

She turned to me. "Ryan still thinks he can save you."

"Shut up," he said, his body tense.

"Let it go, Ryan," she said. "It's time to tell her the truth about Edward."

# Chapter Nine

Gooseflesh pricked my arms as I waited for Gran to speak, and the silence stretched between us. Ryan's face was etched in misery, but he slumped back against the cushions, apparently resigned to listening. The clock measured out the seconds. I sat motionless, waiting for whatever she was about to say.

I always knew there was a locked door inside Gran that guarded a secret room of memory, and I always knew it had something to do with my parents. When I was little, the words "Mommy" or "Daddy" coming from me brought tears to her eyes, so I avoided mentioning them, and never pressed her to tell me about them. Gran was my refuge, my last resort, my only family except for Ryan, and I knew he couldn't take care of me by himself. I needed her, and she needed to keep the door inside her locked. It was a simple equation, and besides, to break down that door would be cruel, like picking a scab and poking the wound underneath.

But I knew the door was going to open now, and I was surprised to realize I dreaded it.

Gran's hair tumbled down like white silk and fell in a firelit halo around her face. Her face softened as she cast her mind back to the past, every·feature smooth and mild as a sculptured marble saint. How beautiful she must have been when she was young, I thought. When she finally spoke her voice was intimately low, soft as Scheherazade's.

"Your father married your mother almost forty years ago. I was only thirty-six then, and your grandfather was still alive. When your parents came to live with us I was sure I would be married to Clarence for the rest of my life. He was a dear man, maddeningly slow·in his speech but affectionate and hardworking. Loyal to a fault. He was wonderful with Caroline when she was growing up, and equally wonderful when she announced she was pregnant and wanted to marry Edward."

I made no comment. I held myself in, building an armor of silence between myself and whatever was coming.

Gran looked down and a brief, pained smile crossed her features. "When Edward came here I was fascinated by his energy. He was the antithesis of Clarence: artistic, eloquent, quick-witted. Very handsome. Caroline was madly in love with him."

She took a deep breath and went on. "Caroline was beautiful, but underneath your mother's beauty there was no complexity, no subtlety. Conversation came as hard to her as it did to Clarence, and she suffered whenever she was forced to leave the farm.

She was the one who insisted that she and Edward should go on living here, with us.

"I believe Edward loved her, but it didn't take him long to realize she was her father's daughter. He would make some silly pun at the dining table and Caroline and her father would just blink, but I would have to smother my giggles with a napkin. It was obvious from the beginning that we were attuned to each other in a way our respective spouses simply couldn't share.

"Edward and I began riding together on Sundays. It was one of the gifts of living here, especially back then, to ride for hours and never come to a paved road. We were restless and energetic, and fed each other's need to talk, to argue, to philosophize. Both of us were avid for ideas and good writing, and eager to compare notes on everything we read.

"Clarence and Caroline were different. They were earth to our sky, water to our fire. But the four of us created a precarious balance, an interchange that filled the gap of what we lacked in our marriages. Of course things weren't perfect. There were some snarls and yips, the minor sharpnesses and inevitable overcrowding of two couples living under one roof, but on the whole we were happy. When Ryan was born we all fussed over him and played with him and shared in the responsibility of caring for him, and for seven years it seemed idyllic, natural and easy for all of us to be together.

"Then your grandfather became ill. We were barely aware that he was sick at first, and it seemed like no more than a bad cold, nothing serious, but it worsened rapidly into bronchitis and then viral pneumonia. After just nine days, he was dead.

"It was a terrible shock. I was devastated by his death, and Caroline was shattered. She was heavily pregnant with you, Brett, and she took to her bed and wouldn't get up, not even for the funeral. I was barely functioning myself. Edward managed the funeral and the disposition of the estate, even though I was the one Clarence had named as executor."

Gran looked at me, her eyes filled with sadness. "You were born just two weeks after your grandfather died."

I cocked my head, waiting, withholding any reaction, as though inscrutability would protect me. Gran paused, and when she began to speak again the words came slowly, reluctantly. "Caroline remained depressed for weeks, so I took over looking after you. Both you children were such a comfort to me, just as close to me as if you were my own. But your mother couldn't be comforted. She remained in bed for what seemed like an eternity, until I wondered if she would ever recover. Caroline kept the shades drawn, and her room was dark as a tomb. It was like living with a ghost. I took meals up to her but otherwise we had almost no contact with her. She insisted on sleeping alone, and wanted nothing to do with any of us. She didn't want Edward. She didn't even want to see you children.

"In those days we barely knew what depression was, and it seemed willful, deliberately invoked. Edward implored her to snap out of it. Treatment for depression was limited, and the doctor we consulted recommended shock therapy, but I couldn't agree to it.

"I was so lonely without Clarence, and Edward was deeply unhappy about Caroline. Caroline refused to look at him or talk to him whenever he went up to her room, so he stopped trying. After seven or eight weeks of this, Edward finally approached me one morning and said there was something he wanted to tell me. He asked me to take a walk with him in the woods. I dreaded hearing whatever it was he wanted to say, but I agreed.

"We walked up to the myrtle woods, and stopped to look at the graves up there. He told me he was going to leave, that he couldn't stand it anymore. I begged him to stay. I couldn't face the thought of being left to cope on my own."

Gran took a deep breath, and her voice shook when she continued. "It was midsummer, when everything on the farm was bursting with life and heat. I remember a thrush was singing in the canopy, pouring out a stream of notes. The sound unleashed a flood of grief in me, as if nature were taunting me with everything I lacked and probably would never have again. I began to weep. Edward put his arms around me to comfort me, and it felt so bitter to be held by a man again, to be reminded of what I'd lost when Clarence died. I—I have no excuse for what happened next. All I can say is that I was desperate to obliterate the present and all its losses.

"I took Edward's face in my hands and I kissed him."

Ryan looked sick. I felt the blood drain from my face, leaving me light-headed and dizzy, but Gran went on speaking.

"There was so much buried hunger in both of us. I couldn't stop. We couldn't."

Frozen, listening in disbelief, I felt a rising nausea. "No," I whispered.

She flashed a look at me. "I was in pain," she said. Her voice was raw.

"So you fucked him?" I asked, and laughed. It was ludicrous, impossible, a dirty joke.

My grandmother looked away, her mouth pressed in a tight line. Then she gathered herself and went on, her voice level, reasonable, as if I might understand. "I'm just trying to explain how it happened."

"How could you do that to your own daughter?" I asked.

Gran looked at the fire and remained silent as the furniture.

"Finish the story," Ryan whispered.

Finally she cleared her throat and resumed speaking. "I knew I'd done a terrible, horrible thing. I knew it was a mistake, but I couldn't stop myself. And Edward didn't want to stop." Her mouth took on a bitter twist. "My son-in-law liked it."

"Did you tell your daughter you screwed her husband?" I asked.

"Of course not," she snapped.

"What about Edward? Did he tell her?"

She didn't speak for a moment. Her eyes were dark, the pupils huge. "After that walk in the woods I swore I would put my sin behind me. I was committed to doing everything I could to help Caroline get better.

"But something evil was released in Edward when we broke that taboo. He changed. He didn't want me to forget that I had wanted him. It excited him. He cornered me in the barn whenever I went out to feed the horses. He would slip his hand under my skirt, as if I were an animal, as if he owned me. 'Give it to me,' he would say, as if my body were an object and I was his slave. Some devil inside him had awakened, and there was no way to put it back to sleep, no way to go back and undo the past. When I went out to collect eggs or cut firewood or weed the garden he was after me, groping me, pinning me against him, whispering, 'Give it to me, Emily, give it to me.' I was miserable. And Edward knew it. It thrilled him, to cause so much torment."

Gran's eyes were bright as ice as she continued. "A thousand times I told him to leave me alone, but he didn't want to surrender his power over me. One night he crawled into my bed after I was asleep. I thought I was with Clarence again, and I began to make love to him while I was still dreaming. When I woke up and saw his face above mine I wept and implored him to stop. He swore he would tell Caroline everything about us if I didn't give him what he wanted, whenever he wanted it. 'Give it to me,

Emily,' he said, over and over. 'I want it. Give it to me.' "

"That sounds like Edward," Ryan said bitterly.

I shut my eyes and felt the wave of nausea roll over me. Ever since I was a little girl there had been a fantasy deep inside me about the father I couldn't remember. He was intelligent and funny and handsome, but above all, he was good. He would never intentionally harm anyone. Now I could feel the dream dissolve like smoke and retreat into nothingness, leaving a hollow feeling in my bones.

"What happened to my mother?" I asked.

"Edward began to spend more time with her, talking to her, petting her, coaxing her back to him. An overwhelming sexual energy had been released in him, and he wanted more than just me. Eventually she responded, and they began sleeping together again. But he wanted both of us."

I smiled bitterly. "How long did you go on fucking him?"

She looked uncomfortable. "It was rape, Brett. Not love. Every time I was with him he coerced me. I couldn't tell Caroline—I knew it would be too much for her. We went on like that for nearly two years, until Edward hired Vincent to help with the haying, that last summer."

"So Edward added a third member to his harem," I said.

A flicker of disgust passed over my grandmother's face. "No. He was completely absorbed with Vincent. He gave up tormenting me."

"How fortunate for you."

Gran ignored my sarcasm and went on. "From the moment Vincent moved here it was obvious to me that he was doing his best to seduce Edward, and Edward was encouraging him. I was relieved in one way, because he stopped thrusting himself at me, but I was terrified of what would happen to Caroline if she found out. After her bout of depression I wasn't sure she could survive such a blow. So I tried to threaten Edward, and swore I would tell Caroline about Vincent. He laughed at me and told me to go ahead."

"Did you?" I asked.

"I did something much worse." Her voice was thick, unsteady, and she shook her head as if to clear her thoughts. "One day Caroline came to me, and she was nearly hysterical. She told me she'd seen Edward kissing Vincent on the mouth. I tried to assure her that it was harmless, a small indiscretion. After all, Vincent was only a boy, and in those days, a mere boy could not be taken as a serious sexual threat. She calmed down a little. I let her complain about Edward while I washed the dishes. He was aloof, she said. Distant, and not nearly as affectionate as he used to be. She claimed he was rude to her whenever she wanted to talk about you children, and he didn't seem to care anymore if he hurt her feelings.

"I nodded and made sympathetic noises and let her talk. Then she mentioned that it had been at least two months since Edward had made love to her. That was so unlike him, she said. He was usually so greedy for sex.

"I remember the moment vividly: I was wiping a plate with a towel, not thinking, in a hurry to get the dishes dried and put away. I said 'I know.'

"There was a sudden, intense silence. When I turned around I could see the suspicion dawn on her face. '*You* know,' she repeated. Her voice was chilly, full of accusation. Guilt flooded through me, and my face must have given me away, because she looked as though I'd stabbed her. I couldn't meet her eyes. Before I could think of something to say she ran up to her room and locked the door.

"She refused to come down for dinner, and that night I could hear her arguing with Edward in their bedroom. She accused him of having an affair with me and he admitted it, then laughed at her for being blind to it. It was like being flayed alive, to listen to them shout at each other. One of them threw a lamp, and I heard it crash against the wall. There was a scuffle and Caroline cried out, but I didn't dare go in. The fighting went on for hours. Finally there was a slamming and banging of closet doors as he packed his things.

"In the morning he and Vincent were both gone." Gran sank back against the cushions, and her face was gray, spent. The next words came out in a whisper. "A week later your mother killed herself."

I couldn't help but feel a pang of pity for my grandmother as I saw the memory tighten her face with pain. Her eyes seemed to gaze inward, toward the past and the ruin of her daughter.

"When I touched her body and realized it was cold I felt closer to being dead than I ever had in my life. I couldn't take it in. She looked like a little girl, dressed in a clean white nightgown with roses stitched around the collar. I sank down on the bed and lay beside my baby and held her head close to my heart, as if I could press her back into my womb and give her life all over again. It was as if the world had stopped spinning, as if God had fallen out of heaven and the universe had dissolved into dust and darkness.

"Edward murdered my child, Brett. He killed your mother. How could I let it go? How could I live in a world where Edward was safe and happy? I made a vow to myself that if he ever came back to this farm I would have my revenge."

Her logic filled me with horror. "What about you? She killed herself because of what you'd done to her."

Gran lifted her hands and let them fall. "It was Edward who manipulated all of us."

I gave my brother a hard look. "Did you know about Edward and Gran, Ryan?"

Ryan slumped at the end of the couch. "I never wanted you to know, Brett. I would have done anything to keep you from knowing."

"Who told you about it?" I asked.

"It was in Mom's suicide note. I read it when I found her body." He let out a long breath, closed his eyes, and let his head fall against the sofa. "We've heard enough. Leave it alone, Gran."

Gran stroked Ryan's back. "I'm sorry, darling. Don't think I don't appreciate what you're trying to do. But it won't work. We have to tell Brett the truth now. All of it."

She sighed as she smoothed the wrinkles in his shirt. "Edward came to the front door, last Tuesday." Her hand stopped moving on Ryan's back. "He told you he would, didn't he?" she asked Ryan.

I realized I didn't want to know everything, after all. I wanted to make time reel itself in, to go backward, so I could avoid whatever was coming.

Ryan spoke. "He was used to controlling people. You. Me. Vincent. He was sure he could wrap you around his little finger."

Gran stared off into the distance, and her gaze held a chilling tranquillity. "Of course I knew him the second I laid eyes on him. He'd lost weight. His hair was thin, and his face was wasted with his disease, but I knew him immediately. I'd waited a long time to see him."

She patted Ryan's back. "You'd already left. Everyone else was gone. Amy was at school, Noah was hunting, and you were at the grocery store, Brett. It was so unusual to be here alone. It seemed like a blessing. A signal, telling me to go ahead."

No, I thought, don't say it, don't.

"I could see the lesions on his neck, his face, and I suspected what they meant. It was obvious he was sick, and it was strange to see him looking so old, so shrunken. He asked me where you were, Brett. He wanted to meet you. I didn't give him the satisfaction of seeing how shocked I was at his sudden appearance, and told him you were probably out behind the barn. He could go on out there, I said, and I told him I'd come out and introduce him to you. I said it would just take a moment for me to fetch my coat.

"I watched him walk across the yard, his gait turtle slow, as if he were an old man, as if he were in pain. There was very little hesitation in my mind. Almost none. I felt a fleeting regret, as if I were leaving home. I was flooded with the feeling that I was saying good-bye to my old life, and wondered briefly if I would be the one to die. I unlocked the gun cabinet, took the Browning from the rack, checked the breech, and put in a shell, then went out to meet him.

"When I opened the barn door Edward smiled at the sight of me, but his face changed when he saw the gun in my hands.

" 'Oh, Emily,' " he said. There was no surprise in his voice, just sorrow, as if he could see I was about to do something that would only embarrass me later. I lifted the gun, fit the stock against my shoulder and sighted through it, aiming at his heart. He made no effort to get away. He came toward me, hands up, palms out.

" 'I only want to talk to you,' he said.

" 'You stole my child,' I said. My voice sounded strange, as if it were coming from the end of a long tunnel.

" 'I loved your child,' he said.

"I began to cry.

" 'Please, Emily' he said. 'Put the gun down. You don't want to do this. Nothing is worth this.'

"I lowered the gun and wiped my face, and when I looked up again he was suddenly close, very close, smiling at me. He grabbed the barrel of the gun.

" 'Give it to me, Emily,' he said. That was when it all came flooding back, how he used to grab me, the way he would say those words.

"He was weak from his sickness. It surprised me, how easy it was, to force the gun away from him. I lifted it and pulled the trigger. It was unbelievably loud. I'd forgotten how loud a gun could be. The shot echoed against the barn walls for a long time. I was glad the horses were all out in the pasture, away from the noise. The dogs barked like mad but there was no one at home to hear them."

I watched my grandmother's mouth move and felt an ebbing of confidence in reality. The laws of physics seemed to waver, as if gravity had quit and we were all left to float unpinned, drifting in a nightmare. The woman beside me had been my model of adulthood for as long as I could remember. She was my parent, my teacher, my guide, and now she was telling me she had murdered my father.

Gran went on, her voice casual and smooth as if she were describing a rabbit hunt. "My aim was too low, and the buckshot hit his belly. He looked stunned, and his mouth moved like a fish flung out of water, his eyes wide with the knowing, finally, that this was how much I hated him. It felt good to watch him struggle. Blood spattered his jacket and poured out of the hole I'd made, blackening his jeans and the shavings on the floor."

I stared at my grandmother, hypnotized, and felt a silent shriek inside me, like the scream of a tree having a limb ripped off.

Gran went on, two pink circles on her cheeks, a slight smile on her face. "I was breathing as hard as if I'd raced to the pond and back, and my heart was going so fast I feared they'd find the two of us on the floor. All I could hear was a sound like wind rushing through leaves, a hissing that lasted for several minutes. I was paralyzed, frightened at what I'd done, but oh God! I was so deeply satisfied, too.

"I dropped the gun and stared at Edward, who was still gasping on the floor. I knew I had to clean up this mess. I didn't want him in the barn. I went to him and tried to lift him by his arms, and he cried out. It was a horrible, inarticulate gurgle of pain. There were red bubbles coming out of his stomach, pouring down his sides, onto my blouse, my apron, my skirt. I tried to drag him again and failed. He was thin as a stork, but he was a tall man, heavier than he looked, and I couldn't budge him." She shook her head. "It was *such* a mess."

Such a mess, such a mess: the phrase echoed in me like a nursery rhyme as I listened to the swoop of emphasis in my grandmother's old-fashioned, upper-class voice.

She shifted slightly in her seat, crossed her legs,

and continued. "The horses were in the south pasture, so I grabbed a rope and saddle from the tack room and stepped outside to whistle for Caledonia. Usually she comes to me at a trot, greedy for the apple or sugar lump she knows I carry for her in my pocket. But she was uneasy about the gunshot and the smell of blood on my clothes and she hung back by the fence, reluctant to come closer. By now I was frantic, terrified of being discovered.

"It was a lovely day, bright and still and warm for November. My chest hurt, and I was having trouble breathing. I threw the saddle on the ground and sat on a clod of mud next to it and picked at the wet stains on my skirt for I don't know how long. I think I was in shock. Caledonia came up and nudged me, and I clung to her and cried a little.

"She let me use her mane to pull myself up. I left the saddle where it was and wandered back to the barn, where Edward was still alive, bleeding to death on the floor. It was as shocking a sight as if I'd never killed him in the first place, but it came back to me in a rush, why I'd done it."

I was seized with impatience at my grandmother's story. "You must have known he was sick," I protested, as if I could change the past by pointing out its lack of logic. "You must have known that he was ready to die. He only had a few weeks left. You could have waited."

Gran's face was cold as an executioner's. "Your father blackmailed me, raped me, forced me to betray my daughter over and over, for nearly two years.

250

My own daughter! The most precious person in the world to me! I could never forgive him for that. I made a vow to myself on the day Caroline died that I would kill him if I had the chance. It kept me going for decades, that hatred. It gave me a reason to live, to work, to raise you children, to go on breathing.

"I was out of my mind with rage at him, even while he twisted and squirmed on the floor in front of me. I told him why I had to kill him. I hope he heard me. I described the way Caroline looked after she murdered herself over his faithlessness, how it felt to see my daughter's cold blue face, to touch and hold the stiffness of her body as I washed her and dressed her for the funeral parlor. I screamed, I kicked him, and I shouted until I was hoarse.

"Finally I staggered outside with a rope, a bit, and a bridle and went back to where I'd left the saddle in the pasture. Caledonia shied away from me at first but eventually she let me fit the bit to her mouth and thread the halter over her ears. I tied her to the railing, threw the saddle over her broad back, and cinched it as tight as I could. My arms were shaking and there was no strength in them, but I was desperate to drag the body away from the barn. I used the fence railing to climb on Caledonia's back, hooked the rope around the pommel, and kicked her toward the barn.

"But she wouldn't go in. She could smell the blood. I had to uncoil the rope thirty feet and take it through the barn door to stretch it to his body. Once

I was standing over him, Edward's eyes flickered and opened as I tied the rope around his chest.

"He tried to whisper something, and I pulled the rope even tighter above the hole in his belly and watched him wince. I felt a savage fury and pleasure, glad for his pain. For thirty years this man had been at the center of my greatest loss, and I knew his return to the farm was a sign that I was meant to destroy him."

Listening to Gran talk about signs made me bury my face in my hands. How could this sensible, intelligent woman carry this mania inside her for so long without ever revealing it? How could it have escaped me? How could she have expressed herself so sensitively, so thoughtfully in her writing without ever betraying the presence of the killer who lived inside her?

Gran cleared her throat, and when she continued her voice was raspy with fatigue. "Once I was back in the saddle, I urged Caledonia to drag him through the yard and over to the driveway. And then I saw his black Mercedes jeep, parked in the center of the drive. It stopped me dead. I'd forgotten about his car. I was frantic now, trying to think. Amy would be home from school any second. I didn't have a moment to lose. I slid off Caledonia and walked over to the jeep and saw the keys dangling from the ignition. I rolled all the windows down and got in. The engine started at the twist of the key, and I put it in drive, aimed the car at the pond and jumped out. It purred across the yard, broke the ice at the edge of the pond and churned all the way into the deep end, its roof covered by water in less than a minute. The mud is so deep at the bottom it will probably stay hidden forever, if no one looks for it.''

If no one looks for it? I thought in disbelief. Of course they'll look for it. Does she believe the investigation of our father's murder will blow over, that the police will simply go away? Does she expect me to lie for her? I seethed under the implication of her words. Ryan's expression was grim, but he didn't say a word to protest her delicate inference. Out of habit, I followed his lead and kept my mouth closed.

''Caledonia was uneasy about all of this, the gunshot, the car vanishing into her drinking pond, the body, the smell of blood. Once I hoisted myself back into the saddle she was ready to leave, even with the corpse dragging behind her. She hustled into a trot before I gave her the signal, and I let her drag Edward down the trail toward the waterfall.

''I was quivering with fear, shocked at the sounds coming out of Edward, shocked at the mess I'd made of his belly, shocked at all the blood. I had no plan. None. I was functioning out of anger and adrenaline and fright. When we were about a mile from the house, I jumped off Caledonia and tried to untie the knot around Edward's chest. There was no reason to dump him there on the trail, except that I felt as though I'd gone far enough from the house. I didn't even think about anyone finding him, or the police coming to search for clues. I never knew there was a will in Edward's pocket, and I didn't think to take away his identification.

"Edward's eyes were open, fixed on me, but unfocused and milky. I was certain he was dead. As I worked on the knot he stared right at me, his eyes just a few inches from mine. It was a terrible sight. It will be a relief to die, just to rid myself of that sight. I tried to untie the knot, which had tightened itself to the point of impossibility, and then I bit the rope, trying to release him. There was blood on the rope, and I tasted the salt of it.

"And then he blinked.

"I screamed and scrambled up to my knees. Crying, whimpering like a madwoman, I gave up on the knot and yanked the rope down over his hips and his legs until we were free of each other. Caledonia carried me uphill, away from the darkness of the woods and his body. When I came back to the barn I hosed the blood down the drain and put fresh shavings on the floor. I wrapped the gun in an old shirt that was hanging on a hook in the tack room, went to the house, and put the gun in the closet upstairs. Then I burned my clothes. If I was thinking clearly I would have burned the rope, too, but I was shaking, slipping in and out of shock. My mind felt frozen."

Gran stopped speaking for a moment and looked directly at me. "I took a long, hot bath and thought about Edward. I thought about who he was and how he'd treated my daughter. I forgave myself, Brett. I want you to know this: it was worth it, to kill him."

The coldness in her voice pressed me back. The

room seemed drained of color. I felt as though I were floating, and noticed my hands were trembling. Let me go back outside your secrets, I thought. I don't want to know. I changed my mind.

Suddenly she laughed out loud. "To tell you the truth, I expected Dan to come right back in here and arrest me after you went to look at the body. I even packed a little overnight bag to take with me to the jail. I had no idea it would take them so long to figure it out. And when that pompous fool Farnsworth started throwing his weight around I suppose I got mad, and I wanted to see if I could get away with it. Then there was all this snow to contend with, and Vincent. But Ryan knew, didn't you, love?"

Ryan rubbed his temple with his thumb and forefinger, refusing to meet her eyes. "I knew Edward would talk to you," he muttered. "I always thought that might be a dangerous thing for him to do."

Gran looked at me. "If you want to turn me in, I won't deny anything. I'll go quietly."

Somehow it sounded like a challenge. Pay attention, I thought. Feel this. Don't be afraid to take your time. Or go ahead and be afraid. I knew my grandmother was not a conventional person. She could drift along behind her beautifully enameled public personality and then be ruthlessly imaginative. Perhaps I was just like her. I killed someone, too, didn't I? I shoved Vincent over a cliff and deliberately left him there to die. What was the difference? Self-defense was just a phrase. It was my anger that killed him, and anger can age for a lifetime with its strength intact. It can grow stronger.

Suddenly I felt heavy as earth. "I need to think about this," I said. "I can't make a decision now."

"Of course," Gran said, and covered up her disappointment in my answer with an uneasy laugh. "Although I must confess it would be easier to live out my days here on the farm rather than jail."

"Do you intend to keep Edward's money?" I asked Ryan.

Ryan had the grace to look ashamed. "He's dead, Brett. We can't bring him back. I think we've all been punished enough. And I can't imagine turning Gran over to the police."

I felt as though the two of them had handed me a burning coal, one I was meant to hold in my bare hands for the rest of my life. Could I turn my grandmother over to the police? The thought was absurd, unthinkable. But could I cover up her crime? Would I become like her if I did? Would I keep the truth about her a secret from Amy, from Noah, from everyone I loved? Would I become another in a long line of liars?

"I have to go to bed," I said. "I'm right on the edge. I can't absorb any more tonight."

"Would you like another Demerol?" Ryan said.

I nodded, desperate to be numb, unconscious. He unscrewed the bottle and shook a tablet into my palm. I put it in my mouth and sipped the tea, which was now cold.

Gran looked at me and her eyes began to fill. "No

matter what you decide to do, Brett, I want you to
know that I'm proud of you. I had the chance to watch
you grow up and become the person you are, and that
makes me rich. So incredibly rich. I love you with all
my heart. I always will, no matter what happens."

I held up my palm. "Don't say any more," I
warned her. My voice was harsh with fatigue. "No
more confessions, no tugging on my heartstrings. I've
heard enough."

Ryan reached out to help me up and I pushed his
hand off my arm. Somehow it was hard to separate
him from her. Vincent was right, I kept thinking.
Ryan wanted the money. Knowing that obliterated
everything else about him. It did not matter that he'd
tried to protect me from our father, or tried to protect
Gran from a murder charge. He was as greedy as
Vincent, underneath his good intentions.

"I'm going to bed," I said.

"Good night," he said. My grandmother kept her
lips tightly pressed together. For the first time, she
looked frightened.

The bed was so frigid it was another fresh suffering to crawl between the sheets. As I waited for the
Demerol to kick in, I held my grief at bay. I didn't
want to cry. I didn't want to feel this jagged hurt.
The minutes passed. Finally the painkiller crept into
my veins and dulled the edges of my misery until it
softened into depression.

Just wait, I told myself. She's old. She'll die. You
can keep her secret for that long. You can wait her
out.

# Chapter Ten

In my dream I was trying to mount a horse that could fly. It was white, like the winged horse on the old gas station sign, but every time I tried to climb up the white, broad slope of its back I slipped and fell into a greasy stream. The stream smelled bad.

My eyes flew open and the dream disappeared but the smell remained. Gasoline. I smelled gasoline. I sat up in bed, listening hard for a moment, my mouth dry from the Demerol, head fuzzy, heart pounding.

It had already been a long and weary night, and I didn't want to get up. But the smell was nagging, insistent. Could Ryan have used gasoline to burn wet wood for the stove? It wouldn't be the first time. Gran kept a can of gasoline under the kitchen counter for damp mornings when the wood wouldn't catch. Maybe it was nothing more than that.

The air felt thick, expectant. Outside the wind was quiet, but I could hear a sighing in the hallway, a breathy murmur that rustled near the door. The smell was pungent now, too strong to ignore, and the whisper in the hallway grew into a burst of crackling as I threw back the covers. In the bars of moonlight shining through the window I could see gray plumes seeping into the room from the crack under the closed door.

Smoke.

I leapt out of bed, ran to the door, and opened it. The hallway was white with flame, bright as magnesium, the walls, paintings, and photographs, all ablaze. The air was thick with smoke, and I winced as the blast of heat poured out to me. Fire rushed at me like a living thing, a bright, hot, searing tongue licking at my hair, my skin, hungry for the oxygen streaming from my open door.

In an instant my nightgown began to smolder. I reeled backward, one hand uplifted to shield my eyes, then slammed the door and ran to the bedroom window. It was frozen shut, and no amount of jiggling and pounding on the frame could budge it. Terrified, I seized the night lamp from my bedside table, yanked the cord from its socket and heaved the lamp through the window. There was a spectacular clash of breakage, leaving a jagged hole in the center of the glass. I catapulted through the knife-sharp edges of the opening and sailed out into the freezing air. The smoldering hem of my nightgown blazed into flames that shot up over my head, scorching my face.

A drift had whipped up in a frozen wave against the house, and when I plummeted into it the snow hissed as it swallowed my burning body. In an instant I was buried. Snow sifted into my ears, fine as powder. My hands and feet tingled, as if from an electric shock. I tried to kick free but sank deeper into the drift. Panicked, I tried to shout and gagged on the snow that flowed into my mouth. Desperate for air, I flailed my arms until I managed to clear a space above my head, and when I tilted my face upward I could finally breathe.

Behind the broken glass in the window I could see my curtains were on fire. The open window was spitting sparks that spiraled upward into the sky, and I could hear the fire suck in fresh air with a sound like a giant intake of breath. The dogs were barking inside, and I could hear an unmistakably familiar voice shouting and laughing toward the back of the house.

It was Vincent.

No, I thought. Vincent is dead. I killed him. I saw him go over the cliff and fall sixty feet, and no one could survive a fall like that. Surely he was still lying at the bottom of the gorge. Then I thought of my own flying leap out of the bedroom window. The snow was deep and soft, soft as down, soft as a feather bed. People leapt out of tall buildings onto inflated mattresses, so why couldn't the snow have provided Vincent with the same escape? How else could he be here?

My nightgown was a charred rag that disintegrated into wet, blackened strips as I struggled to escape the icy drift. My arms and legs were numb, and when I pushed the snow away I saw that the broken glass from the window had sliced my skin like a razor, and blood was darkening the snow around me. Grunting with effort, struggling against the freezing embrace of the drift, I finally worked my shoulders free.

The heat of the burning house and the warmth of my blood spreading in a dark stain around my body condensed the surface of the snow, and a denser, slick skin of slush formed over the sugar-fine granules underneath. Finally I gained enough purchase with my arms to slither out of the hole I'd created by jumping from the second story, and I slid head-first down the slope to an awkward landing in the trough beside the drift.

The conflagration radiated a dazzling light that glared against the barns, the humps of snowed-in cars, and the black pines that lined the driveway. The sky itself looked pale in the glow from the house; stars and moon were erased by the flashbulb brightness of the fire. A window exploded in the heat, and I whipped my head around when I heard the rifle crack of glass breaking.

Bleeding, burnt, freezing, and clothed only in the nightgown that hung in blackened tatters from my neck, I floundered toward the sound of Vincent shouting at the back of the house. The towering drifts were a maze that offered no clear path, and I staggered and fell again and again. There was no refuge from the cold, which burned as much as fire. My feet felt like blocks of iron.

"Brett!" Noah's voice came from behind me, and I was filled with a rush of hysterical relief to see him. We wallowed toward each other and I buried myself in his arms, suddenly aware that I was overwhelmed and exhausted and my reserves were perilously low. This is how people go crazy, I thought. They fill themselves up with too many unbearable things and then they check out, they leave, they say no, I won't take any more of this. I was shivering uncontrollably, and not just from the cold.

"Take my coat," he said, stripping it off. He hurried my arms into the sleeves, into the imprint of his warmth in the fleece, into the welcoming protection of the long, heavy sheepskin.

"Amy," I said, and lifted my arm toward the glare and let it fall. My face felt like a singed piece of meat. I shook my head, unable to say what I meant.

"It's all right, Brett, she'll be all right," he murmured. "Let's go find her."

"Vincent is here," I said. "I heard him, around the back."

"I know," Noah said. "I heard him too."

"He must have set the fire. I smelled gasoline. He could have gotten it from the pump in the pole barn. We don't keep it locked."

"Let's find out," he said, and looped my arm around his neck and half carried me, pushing through waist-high snow toward the back of the house.

"Have you seen Amy?" I asked. "Is she out of the house?"

"Look," Noah said, and gestured with his chin toward the porch, where the kitchen door opened and Ryan and Amy tumbled out in their bathrobes, followed closely by the dogs. The dogs ran into the yard and barked in high, fretful voices at the figure crouched by the steps.

It was Vincent, and I knew in an instant that he was waiting for Ryan.

In a flash Vincent hurled himself at Ryan, who was completely unprepared for the flying tackle that threw them both to the floor of the porch. They struggled, rolling until Vincent pinned him and hit him in the face. Ryan went limp. Vincent grabbed something from the pocket of Ryan's robe, then staggered to his feet, the will clutched in his fist.

"I knew it!" Vincent crowed. He tore the paper into scraps and threw all the pieces into the air.

You bastard, I thought. You knew I'd give the will to Ryan. And you knew Ryan would take the will out with him if you set fire to the house.

Ryan's voice rose above the noise of the fire as he pulled himself up and charged Vincent. "You son of a bitch! I'll kill you!"

Vincent's face was illuminated by fire, his mouth stretched into a grin that bared his teeth. He seized Ryan by the throat and shoved him back. "It's all mine now," he shouted, and let out a high-pitched crazy laugh. Vincent pushed him backward until Ryan tripped over the rocking chair and fell heavily on the floor of the porch. Vincent kicked him, over and over, solid, booted kicks that made Ryan writhe helplessly under him. I saw Vincent's boots in the glare of the flames. Black leather. Tips reinforced in silver. Boots that could kill.

Noah and I floundered through the deep snow as fast as we could, but it was like moving through glue. The fight on the porch occurred in seconds, so fast it was hard to believe it was really happening, but I couldn't get my legs out of slow motion.

Amy danced around Vincent, agitated, screaming, "Stop it! Leave him alone! You'll kill him!" while the dogs whined and yipped but were held back from attacking because of their fear of the flames that crackled behind the windows. Amy leaped on Vincent's back and clung there, her legs wrapped around his body, her hands clawing his eyes. For a brief moment I was torn between admiration for her courage and terror that she'd be killed, until Vincent lurched back from Ryan and slammed Amy's body against the wall of the house. I could see her drop to the floor, limp as a sack of wheat.

I was almost there. Noah struggled on ahead of me, determined as a linebacker, forcing his way through the snow to the porch steps.

"You're dead," Vincent snarled at my daughter. He grabbed the rocking chair and lifted it over his head, aiming for her.

Noah scrambled up the steps and seized the heavy black cowbell by the railing, then swung the bell in a full arc that connected with the back of Vincent's head. There was a dull clank of iron on bone. Vincent grunted as the chair fell harmlessly to one side, and then he dropped in a heap at Noah's feet.

I struggled up the steps and ran to where Amy was lying. "Are you all right?" I asked, cradling her head.

Amy was white with shock, hyperventilating, but her eyes were focused. "Gran is still in there, Mom."

I helped Amy to her feet. "Go out in the yard. I'll be right back."

"No," she said, clinging to me. "Don't go in there. It's too hot."

"I have to, honey." I shoved her away and ran to the door, but when I touched the knob it was too hot to hold.

Noah had his arm around Ryan, who sagged against him, limp as laundry while they struggled down the steps. Noah looked back wildly at me. "No!" he shouted. "Wait for me!"

I used the sleeve of Noah's coat as a potholder to turn the knob, then pushed the door open and entered the inferno.

Being inside the house was like being in a cauldron. The heat was unbearable, and I knew I'd die if I didn't turn around and go back outside within the next few seconds. Every instinct urged me to run out as fast as I could, but I turned up the thick collar of the coat and forced myself to go deeper into the house, toward the staircase. Fire glared white and blue from the living room as the flames licked up rugs, furniture, books, and curtains. Even the logs piled next to the woodstove were blazing in their brass basket. The handles of the antique farm tools that covered the walls were burning on their hooks. Walls groaned and sang around me as steam escaped wood, and a beam in the ceiling hissed and cracked like a pistol shot.

The furious heat cut into me like a sword, in spite of the shield provided by Noah's heavy coat. I buried my nose in the collar but my face, throat, and lungs were cooking. My feet were beyond sensation, and I ordered them to move even though I knew the heat from the floor was blistering the soles. I would feel the pain later, when I could afford to. Now I had to be a machine. I had to keep pushing.

Gran was barely visible in the haze of smoke, crouched at the top of the stairs, obviously petrified at the sight of the smoking steps below her. The banister was on fire. She was perched between two impossible places, the bright dancing flames of the hallway behind her and the inferno below. I was amazed she'd been able to crawl from her room through the glare of the burning hallway. Her kimono was smoldering. I could hear her cough.

I screamed through the smoke. "Come down!"

She shook her head. "It's too hot." Her voice was choked.

I ascended the first five steps of the stairs, walking barefoot on the scorching wood. "See?" I said through gritted teeth. "It's easy. You can do this." Now I was close enough to see her face, and thought I saw a glimmer of hope there. Her head came up.

She rose to her feet, took two tentative steps down toward me. She was almost within reach.

The step underneath me let out a groan of warning and buckled, releasing a blast of heat. I sprang back to the bottom before it broke and watched in horror as the entire staircase collapsed and fell into a heap of blazing rubble, a bonfire within a bonfire. Gran scrabbled her way back to the top of the landing and knelt there, crouching below the thickest layer of smoke.

I could see her through the flames. "Go back!" she called to me. "I'll find another way out!"

"Jump!" I begged, then coughed as the smoke seared my lungs. "There's no other way!" I held out my arms for her.

She shook her head, paralyzed, just ten feet above the heap of broken, burning steps. "I can't, Brett." Her eyes were fixed on the fire below.

"Don't think about it!" I yelled. "I'll catch you."

"No," Gran said. Her voice was suddenly calm. "Brett, get out while there's time."

I held my arms outstretched, the tips of my fingers straining upward. I couldn't breathe. The heat was too great, the smoke too thick. A beam in the ceiling shrieked, the wood tortured by flames until its weight was too much to bear, the sucking fire too great to resist. The beam fell as I watched, horrified, unable to move. It came directly toward me. I heard Gran scream.

The floor shuddered as the timber fell to one side of me, bounced on a chair, broke it to kindling, and set it on fire. The ceiling sighed and a huge scrap of plasterboard peeled off and dropped a wall of fire behind me. Gasping for air, swatting out the flames that clawed at Noah's coat, I waved at the smoke and shouted at Gran.

"Vincent set the fire," I gasped. "He's alive. Do you want him to win? Do you want to die?"

I jumped back as another beam fell with a splintering crash exactly where I had stood a moment ago. Seizing the new fuel, the burning rubble of the staircase roared higher and hotter than before.

Gran shook her head, leaned back on her knees, and called to me through the flames. "I wish I could kiss you good-bye." Her voice was as tranquil as if she were stepping out to weed the garden.

No, I thought. I won't leave. I can't let you die. Time slowed itself and expanded then, like the spiral of a watch spring unwinding, until a whole lifetime of moments filled the space between us. My heart was loud in my chest, and between one beat and the next I saw her as I always remembered her whenever I was far from home, with a pencil stuck in her hair, her hands moving like birds as she described the hepatica budding in the woods, or the praying mantis she found in the raspberries, or the taste of a daylily. Another beat of my heart and I saw her shelling peas in the kitchen, hair piled on her head in a graceful knot, her face animated, rosy, disarmingly youthful and confident. Again the sluggish squeeze in my chest came and I saw Gran laughing, looking at me with a face full of love when she held Amy for the first time. I knew she would forgive any mistake I ever made. I knew she would always protect me. I remembered seeing her skinny-dip in the pond before dawn one morning in late September, just a few weeks ago. Her body was a silhouette in the mist, and I could see the slender violin-shape of her back as she walked into the cold water without pause. She had always seemed immortal. For all of my life she had been there, a luminous, loving, good-humored presence.

The fact that she killed my father didn't even seem important now. I never knew him, never loved him. He raped Gran, blackmailed her, drove her child to suicide. Perhaps I would have killed him, too, in those circumstances.

It seemed so clear, there in the heat of the burning room. I would put the murder behind me. I would never speak of it to anyone as long as I lived.

"I'm not going without you," I said, but my voice was no more than a whisper and I knew she couldn't hear me.

Gran stood and walked back along the hallway. Instantly her long white hair caught fire, and her kimono blazed in a brilliant outline of her body. For a moment she was dazzling, haloed by fire, and then she disappeared into the smoke.

I sank down on the floor and put my head down on the scorching hot boards. I was so tired. Maybe I'm still dreaming, I thought. That would be good. I wanted to go back to sleep. It was too hard to breathe, hardly worth the effort, and besides, it only made me cough.

The floor shook with the weight of someone running across the room. I tried to raise my head but it was too heavy, and then the room tilted as I was lifted and heaved over someone's shoulder. It was Noah, I realized. Noah, my protector, my bodyguard. Noah loved me. We lurched toward the door as he ran, stumbling, carrying me.

My lungs were ready to burst by the time he staggered outside with me slung over his shoulder. I gasped and coughed and retched at the shock of fresh air. Vincent was still unconscious, sprawled on the porch, and Noah stepped over him, then pitched forward down the steps and into the yard, where he dumped me unceremoniously in the snow. He knelt above me, choking, coughing, fighting for breath.

The porch roof burst into flames, and the windows popped and shattered as tongues of fire licked out of every opening. We watched helplessly as the house exploded in a single burst of incandescence, and I realized the kerosene and gas tanks that were stored in the cellar had become a bomb. Every timber glowed red, then collapsed outward, releasing a rolling fireball that shot the burning debris of the roof into the sky. Fire rained down on us. Noah threw himself over me, his head buried in his arms to avoid the blinding glare. Snow sizzled around us as bits and pieces of burning shingles, boards, masonry, and metal fell in glowing hot fireworks from the sky.

I sucked in air, my head reeling with oxygen, my

chest filled with a deep, soul-wrenching sorrow, a void so great I couldn't feel it, couldn't admit it. She was gone. The house she'd loved was no more than a column of heat and light that would leave only charcoal behind. Gran was dead. The thought was unbearable to contemplate, like looking at the sun.

Noah rolled off me and Amy and Ryan staggered over and helped us to our feet. We were silent, stricken by the sight of the burning house and all that we had lost.

I stood and swayed between them, shaky, coughing, alive.

As I stared out the window of Noah's cabin I could see the smoke from the burning rubble turn the color of blood as dawn streaked across the sky. The fire had died to a scattering of smaller blazes that paled when the light touched them. I couldn't absorb it. I felt like a sleepwalker, exhausted, numb, caught in a bad dream.

"Is he alive?" I asked Ryan.

"Barely," he said. Vincent was stretched out on Noah's bed in the cabin. Ryan dabbed at Vincent's exposed wounds with a mild solution of soap and water. Noah's emergency medical kit was open on the table beside him. Vincent's face was a mass of charred pulp, and there was an unmistakable smell of cooked meat emanating from him. He had been unconscious ever since we carried him from the porch, where the burning roof had collapsed on him. Vincent was wearing a black turtleneck, and I could tell from the charred and viscous pulp around the neck that removing the shirt was going to be extremely unpleasant. Polyester didn't burn; it melted, and when you pulled it away, it took a lot of skin with it.

"Should I try to wrap him up?" Ryan asked me.

"No." My voice was hoarse, almost gone from smoke inhalation. "With burns that severe he's better off without any bandages. Just clean the wounds as well as you can." I would have treated Vincent myself but my hands and feet were heavily bandaged, and I couldn't walk. My lungs ached, as if a thousand slivers of glass were stuck in them. But Vincent was in far more critical condition.

Ryan looked at me. "His pulse is weak. I don't think he'll last long."

I nodded. "It looks like third-degree burns over most of his face, right through the epidermis and the dermis. They'll know more when the areas of third-degree depths demarcate. The nerve endings are probably destroyed. After the initial pain he didn't feel a thing."

Eventually, if he lived, they'd begin to debride him, strip the blackened flesh and leave him flayed, raw, suppurating. I wasn't sorry, and it didn't seem as though Ryan cared much, either. But I felt the old pull, to read the symptoms, make a careful diagnosis, and treat the patient. "He needs fluids. He should be on an IV. In fact we should all be drinking water right now."

Ryan went to the cupboard and pulled out two

glasses, then filled them with water from the tap. "Are you sure you'll be okay riding over to the Arsenaults'?"

"I'm not staying here," I said, looking at Vincent. We were all going over to our nearest neighbor to use their telephone. Noah had given us jeans, shirts, sweaters, socks, and shoes that fit none of us but protected us against the fierce cold. He and Amy had gone out to saddle up the horses.

"What will we do with Vincent?" Ryan asked.

"We'll have to leave him here until the paramedics come and get him. No ambulance is going to make it up here today, not with this much snow on the ground. Cover him in blankets. Leave the heat on, and water next to the bed in case he wakes up." But he wouldn't be waking up, I thought. Not this time.

"We could carry him with us, take him in for treatment."

"Ryan, it's fourteen miles to the hospital," I pointed out. "Bumping over these drifts would kill him."

We looked at each other. "I know," he said, and shook his head. "I just don't know what to do." He stood by the couch, dazed and gray. Inside the clothes Noah had given him he looked limp, and his arms hung down from his shoulders as if his brain had forgotten they were there. His eyes were stark with shock. I touched him and without warning his eyes filled and a terrible heaving, rasping noise came out of his mouth. He looked helpless, like a small boy.

"I should have saved her," he said. "I should have checked her room."

"Hush," I said, and put my bandaged hands around my brother. His arms were taut as wire, his back rigid with tension.

"It's okay," I said, and lay my head gently against his chest. "Everything will be all right."

His arms began to tremble. I could feel the air go out of him, hear the rough sob as he tried to swallow his grief, and the ache in me swelled with the guilt we shared. We should have saved her.

"Let it go," I said. "Let it go."

# Chapter Eleven

The next few months passed slowly, like a long illness. Amy and I settled into a three-bedroom apartment in Ithaca, near the high school. Everything in the apartment was new: new rugs, new furniture, new appliances, dazzling in their rich, clean, unstained newness. It cost a fortune to cover the expense, but I dipped into my savings and begged the hospital to rehire me. They gave me a job in the ER, and I worked sixty or seventy hours a week right through Christmas. Work was numbing, and I liked numb more than anything. Being at the hospital was like taking heroin all day long, and I stitched up gunshot wounds and set the bones of car wreck victims like a junkie shooting up, again and again.

I thought of this as my afterlife, a purgatory without a future. My white coat was my uniform, and it gave my days a reassuring sameness that helped me feel distant and self-contained. When I wasn't working I stayed in bed and watched TV, or else I was in the bathtub, reading books from the library. The days passed in a blur, in the bubble of urban routine. The world of nature that is so inescapable on a farm, where every season is distinct and weather is a constantly shifting omen of prosperity or ruin—this world left me. I was rarely outside, rarely saw the sky. I worked in concrete hallways and windowless rooms. In some ways I forgot I was alive.

After a week in a coma at Tompkins County Hospital, Vincent died. The only beneficiary listed in Vincent's will was the Metropolitan Museum of Art in New York, and Edward's estate went to them. Whatever relatives Vincent had were dead, and that made it easier to lie when Farnsworth questioned us about Edward's murder, the fire, and our grandmother's death. Ryan and I told him the same carefully rehearsed story: Vincent confessed that he killed our father right before he lost consciousness. According to this mythical confession, he was the one who drove Edward's car into our pond and set fire to the house, and the fire destroyed the will and killed Gran. Eventually Farnsworth stopped calling without ever actually saying he believed us, and I suspected that Dan probably had something to do with that.

Gran's body was cremated in the conflagration of the house, but the medical examiner found a few teeth and charred bones in the ashes. When those fragments were finally released from the forensics lab, Ryan scattered them in the myrtle woods, near the other graves.

The farm wasn't insured against arson, so the bank foreclosed on the property in January. It was big news in the county, bigger than we expected. Emily McBride was a small legend in the town, a source of civic pride, and after the foreclosure her farm became the beneficiary of a month-long fundraising effort by the Finger Lakes Land Trust. By March the trust had made a modest bid on the farm in order to create a wildlife sanctuary, and since real estate values had been more or less flat for three decades, the bank jumped at the offer. Now the farm was public land, a refuge for trees, plants, and wildlife; off-limits to development, hunting, and logging.

Ryan went bankrupt and moved back into town to start up his practice again. The horses were sold or given away. I had a hard time talking to Ryan these days, and pleaded fatigue or a strenuous schedule at work whenever he wanted to connect with me. I hadn't seen him since Gran's memorial service.

Noah called me almost every day for weeks after the fire, but I kept my voice cool and remote when we talked. He told me he was working in the stables at the vet school at Cornell and taking classes part-time, and he was eager to see me, talk to me, take me to dinner. Each time he called I told him I was busy, and gradually he gave up calling. Detachment was what I craved, what I needed. It felt safer to live on the outside of things, to bury myself in work. Besides, I reasoned, Noah was better off without me, and I could certainly function more easily without him.

I didn't tell anyone that Gran had murdered my father. I couldn't tell anyone, not even Amy. The secret my grandmother carried to her grave was mine now. It was all I had left of her, and it was going to stay buried in me, exactly where she'd left it. I avoided conversations where my guard might slip, where someone might see the truth behind my efficiency. Most of the time I kept my distance from everyone I'd ever loved, and that included Amy.

One night on the way home from the hospital it occurred to me that I never saw the sun anymore. It was late; I'd left the house at five, an hour before dawn, and now it was eight in a black-dark evening. By the time I changed out of my hospital clothes into jeans and a sweater I was exhausted, and wanted nothing more than to lie in bed with a glass of wine and watch a little CNN.

Amy came up to my room and stood awkwardly in the doorway, watching me. Our interactions were limited these days, and I liked to think I was giving her space, letting her grow up in her own way, without any nagging or interference from me. It was unusual for her to come to my room, and I looked up, expecting bad news.

"What is it?" I asked.

"I've been having dreams about the fire," she said.

I didn't want to talk about it. I wanted the memory of the fire to remain safely buried, along with all the other circumstances surrounding Edward's murder, but I didn't want to admit that to her. I slipped into a patient tone of voice that I put on like a hat. "That's natural, honey. Give it some time."

"You never talk about it."

"I know." It was the closest I'd ever come to an admission of the truth. I lay down on the bed and picked up the remote, aimed it at the TV, and pressed buttons until the sound of canned laughter filled the room.

Amy heaved a monumental sigh. "You're not happy," she said.

I kept my eyes on the television. "I'm just tired."

"You never used to watch TV, and now you watch it all the time. It's like you're living on some other planet, and we never connect anymore, or laugh, or talk. You never even smile, did you know that?"

She was accusing me of something I didn't want to change, and my fear of being exposed began to take shape as anger. "I'm sorry," I said flatly.

"I don't want you to be sorry. You're depressed, Mom," she said. "It scares me."

It was unnerving to be this girl's mother. What surprised me about Amy, what had always surprised me about her, was how direct she could be, how unafraid of confrontation. I saw her eyes dart around my room, as if she could find whatever was wrong with me and pluck it out of my life. I felt a spark of resistance. What did she want? I went to work every day, I made money, I gave up Noah. What else could I do? We stared at each other aggressively for a long minute, and then I softened and sank back into the pillows as I realized she was simply lonely for the person I used to be. Teenage loneliness: it struck me with the force of a blow. Loneliness never stopped; it was a lesson I had to learn again and again. And no matter how much I tried to shield her from the truth of what had happened, it would become her punishment, too, because knowing Gran's secret had changed me. It made us both lonely.

"You worry too much," I said. I turned off the TV and held out my arm to invite a hug.

She walked to the foot of the bed but no farther, her arms crossed against her chest, a strangely adult mixture of fear and determination on her face.

"You need help," she said.

I made myself speak in an even voice. "Amy. I'm tired. I want to watch TV. Stop worrying about me. I'm fine."

She backed away toward the door, looking younger now, and a little scared. "There's someone here to see you. He's downstairs. I want you to tell him whatever it is you can't tell me."

I glared at her. "If you called your father, so help me . . ."

Amy opened the door and went out to the living room. "She's coming out," I heard her say to whoever was waiting. Then I heard her bedroom door open and close.

My heart hammered in a new kind of anger, the anger that comes after fear and begins to line up the excuses, the reasons, the extenuating circumstances. I threw the remote down on the bed, my mind racing with thoughts that tumbled and scurried over each other like rats. I was doing my best, wasn't I? I was trying so hard I felt invisible, as if I'd parceled out every piece of myself, until there was nothing left.

Dan had better understand I didn't have anything left to give, no time in my schedule for therapy or exercise or whatever the magazines were prescribing these days for fulfillment. Charged by my own self-righteousness, I stalked out to the living room to defend myself.

Noah was sitting stiffly on the couch, and when he saw me he jumped up. "Amy asked me to come over," he said quickly, as if I might yell at him.

All the air went out of me. He looked so good. Weathered, lean, loose-limbed. He looked whole, unscathed by the fire and its aftermath. He hadn't been touched by any of it. He didn't even know about any of it.

"Would you like a drink?" I asked. "Coffee? Tea?" I hoped he would want something complicated, so I could busy myself with cups, spoons, running water into a kettle. Anything to avoid looking into those eyes.

"No, thanks," he said, sitting down again.

"What brings you out here so late?" I stood by the wall, unwilling to sit.

"I went to see Ryan."

"How is he?"

"He said to tell you Billy took him back."

That surprised me. Ryan must have stopped gambling if Billy was risking a relationship with him again.

"I asked Ryan about your grandmother," Noah said.

Just the thought of Noah asking about her made me feel as though I'd swallowed a stone.

"What did he tell you?"

"Everything."

My mouth was dry, and the room seemed to pulse with my breathing. It astounded me that Ryan could so casually betray her. Not even Dan knew the truth.

"I don't believe it," I said, automatically shielding myself from the possibility that Noah knew what I had refused to reveal.

"I can see why she killed him," he said softly, looking right into me.

I felt a small, chilled, blossom of surprise. That he knew about the murder and dismissed it so swiftly unnerved me, as if something intensely private had suddenly been exposed and discussed by people I barely knew. I stiffened, expecting to be judged in spite of his words.

"Your grandmother wouldn't want you to keep her secret if it cost you this much, Brett. Amy told me you're not happy. She said you have no friends, no one to talk to, no social life at all."

My face burned at his assumptions. Didn't he know I was working my butt off? People needed me. I saved lives every day. The tasks never ended, and there was no limit to my schedule. A headache pushed up and swelled to fill the space behind my eyes.

"I'm fine," I said. "I'm just fine." He met my gaze, and I could tell he knew I was lying.

He spoke softly, taking direct aim. "We had something once. You know we did. It happened at a complicated time in your life, but it was real. I know it was real."

"You don't know what my life is like now," I said, wishing he would disappear. I couldn't afford to feel this hollow about my own life, and that was how I felt when his eyes were on me. I was lost in the stumbling, clumsy sensation of being pulled into those eyes and held, so easily caught it seemed as if I had been waiting for him all this time. I looked at his lips and tried to resist the memory of how they once had fit against my own.

He stood up and moved toward me. "I know what it's like to lose the only parent you've got. I know how it feels to want to check out of wherever you are and cut yourself off from the people who love you."

"You don't love me," I said, putting the words between us like a fence. He was only inches away from me now.

"You're wrong about that," he said.

Pity isn't love, I thought, but let it ride.

"Have you been back to the farm?" he asked.

"I'm never going back." The words shot out of me before I could disguise the feeling behind them.

Noah's gaze was soft but insistent. "The land trust people have already cleaned out the rubble from the fire. The chimney's still standing, and there's a plaque next to the foundation, dedicating the property to your grandmother's memory. It's still beautiful, Brett. The land, the pond, the woods. It's all safe."

I stared at the ceiling and felt tears needle my sinuses as my eyes swam and blurred. I swallowed. That land was like my own child, so familiar and dear I didn't know if I could bear to see it at all, if it belonged to someone else. But at least it was safe.

"I want to take you there," Noah said, and took my hand in both of his.

"No," I said, quickly, reflexively.

"Please," he said.

I wanted to push him away; I wanted to pull him close. I could feel my heart expand and contract, then expand again, stirring like a seed struggling to open. It was terrifying to realize he could see right down into the bottom of me, into the feelings I still had for the farm. Right down into the feelings I still had for him.

"We'll see," I whispered.

We went back to the farm on the morning of my next day off, a Tuesday. I emerged slowly from Noah's truck and averted my eyes from the chimney standing like an obelisk over the black square of the burnt foundation. The forsythia was in bloom on the south lawn, a mass of yellow against the green grass, and the sun caught the petals and set them aflame. A mist was rising from the pond, and it seemed unnaturally quiet without the baying of the dogs. Noah caught my hand and held it as we walked toward the pond. The air was chilly, and full of ghosts. His hand was warm. I looked toward the woods and wondered if the buck had lived through the winter.

"Narcissus," Noah said, his eyes on the delicate survivors in Gran's flower bed. Their trumpets bobbed and nodded in the faint wind, next to the sturdy candy-colored curls of hyacinths. Beyond them the blackened stones of the foundation contrasted with the bright blossoms. By June the garden would come into its full glory, if anyone bothered to weed the rows.

I stood in the sunlight, peered into the dark envelope of earth under the blooms, and felt a tight heat escalate in my chest. It was almost unbearable to be here. I couldn't walk anymore. I could hardly breathe. I dropped Noah's hand and he turned toward me, his face composed and patient.

"I can't go on," I said.

"All right."

"I loved her," I said.

He nodded, his eyes holding mine. "I know."

"I should have saved her."

"No. You couldn't do that, Brett."

The grief boiled up in me like an epileptic fit, a seizure I couldn't control. My shoulders shook and my mouth opened as my lips stretched in a grimace of pain.

He stepped forward, took me in his arms, and held me. Underneath the cage of my ribs my heart was beating like a bird with a broken wing, and a terrible noise came out of my mouth as I cried for the future I had to face without her. I had tried so hard to be the woman she wanted me to be, the doctor, the wife, the mother, because of her eyes, watching me. Who was I without her presence, steering me, encouraging me? Where would I find my courage now? Who was watching?

# *Epilogue*

It's hot. I struggle to hold the calf firmly pinned with one knee while Noah sticks the needle full of vaccine into its hip. My hat is sliding off again and it's a relief to get up, set it right, and watch the calf run kicking and bawling back to its mother while I wipe the sweat from the back of my neck.

Noah glances up at me and grins. "You need a new hat," he says. "That one's too big."

It's true. Ever since the fire burned my hair I've kept it short, no longer than a couple of inches, and it forms a sleek cap of auburn streaked with blond from the New Mexico sun. Here in Abiquiu it's sunny all the time, from January to December, and even on the days it snows you can see the sun up there somewhere, flirting through the gray skirts of clouds.

I run my own clinic in the village three days a week, but since I'm the only doctor for fifty miles, the neighbors think nothing of getting me out of bed for any emergency, day off or not. Often I'm paid with bushels of chile, pinto beans, or livestock instead of actual cash, but Noah and I do all right. The neighbors treat me like an adopted daughter, one who must be corrected from time to time, and they complain I'm too honest with those who are going to die, and if I must speak about death at all I must speak of it in Spanish, which is so much softer to the ear. The men grumble that my clinic is too free with information about birth control, and the women tell me I'm too skinny for my own good.

On our one birthday in late August Noah and I are overwhelmed with their homemade, lopsided cakes, as well as the harvest from their gardens, and they always insist that we dance until midnight at the local bar, where everyone can enjoy our happiness. We dance obediently, and pay for many rounds of beer, which contributes a great deal to our popularity.

Noah's advent in my life is still a mystery to me. He is an honest man, and his honesty gives me confidence, but I still don't understand the faith that he always had in me, in us. His obstinacy infuriates me from time to time, just as he told me it would, but it's also a mark of his loyalty to the choices he makes, and since I am the one he chose, I trust him because of it.

In New Mexico anything less than a thousand acres is barely considered a ranch, but our parcel of a hundred and fifty acres presses up against ten thousand more of uninhabited, undeveloped land owned by the Bureau of Land Management. Our house is made of earth, built from bricks of clay and straw, each brick baked in the sun, then stacked and plastered with mud. The lines of each room are hand-made, stroked and filled in and replastered every few years. We mend the cracks as they appear, working with our hands in the way our neighbors advise, with a wheelbarrow, hoe, dirt, and water. The walls aren't plumb or square, but curve in and belly out, oddly animate and graceful.

Amy is enrolled at Syracuse University, majoring in broadcast communications. I miss her, but the semester is almost over and next week she's coming to spend the summer with us. When Amy and I moved into our apartment in Ithaca five years ago, Dan moved to a house within walking distance, and for two and a half years Amy bounced between our households while she finished high school. It was a relief to share custody with him. When Dan found out she'd been suspended from school for stealing, he took her downtown to police headquarters one weekend and explained exactly what would happen to her if she were caught shoplifting. One of his buddies fingerprinted her, took her mug shot, and showed her the cell and the roommates she'd have if she were ever arrested. Whether she understood that stealing was wrong or not I'll never know, but she understood the shame involved in getting caught, and never stole from us again. Dan and I pooled our funds to get her a used car for her sixteenth birthday, and she found a weekend job soon after that, teaching riding to kids under ten at Anyday Farm.

Ryan contested our father's will, but without any hard evidence to support his claim that Edward wanted to leave everything to him, the case was dismissed. Eventually the medical examiner released Edward's body from the morgue and Ryan had it cremated, then scattered the ashes in the myrtle woods, near the other graves.

After one trip to New Mexico both Ryan and Billy refuse to visit us again. They consider New Mexico a barbaric, desolate, and dusty hell, and plead with us to move back to New York. Once a year I fly out to spend a weekend with them, and the densely wooded green hills around Ithaca are visible from the airplane, awakening a thousand memories in me: the bracing summer chill of floating on my back in the pond; the exotic scent and texture of Gran's clothes; the homely odor of manure rising from the stalls in the barn; the deep cold of waiting for the school bus in the darkness of winter.

For two or three days in the city I eat well, realize all my clothes are years out of date, and exhaust myself walking through museums. Ryan looks more and more prosperous every year, and Billy confesses that while Ryan's fortunes were in free fall after the bankruptcy, Billy's investments in the stock market have lifted them into a higher tax bracket. It pleases me to see them and talk late into the night over expensive bottles of wine, to rehash the past and all its complications, but when I come back to New Mexico, I know I'm coming home.

There's a hawk that circles our ranch every morning, a large red-tail I've come to think of as Gran's hawk. I feel her here, even more than I did back East after she died, and I know she's watching, hovering over us with her lofty, clear-eyed presence. I miss the years we lost and often think that if she had resisted that single act of violence, she'd be alive; Vincent would never have come to visit, and the fire would never have happened. But I saw the satisfaction in her eyes, the night she confessed to killing Edward. Even now, if she exists at all, if she is aware and some part of her is up there in a blue sky, circling our farm, I doubt she feels regret.

Sometimes it seems as though I've left childhood and Gran behind with the farm, to come to this wind-scoured place where there is so much light. But the darkness is everywhere, as close as the local news. That was Gran's gift to me, to expect the shadow, the dark underside of anything that looks like serenity. I see the darkness in Noah, exactly where he told me it would be, in his stubbornness, in his judgments about other people, in his self-righteousness. And I see the darkness in me, in my willingness to kill, in my willingness to be a victim who is more comfortable with lies, because the truth is sometimes exhausting, and difficult to face.

A river flows past our property, carrying unknown quantities of pollution from the lab at Los Alamos and the pesticides leached from the farms above ours. But the river also brings enough water to irrigate our peaches, apricots, corn, beans, chile, and alfalfa. Without it our garden wouldn't exist, and the desert would take over.

Gran reminds me of the river, the poison of her secret hate suspended in the love she bore for Ryan and me and the farm. She made us bloom. She taught me to go to Africa, toward the place I feared, and her dying taught me to see the darkness in others, to allow it and try to love them anyway.

I can only wonder about my father, and what his attention might have felt like if Gran had let it flow toward me. There must have been a sweetness in him, somewhere. By now I've visited three of the homes he designed, and they all make me immeasurably sad, the way an aria or a painting can make me feel the exquisite, lonely pain of being human. Clean, light, and uncluttered, his houses have a purity, a harmony in the smallest details, a soaring individuality. Walking through one of his homes reveals my father's longing for order, for healing space, and it cuts me to know that he built sanctuaries for others, but found none for himself.

When Noah and I finish vaccinating the calves, we walk back to the house from the corral. In preparation for Amy's arrival next week, Noah repainted her room this morning. The windows are open to get the smell of latex out of the house, and the carpets and blankets are all out on the grass to bake in the sun. The yard is strewn with bedding, our mattress flung across the lawn.

"Come here," I say to my husband.

"Yes, dear," he coos, cupping my ass.

"I think I love you," I say.

He throttles me with a kiss, bends me over in a Fred Astaire dip, and I realize we have danced through five birthdays together, and all that practice is paying off. He dances me backward, toward our mattress under the blue sky.

We fall.